THE ISLAND OF DREAMS

HELEN MCGINN

Boldwood

First published in Great Britain in 2024 by Boldwood Books Ltd.

Copyright © Helen McGinn, 2024

Cover Design: Alice Moore Design

Cover Photography: Shutterstock

A CIP catalogue record for this book is available from the British Library.

Paperback ISBN 978-1-80280-611-3

Large Print ISBN 978-1-80280-612-0

Hardback ISBN 978-1-80280-610-6

Ebook ISBN 978-1-80280-614-4

Kindle ISBN 978-1-80280-613-7

Audio CD ISBN 978-1-80280-605-2

MP3 CD ISBN 978-1-80280-606-9

Digital audio download ISBN 978-1-80280-609-0

Boldwood Books Ltd
23 Bowerdean Street
London SW6 3TN
www.boldwoodbooks.com

For my sister, Alex (still funny)

1

Martha Williams had a feeling today wasn't going to be her day.

It had started quite promisingly. She'd bagged the last almond croissant at the café she always stopped at on her way to the station, before getting a window seat on the train.

Then things had started to go wrong. Crossing her legs as she sat on the train trying to read her book, she'd noticed a mark on her dress. Scratching it had only made it worse. She'd gone to put on her favourite lipstick only to find the lid had come off, leaving sticky red smears across the contents of her handbag. By the time she got to Waterloo, the sun that had been shining so brightly when she'd left her flat barely half an hour before had disappeared behind thick dark clouds.

As she stepped out onto the street to make the short walk to work, the heavens opened. Martha rummaged through her handbag for her umbrella, resulting in more lipstick on her fingers, only to find she'd left it at home. Instead, she pulled her trench coat over her head and made a run for it.

She crossed the small courtyard of the old red-brick school that was her workplace, fat raindrops falling down her face.

Deciding to avoid the staffroom, Martha headed straight to the staff loos to survey the damage in the mirror. Her dark hair hung heavily, strands sticking to her damp skin. She took off her glasses and wiped the smudged mascara from under her eyes with a paper towel. Shrugging off her coat, she shook her head under the hand dryer to get some of the water out.

'Morning, Martha,' said a slightly-too-cheerful-for-that-time-in-the-morning voice.

Martha didn't even have to look up to know who it was. 'Morning, Janet.'

Janet was the school receptionist with a habit of stating the obvious with a side order of smug. 'Someone got a soaking this morning. I left a little earlier when I saw the forecast, managed to miss it.'

'Well done you,' Martha said without a smile. 'So organised.' She stood upright again and pulled her hair back into a ponytail. 'Right, I'd better get going.'

'Ah yes, big day today. Last day of term. Always so sad to see them go.' Janet sighed.

'Well, not all of them,' said Martha, laughing.

Janet looked blank.

'I mean, they're great kids. It's just, you know...' Martha tailed off.

'It's been a long year, I'm sure you're looking forward to the summer holidays just as much as they are.' Janet smiled tightly and turned, disappearing into a cubicle.

Martha took one last look at her still slightly bedraggled appearance in the mirror and left, making her way down the long, still empty corridor to the staffroom. She scanned the room for a familiar friendly face. Over on the other side she spotted her fellow teacher and beloved friend, Joanie.

'What the hell happened to you?'

'Morning, Joanie, nice to see you too. How can you eat those this early in the morning?' Martha gestured at the packet of pickled-onion-flavoured crisps in Joanie's hand.

'Easy,' she said, popping a few in her mouth. 'You sure you don't want some?' She proffered the packet.

Martha sat down next to her on the old, battered staffroom sofa and shook her head. 'You're all heart. But no, thanks.'

'Are you coming out for drinks later?' Joanie licked her fingers, the smell of the crisps wafting over to Martha.

'I wish I could, but I can't. Got to run for a train straight from here after school. I'm heading down to my parents' house tonight.'

'Oh yes, you did say. The big pre-wedding dinner.' Joanie's eyes widened. 'Clearly you decided not to tell your sister she's marrying a total dick, then.'

Martha scowled at her friend. 'Really? You're going there.'

'What's his name again?'

'Toby.' She'd gone over this so many times in her head but somehow it didn't feel right to tell her older sister Iris that, in Martha's opinion, she really wasn't sure about him.

Toby and Iris hadn't even been together for that long, but Iris had insisted that he was, without doubt, The One.

'When's the wedding again?' Joanie asked.

'A week tomorrow.' Martha sighed. 'It's weird, Joanie. I hardly know him. But there's just something about him... I don't know.' She shivered slightly.

The rest of the family were seemingly really keen on Toby and the wedding was all anyone had talked about for months. Martha's eldest sister Liv's wedding just a few years before had been a very quiet affair, a handful of close friends and family only at a London register office. Liv and her husband, Jimmy, already had a toddler and a six-month-old baby by the time they'd decided to get married and the whole day had been utterly perfect.

Iris' impending nuptials were a totally different story. There was to be a big marquee in the garden of their parents' house in Devon with well over a hundred guests invited. The band had been booked, the wedding breakfast discussed and changed so many times Martha had lost count, not to mention interest.

'And you're not going to say anything?' Joanie looked at Martha and raised an eyebrow.

'I can't, Joanie. Can you imagine? Iris says she loves him.'

'But you're all so close, aren't you?'

'It's complicated. I love my sister dearly but if I just throw that in without anything to back it up, and then she marries him anyway, it just sits there forever. If I'm honest, I think she must know I'm not his biggest fan.'

Joanie shrugged. 'Oh well, promise to let me know how it goes.'

Martha smiled. 'I will.' She stood up and offered her hand to Joanie, pulling her out of the sagging sofa. 'Ready for one last assembly?'

'Can't bloody wait,' said Joanie, scrunching up the empty crisp packet with her other hand.

'Martha, can I have a quick word with you?'

Martha turned to see her boss, the school headteacher, an imposing woman called Mrs Browning. 'Yes, of course.' Martha raised an eyebrow at Joanie then turned and followed Mrs Browning back down the corridor towards her office, the head-teacher's sensible shoes squeaking on the shiny blue floor below as she strode ahead with purpose. Martha glanced at her own battered Chelsea boots, socks poking out of the top, wishing she'd worn something a little smarter. Mrs Browning opened the door and gestured for Martha to take a seat.

'Please, sit down, Martha. Now, I realise this is a little last minute and not quite as I'd hoped to do things, but it seems we're going to have a vacancy in the English department. Head of English, in fact.'

Martha's stomach flipped. 'What about...?'

'Mr Bentley is leaving us, after today. He's been poached by the lot down the road.' Mrs Browning tilted her head a little. Martha presumed she was referring to the nearby private school. They were always trying to pinch the best teachers. 'Anyway, with the holidays coming up I'd like you to consider taking the position at the start of next term. If you want it, the job is yours. I'm aware that you basically run the English department anyway. The hours are longer but the pay not much better, I'm afraid. Anyway, I wanted you to have the chance to give it some thought and I'll be in touch.'

Martha sat open-mouthed for a moment, lost for words. Her job was all-consuming, exhausting, relentless and stressful. But she loved her subject and most of the time she loved teaching it to her students, even if they sometimes annoyed the hell out of her. 'Um, thank you. Quite unexpected.' Martha nodded and smiled, trying not to let her emotions get the better of her. She was so happy she could have cried.

'Wonderful. Thank you, Martha. Right, we'd better head down to the hall.'

Suddenly, Martha's day was looking up.

* * *

The day passed in the usual chaotic manner, as all last days of term did. There was a sense of excitement in the air as Martha's pupils hugged and signed each other's shirts. As they left her classroom, she collected up the textbooks left on the tables and piled them neatly on her desk at the front. She wiped the board clean and sat down, enjoying the silence of the empty room for a moment. She thought about the weekend ahead, her heart lifting at the prospect of getting out of town and escaping to the familiar comfort of her childhood home for a few days.

She assumed her sisters would already be there by the time she arrived. Liv and Jimmy lived near to her parents' house, having moved back to Devon a few years before. Iris was travelling down with Toby in the car and had offered Martha a lift, but Martha had insisted they go without her saying she couldn't be sure what time she'd be able to get away. The truth was she didn't want to be stuck in a car for three hours with them talking wedding plans when she'd rather travel on her own with nothing but a book and some music in her ears for company.

She thought about what Joanie had said to her earlier in the staffroom. Maybe she should have said something to Iris? But it was complicated.

Martha had grown up watching and observing her two older sisters, just a few years in age between them. Martha had come along almost eight years after Iris. The age gap was such that growing up she'd sometimes felt like an only child. Even now, she felt they treated her more like a teenager than a woman in her mid-thirties.

Martha's phone vibrated in her pocket. She looked at the screen, a message from her mother asking what time her train got in. She knew her father would be there to collect her as he always was, usually waiting on the platform in his usual navy jumper with holes at the elbows. She gathered up her coat and bag from the back of the chair and made her way to the door. No, she couldn't risk saying anything to Iris. It was just a feeling, after all.

An hour later, as the train raced away from London and headed deep into the countryside, Martha felt her shoulders drop as green fields flew past the window, the early evening sun casting its golden light across them. She tapped at her phone and put on a favourite playlist that reminded her of home, music she'd grown up listening to. As familiar seventies folk songs flooded her ears, she picked up her book from the table in front of her and started to read. Soon she was lost in the words on the page, the characters speaking so clearly in her mind it was as if they were sitting right next to her.

The hours whizzed by as fast as the scenery outside. By the time the train pulled into the station near her parents' house the sun had dipped almost to the horizon, streaking the sky deep orange and pink. Martha reached for her bag above her seat and made her way to the door. She heard her father's voice as she stepped onto the short platform.

'Hello, darling.' Martha's father held his arms out as he walked towards her. He was tall and a little stooped with age. He still had a full head of hair, now grey rather than very dark brown as it once was, and his eyes were bright like Martha's.

Martha dropped her bag and hugged him tightly. 'Hi, Dad, how are you?'

'Thrilled you're here.' He held her by the shoulders. 'Everyone's so looking forward to seeing you. Here—' he picked up her bag '—I'll take that. How was your journey?'

'Oh, fine.' Martha sighed. 'Nearly finished my book.'

'And how was your last day of term?'

'Well, it's not quite my last day. We're back in next week to wrap up the year and start planning for next term. Oh, and I have news. I've been asked to apply for Head of Department. Well, it's mine if I want it, apparently.'

'Oh, Martha, that's fantastic news!' Her father beamed at her, his eyes glistening with tears.

'Thanks. I wasn't expecting it. It does mean more work for not much more money but I'd be mad not to take it.'

'Absolutely, you must. Car's this way.' Her father gestured to an old blue estate car.

'Crikey, is that still going?' Her parents had had it for as long as Martha could remember.

'Most of the time.' He laughed.

'Are Liv and Jimmy at home?'

'Not yet. It was just Mum, Iris and Toby when I left but they might have arrived by the time we get back. You made good time, though.'

'And how are the wedding plans?' Martha tried her best to sound bright and breezy.

Her father hesitated for just a moment. 'All good, I think. I'm staying out of it as much as possible, to be honest. I don't really have strong feelings when it comes to whether they have a cake or croquembouche, whatever that might be.'

'Very sensible.'

'You've met Toby a few times, haven't you?'

'Yes, why?' Martha glanced at her father, seeing what she could read from his face.

He kept his gaze ahead. 'What do you think?'

'I... er, he's fine. I mean, I don't really know him very well to be fair and Iris seems very happy so...' Martha couldn't think of what else to say.

'Yes, she does.'

There was another brief silence between them. She wondered whether he too wasn't sure about his prospective son-in-law but didn't want to say it out loud. Martha's father started the car and nosed out of the car park and back onto the main road. After about half a mile they took the small turning towards their village. High hedges on either side kept the sea just out of view as they followed the narrowing track, twisting and turning their way down the steep hill towards the house.

'I can't believe Liv's never met him either. She used to practically interview all of Iris' boyfriends when they lived together.' Martha's sisters had shared a flat in London for years when they'd both worked there, before Liv met Jimmy.

'Well, I'm sure he'll be able to hold his own.' Her father laughed gently.

They turned into a driveway marked either side by old staddle stones and drove up to the front of the house, a beautiful wisteria-covered pale stone building overlooking a gently sloping lawn bordered by huge rhododendrons. Behind sat a backdrop of beech woods.

'Home,' Martha whispered, suddenly grateful to be out of her tiny, damp flat at least for the weekend ahead. She knew her parents would be horrified if they knew where she was living. They'd never seen it and she hoped they never would, but it was all she could afford to rent on her salary.

Her mother appeared at the door on the side of the house, hair up and apron on, followed closely by an old black Labrador and two small brown spaniels. 'You're here!' she cried, opening the car door.

'Hi, Mum.' Martha stood to hug her mother.

'My goodness, let me look at you.' As ever her mother looked quite beautiful, her grey hair held back from her face with a bright blue silk scarf. Her piercing eyes, the same colour as the scarf, swept over Martha. 'You look wonderful, darling!'

Martha laughed. 'Mum, you always say that. I'm knackered.' She knew she looked tired, and her hair had gone frizzy at the ends having never quite recovered after the soaking that morning.

'John, did you get my message?'

Martha's father looked at her blankly.

'I messaged you – we've run out of milk. I wanted you to pick some up from the garage shop on your way past.'

'Sorry, Pen, I didn't. Can we ask Liv to bring some?'

'No, they're already here. Never mind, we'll make do without. Martha, come and say hello to everyone. I've just got to go and check on the potatoes.'

Martha followed her mother into the kitchen. The old farm-house table was already set for dinner, a multitude of flowers from the garden spilling out of a huge vase in the middle. Along the wall behind sat an old, crowded dresser, its shelves covered with mismatched crockery, dog-eared photos, old invitations and postcards propped up wherever there was space.

'You go on through, Martha,' said her father. 'I'll put your bag at the bottom of the stairs and bring you a drink. Gin and tonic?'

'Yes, please,' said Martha. 'Are they through there?'

'Yes, in the sitting room.' He let her go ahead.

Martha headed down the hall. She loved the way the house always smelt the same, a mix of cooking and dogs and woodsmoke. As she walked into the sitting room at the front of the house, her sisters cried her name in unison.

Liv was the first to leap up and reach her for a hug. 'You're here! How are you?'

'Ah, it's so good to see you.' Martha squeezed her eldest sister tightly. She looked across at Jimmy, standing just behind. 'Hi, how are you?'

He waved and nodded, mumbling his usual cheerful hello. Martha always thought his unruly grey curls made him look part mad professor, part ageing rocker.

'My turn.' Iris tapped Martha on the shoulder, smiling.

'Iris!' Martha kissed her on both cheeks. Unlike her sisters, Iris wasn't really a hugger. With the same bright blue eyes as their mother, Iris was tall with long blonde hair. She wore a beautiful floor-length red silk dress with huge gold hoop earrings. Not for the first time that day, Martha glanced down at her rather crumpled black pinafore dress and scuffed boots, feeling a little self-conscious.

'And Toby, of course.' Iris reached out her hand to pull Toby forward.

'Yes, of course. Lovely to see you again.' Martha tried her best to give a friendly smile.

'Can't believe we have to come all this way to see you when we only live about a mile apart!' Toby laughed, loudly. Martha had forgotten about that laugh. He bent down to kiss Martha on both cheeks as Iris had done.

'Getting my little sister out on a school night is impossible,' said Iris. 'Too much homework, I say.' She grinned at her sister.

'Ha, very funny.' Martha turned to Liv. 'Are the kids here?'

'Left them with a babysitter. You'll see them tomorrow, though. We could go for a walk down at the beach?'

'Definitely.' Martha smiled at the thought of the small stone beach they'd played on as children, just a short walk from the house. Hidden from the road, it was still a well-kept secret and most of the time they had it to themselves. 'So, Iris, how's it all going? Can't believe this time next week...'

'I know, me neither.' Iris looked at Toby. 'I feel like the luckiest girl in the world.'

'I think I'm the lucky one,' said Toby, planting a kiss on her forehead. He turned back to Martha. 'Iris tells me you're single. I hope this wedding stuff doesn't bore you too much.'

Martha couldn't keep the look of surprise from her face. 'Erm, yes. Currently.' She felt her cheeks begin to burn.

'Don't put her on the spot like that,' chided Iris, poking her fiancé gently in the ribs with her fingers.

'No, it's fine. Really.' Martha shrugged. 'But yes, still resoundingly single.' She wondered exactly what Iris had told Toby.

'Here's your drink, darling.' Martha's father crossed the room and handed her a tumbler, ice clinking in the glass as he did so.

'Thanks, Dad.' She took a large gulp of the contents, the taste of juniper hitting her palate with force. She was grateful for the diversion.

'What have I missed?' Martha's mother appeared and sat beside Liv on the sofa.

'I was just asking how everything was going,' said Martha, before taking another sip.

There was an awkward silence. Liv shifted in her seat. Jimmy stared at the floor.

Martha looked around the room, no one quite able to meet her gaze. She glanced down at her drink, watching the bubbles rise.

'I'm sorry, Martha, I didn't mean to—'

Martha cut Toby off. 'No, it's fine, really. I know it's the elephant in the room.'

'Toby didn't mean anything by it. Really, Martha, he doesn't know,' said Iris.

Martha stood up. 'Listen, I'm fine. Please don't think we have to avoid talking about weddings when I'm around. I'm not the first person to call off a wedding at the last minute and I'm sure I won't be the last.' She looked at them, smiling as convincingly as she could. 'Now, Mum, there must be something I can do in the kitchen to help.' She got up and moved to the door, pushing down the feelings in her chest, willing them back into the dark corners of her body. That way she could pretend they weren't there. Most of the time, anyway.

2

THREE YEARS EARLIER

Martha sat at her parents' kitchen table in an old T-shirt and leggings, squinting at the screen of her laptop.

'Where are your glasses?' Her mother placed a cup of tea in front of her.

'I left them upstairs, but I'll wake Joe if I go in there again and I want to leave him to sleep. He's shattered. Work seems to be relentless at the moment.'

'How's the list coming along?' Her mother sat opposite her. She was dressed in her gardening clothes, having been up early, as ever, to potter in her vegetable garden.

'Fine,' Martha lied. She was, in fact, staring at a blank screen. She shut the laptop with a snap.

'How many are we up to?' Her mother picked up an apple from the bowl on the table and bit into it.

'About eighty, we're trying to keep the numbers down.' Even saying the words made Martha feel nauseous. She tried to ignore the now familiar sinking feeling in her stomach.

'Everyone's so excited, I can't even pick up a pint of milk from the shop without someone asking me about it.' Martha's mother smiled to herself, then looked at Martha.

'Mum, you know what? I might go down to the beach and have a quick swim before everyone's up. I've got this on under-neath—' she pulled at the strap of her swimming costume '—and I grabbed a towel from upstairs.' She gestured to the tote bag at her feet.

Her mother looked at the clock on the kitchen wall. 'Perfect timing; tide's almost in. It'll still be nice and quiet, too. You go, I'll make you some eggs when you're back, when Joe's up.'

'Thanks, Mum, I'll be half an hour.' She slipped her feet into some old trainers by the back door and headed down a path through the trees towards the beach. The sun was already warm on her face as she walked. Before she even saw the water, she could hear it. The gentle lapping of waves on stones, a sound so familiar she sometimes heard it in her sleep.

The small cove was empty, the sky above the clearest blue. Martha took a deep breath, wanting to enjoy this perfectly still, early summer morning. She balanced her mug of tea on a rock and slipped off her trainers before peeling off her leggings and T-shirt.

Picking her way across the stones towards the stretch of sand by the shore, she stood for a moment, letting the water lap around her ankles. It was cold at first, but soon her skin had adjusted to the temperature. She walked until the water was up to her waist, then stood for a few seconds looking at the horizon. Breathing in deeply, she launched herself forwards, taking a few strokes before coming up for air, her bare feet finding the bottom. She loved being in the sea but hated not being able to stand, fearing what lay beneath. Turning back towards the shore, she looked beyond and up to the house, just visible over the top of the hedges. She thought of Joe, sound asleep in her old bedroom.

It was barely a month before they were to be married. A fairy-tale wedding, so everyone kept saying. But as the date grew closer, Martha felt a creeping sense of dread. Worse, she didn't really understand why. She and Joe had been together since their early twenties. His parents lived just a few miles away in a nearby village. They'd been good friends all through their teenage years but only got together once they'd moved away. Reunited at a mutual friend's New Year's Eve party, Martha and Joe had bumped into each other at the bar and not stopped talking until they found themselves kissing at midnight as fireworks lit up the dark sky above them. It had all seemed so perfect: two old friends, so much shared history and none of it complicated. Everyone loved Joe, especially Martha's family. As for his family, they were mad about Martha.

She soon found herself moving into Joe's (much bigger) flat in London, not far from her job at the time as a teaching assistant at a large secondary school. He had a good job in finance, was paid ridiculously well for someone his age. They threw supper parties for their friends, went on mini breaks to cities all over Europe and spent endless weekends at various friends' weddings and birthday parties. Some of the people around them got married and before long started having children and one evening Joe looked at Martha as they sat on the sofa eating their Chinese food straight from the takeaway box in front of the television.

'Can you put your food down for a moment?'

Martha looked at Joe. 'Are you okay? You've gone pale.'

'Please, Martha, put your box down for a moment.'

Martha did as she was told, reaching forward to put it on the small pine coffee table in front of them. She balanced her chopsticks carefully on the top and sat back, turning to Joe once more.

He reached for her hands and took them in his own. 'Will you marry me?' His voice shook a little.

Martha looked at his kind, familiar face. She hesitated for a moment, not able to move her mouth. It felt as if it were clamped shut.

'Martha?'

Martha took in a deep breath. 'Yes, Joe. I will marry you.'

His face crumpled with emotion. 'Thank God for that!' He reached forward and wrapped her in his arms, knocking his take-away onto the floor as he did so. 'Thank you, Martha. You have made me the happiest man in the world.'

Martha hugged him back. 'And me. Happiest woman.' But as she said those words, something shifted inside her. At first, she couldn't work out why she was feeling like this when she should have been so happy. But with a creeping sense of dread, she had to admit to herself that she was sleepwalking into a life everyone expected her to have. The problem was Martha couldn't face disappointing everyone around her. Not Joe, not her parents, her sisters or friends. Even if it meant disappointing herself.

In the months that followed Martha felt as if she'd stepped aboard a train, speeding towards a destination she didn't really want to go to but knowing it was too late to jump off. Her parents were over the moon, as was Liv. At the time Iris had just extri-cated herself from a particularly exhausting relationship and was telling anyone who'd listen that marriage was a terrible idea but she, like everyone else, loved Joe.

Joe told Martha at every opportunity how much he loved her, how they were going to have the most fantastic life together. Martha smiled and returned similar promises. But she knew she didn't mean them like he did and the more she said them, the more she hated herself for doing it.

It was on a night out with Joanie, after too many tequilas – the only way to do a night out as far as Joanie was concerned – that Martha admitted how she really felt, out loud, for the first time.

As they'd sat waiting for the night bus, sharing a bag of salt-and-vinegar-drenched chips, Martha had been answering Joanie's questions about Joe and whether they were going to stay in London or move out to the suburbs or, worse, the countryside and desert her (Joanie's words) when Martha found herself saying she wasn't sure she was doing the right thing.

'What do you mean – moving out?' Joanie held a chip between her long fingers, stopping before it could reach her mouth. 'I'd say that's definitely not the right thing to do. You'll be thinking it's acceptable to wear a fleece in no time.'

Martha took a deep breath. 'No, I mean marrying Joe.'

Joanie's mouth fell wide open.

Martha saw the look of shock on Joanie's face. 'I know. I can't believe I'm saying it either.'

'Since when? I thought you two were, like, the real deal. What happened?'

Martha shrugged her shoulders, her eyes now studying the cracks in the pavement. 'I said yes because I thought I loved him. I do love him. The problem is...' Martha hesitated '...I don't think I love him enough.'

'Shit, Martha. The wedding's in a month's time. You have to tell him!'

'I've been trying to convince myself that I'll love him more as time goes by, but I know I can't do that to him. It's not fair. God, Joanie. What have I done? I thought it would be all right.'

Joanie sat back down and put her arm around her friend, still holding a chip between her fingers. 'Listen, worse things have happened. Nobody died. But you've got to tell him now. Well, tomorrow when you're sober might be better, to be honest.'

Martha wiped at the tears that had started to fall. 'I feel horrible about it.'

'Is there someone else?'

'No!' Martha looked at Joanie, her eyes wide. 'I promise, absolutely not.'

'Just checking.' Joanie took Martha's hand. 'You need to tell him, Martha. Leaving it any longer will only make it worse.'

'I will, I promise.'

But Martha didn't tell him. Not that night, or the next day. She just couldn't bring herself to. And the longer she left it, the worse she felt. And the harder it became to live a lie.

* * *

That morning, as Martha swam back towards the shore, Joanie's words ran round her head. Martha and Joe had come down for the weekend to stay with Martha's parents and his parents were due to come for dinner that evening. The thought of what she was about to have to do made her feel physically sick, but she knew it was time. She had to say something now, before the dinner.

Martha headed back up to the house from the beach. She knew Joe would be devastated but she had no choice. She took him his tea, then asked him to get dressed and meet her in the garden so they could talk. He looked at her quizzically but simply nodded and said he'd be down in ten minutes.

Martha headed out into the garden by the back door to avoid having to face her mother, sat on a bench by the side of the beech wood behind the house and waited for Joe. He appeared shortly after, having thrown on his T-shirt and shorts. His hair was still ruffled from sleep. As he walked towards her across the lawn, Martha wished she could turn and run into the woods, disappear into the trees and not have to say what she was about to say, ever.

'What is it?' He sat down beside her.

'Joe, I'm so sorry.' Martha forced herself to look at him, desperately trying to keep her voice steady. 'We can't get married.'

'What?' His voice was barely a whisper.

Martha shook her head slowly. 'I'm so sorry.'

'I don't understand... what do you mean? Why?' He stared at her in disbelief.

'I thought the feeling would go away but I...'

'What, Martha? Just say it.'

Even though she'd thought about this moment repeatedly since admitting how she felt to Joanie, words now deserted her. 'You deserve better.'

He shook his head and laughed. 'Oh, come on, please don't do that. Give me a proper reason.'

Martha dug her nails into her palms. She hadn't wanted to say the words, but she knew she had to be honest. 'Joe, I'm so sorry. I don't love you enough to marry you.'

He screwed up his face. 'What does that even mean? You said yes!'

'I know, and I shouldn't have.'

'What the... so why did you?'

'Because I thought it was what I wanted too. And I'm so sorry, I wish I didn't feel like this. I've been willing it to feel right but I know it's not. It would all be so perfect, us getting married, but I'm not being honest with you.'

'I think you're being very honest, don't you?' His face was drained of colour.

'I'm so sorry.'

'Yes, we've established that.' He let out another laugh, this time a hollow one. 'Well, I just wish you'd thought to tell me this before now. But thanks for your "honesty", Martha.' He spat the word out. 'How do you know?'

'What do you mean?' Her voice shook.

'How do you know you don't love me enough?'

'Joe, please...' Martha tried to reach for his hand, but he moved to stand.

He turned to face her as she sat on the bench. 'Well? How do you know? Is there someone you love more? Is that how you know?'

'No, I swear it's nothing like that. Joe, I do love you, but I know it's not right. To marry you, I mean.'

'Fuck you, Martha.' Joe stared at her, his eyes burning with fury now. 'Really, fuck you.' He started walking back towards the house.

She got up to follow him, reaching out for his arm.

He shook her off without looking back. 'Please, Martha, do me a favour and leave me alone. I've heard enough.'

'Please listen to me, I—'

'I said *enough*!' Joe turned towards her and held up his arms. 'I don't want to hear it, Martha.' He carried on walking back to the house, turning to look at her one last time before he disappeared inside.

* * *

Martha knew the fallout was going to be bad, but nothing had prepared her for just how awful. Her parents, after getting over the initial shock, offered words of comfort, reassuring Martha it was better to be truthful, but they were obviously devastated. Liv tried to talk Martha round. Iris simply rolled her eyes, telling Martha she was far better off not getting married anyway.

Joe refused to answer his phone or respond to any messages at all, so Martha tried to speak to his parents, calling them on their landline. Joe's mother put the phone down as soon as she heard Martha's voice.

Un-arranging the wedding was a truly hideous experience. The guilt she felt was crushing but, as far as she was concerned, she deserved to feel terrible for what she'd done. She insisted on doing everything that had to be done herself – telling the vicar, cancelling caterers and flowers and the wedding singer, a local Elvis impersonator (that had been Joe's idea). When it came to emailing the guest list telling them the wedding was off, Martha stared at a blank screen for what seemed like hours, wondering what to type. How could she tell her friends and family that she didn't love the person she'd agreed to marry enough to go through with it? That she hadn't said anything until the last minute because she'd been too scared to admit her true feelings? How it had been easier to go along with everything because she'd felt that was what was expected of her?

That Sunday afternoon Martha typed a short email stating that the wedding had been cancelled due to unforeseen circumstances. She pressed send only for her phone to light up with messages from friends asking her what had happened. She ignored them all, unable to face answering their questions.

She moved her things out of his flat the following week. After she'd sent a few more messages that had gone unanswered, Joe had replied saying he would be out on the Monday evening so she could collect her things then. She let herself into the dark flat. The curtains were undrawn, dirty plates were piled up in the sink and the bed was unmade. It didn't take Martha long to load her clothes into a few bags and clear out her things from the bathroom. She picked up a few of her photo frames, grabbed her pile of unread books from her side of the bed and rummaged in the kitchen cupboard for her favourite mug, one she'd had since she was a student. Everything else, she decided, was replaceable.

An hour later she pressed the doorbell of Joanie's flat, bracing herself for Joanie's questions but instead her friend simply met her with a hug.

'Hello, you.' Joanie squeezed her.

Martha felt the tears coming again. 'I'm a horrible person.'

'No, you're not. You've been honest. I mean, yes, technically it would have been easier if you'd not said yes in the first place but at least you got there. In the end. You've done what lots of other people are probably too scared to do.'

'What do you mean?'

'Not pick the easy option.'

'You really think so?'

'Absolutely. You haven't settled for something just because it's better than nothing.'

'I really do love him, but not as I should. It's not even like I've loved someone else more than him, ever. But I just know it's not enough.'

'Exactly, and that's why you've done the right thing. Martha, listen to me. Most women our age are freaking out about whether they should get married and if they leave it too late does that mean they'll miss out on having kids. But you've got to put yourself and your own happiness first. Work out what you want in life, not do things because you think it's what everyone else wants.'

'He won't even speak to me.'

'You've just broken his heart.'

Martha winced.

'You need to leave him alone until he sees life does go on. Yes, it's an awful thing to happen but, like I said, you've done the right thing. And the braver thing, too. So, stop feeling sorry for yourself, get in here and make yourself useful. Open the bottle in the fridge door and let's have a glass of wine.'

'On a school night?' Martha raised an eyebrow.

'I know, I'm making an exception. Now bung your bags by the sofa, you can stay as long as you need to.'

'Thank you.'

Joanie smiled. 'Come on, chin up. You've done the hard part.'

Martha nodded. 'I still feel wretched.'

'Enough, you're boring me.' Joanie laughed and kissed Martha on the cheek. 'Let's drink wine, watch telly and judge people. That's always a good distraction.'

3

PRESENT DAY

The quiet of the kitchen was a welcome relief. Martha stood by the back door breathing in the cool evening air. For a moment, she was tempted to rifle through the pockets of her old coat that hung on its usual peg to see if the emergency packet of cigarettes was still in there. Strictly speaking she didn't smoke, but a solitary ciggy smoked on her own hidden in her parents' garden from time to time was her guilty pleasure. It made her feel like a teenager again.

Martha knew how lucky she was, to have parents who were still married and clearly devoted to one another, even after half a century together. So many of her friends' parents were divorced or in some cases still together but evidently unhappy. She remembered once, when she must have been about six or seven years old, finding her parents sitting in the car in the garage together. It was an old sports car they'd owned before she was born but hadn't been used for years. She'd gone to find them only to see her father pretending to drive with one hand whilst holding a glass of Scotch aloft in the other. Her mother wore a pink silk headscarf around her head, glass of wine in hand. Music blared from the radio and they both sang at the tops of their voices.

Laughing, Martha asked where they were going. She remembered her mother looking at her, blue eyes shining.

'Wherever your father wants to take us. Are you coming too?'

'Yes, hop in, little one,' called her father without looking round.

Martha clambered in, her mother helping her over the side of the car and into the back seat.

'Ready?' Her father turned up the music even louder. 'Let's go!'

'To the South of France, please, darling,' shouted her mother.

'Right you are, madam. We should be in Monaco in time for lunch if I put my foot down.'

When she thought about it now, Martha realised her parents had always made marriage look so easy. She knew they'd had difficult patches, remembered hearing raised voices downstairs when she was little on a few occasions. Arguments about money, usually, at least the lack of it. But never in front of them. What Martha remembered most was how her parents clearly loved each other's company. They were always talking, making each other laugh, forging plans. When they saw one another, their faces lit up; it sometimes made Martha wonder whether her own expectations were just too high.

Take Liv, for example. Jimmy was hardly the most exciting man on the planet, but he was kind and gentle and evidently adored Liv and their children. Theirs wasn't a great passion, at least from what Martha saw, but their love was seemingly uncomplicated.

Iris on the other hand was a completely different story. Martha's middle sister had lurched from one great love affair to the next, always leaving first, never looking back. Somehow Iris was able to pack up her feelings as soon as one came to an end, moving neatly on to the next. Her stop-and-stare beauty and irresistible charm had attracted a great many devoted lovers in the past but none of them had been anything like Toby.

Ah, Toby. Martha shuddered a little. Compared with his predecessors Toby wasn't exactly what Martha would describe as Iris' usual type. Normally they were extremely handsome – and wealthy. Toby was certainly the latter according to Iris – and judging by the rock the size of a small island now residing on her left hand, she wasn't wrong – but looks-wise he was not what Martha was used to when it came to Iris' boyfriends. First, there was his hair. Bouffant was the word that came to mind when Martha first saw it. Then there was that unexpectedly high-pitched laugh. When Martha had first heard it, she'd assumed it was put on. But then on second and third hearing she'd realised that it was, in fact, his actual laugh. Iris didn't seem to even notice.

'Are you all right, darling?'

Martha turned to see her mother in the kitchen, reaching for a glass from the cupboard. 'Sorry. I know everyone's worried about talking weddings in front of me, but knowing everyone's watching what they say makes me feel worse.'

'They just don't want to upset you, that's all.'

'Mum, it was a long time ago now. I've moved on. Even Joe's moved on, apparently.'

'Yes, I heard from his mother when I bumped into her in the post office. I wondered if you'd heard.'

Martha looked up at the pale evening sky through the half-closed kitchen stable door. 'Yes, I did. Andrea whatshername.'

'Jeffreys.'

'That's it, Andrea Jeffreys. We were in the same class at school. She always had a thing for Joe.' She sighed. 'Deserves him more than I do, anyway.'

'You didn't want him, remember. You can't feel sorry for yourself now.' Her mother nudged Martha gently.

'Thanks, Mum, now I feel a whole lot better.' She rolled her eyes at her mother and sighed. 'But I suppose you're right.'

'Well, then. Stop feeling sorry for yourself and come and help me put supper on the table.' Her mother signalled to the dresser. 'Can you hand me some plates and I'll stick them in the oven for a bit? Nothing worse than cold plates.'

'I'd say calling off a wedding at the last minute is worse.'

Her mother waved the words away with her elegant hand. 'Old news, Martha. Hand me the plates.'

'Mum, can I ask you something?'

'Of course.'

'Do you think I made a mistake, leaving Joe?'

'Only you can answer that one, darling, but I think the very fact you're asking tells you all you need to know.'

'What do you mean?'

Martha's mother put down the cutlery she was holding, letting it clatter gently onto the table. 'All I can say is when you know, you know. There's no question. You shouldn't be having to ask me.'

'Is that how it was with you and Dad?'

'He drives me mad sometimes, but I can't imagine life without him. It really is as simple as that. I promise you, when it happens you really won't be asking me if you're doing the right thing.'

Martha picked up the cutlery and started placing it around the table. 'Do you think I'm expecting too much?'

'I should hope so! Nothing wrong with high expectations, darling. But you learn to compromise too, that's what sharing your life with someone is all about.'

'So...' Martha glanced behind her and lowered her voice '... what do you think of Toby?'

Her mother didn't miss a beat. 'If your sister's happy, I'm happy.'

'He's not what I expected.'

'Martha, stop it.' Her mother raised an eyebrow at her, a sure sign that she thought Martha was about to say something she really shouldn't.

Realising she wasn't going to get anything out of her, Martha carried on laying the table. 'I just wondered what you thought, really.'

'Thought about what?' Iris breezed into the kitchen, picking up a wine bottle from the side and filling her glass.

'I was just asking Mum what else we could do to help before the big day,' Martha replied airily.

'Don't you worry, there'll be plenty to do, I'm sure. What have you been talking about in here? Have I missed anything?'

Martha picked up an empty wine glass from the table and held it out towards Iris, who duly filled it from the open bottle still in her hand. 'Funnily enough I was asking Mum the secret to a happy marriage.'

'I'm not sure I want to hear that from my mother.' Iris screwed her nose up.

'Communication,' said their mother, standing and turning to face them, holding the huge orange casserole dish she'd just retrieved from the oven. 'Talking of which, can you tell the others that the food is on the table?' She put the dish down in the middle, taking the lid off. The smell of warm herbs and spices filled the air.

'Ooh, is that Ottolenghi?' Iris peered into the dish.

'Who?'

'Mum, please tell me you know who Ottolenghi is!' Iris laughed.

'Never heard of them. Martha, go and get the others, please.'

Martha made her way down the corridor towards the sitting room when the door to the downstairs loo suddenly flew open, almost hitting her in the face.

'Whoa!'

'Sorry,' said Toby, lurching to one side then back again.

'No problem.' Martha looked at him, his eyes glistening. His face was uncomfortably close to hers and she could smell the red wine on his breath. Martha tried to pass him, but he moved the same way at the same time, forcing them to do an uncomfortable dance until a gap appeared. 'I'm just going to...' Martha pointed to the sitting room.

'Yes, right. I'll see you in the kitchen.'

She'd suspected he was an idiot. But, she thought, it takes a certain kind of idiot to get completely pissed before a dinner to celebrate their impending wedding when at their in-laws' house. As far as she was concerned, the less she had to do with him, the better.

Martha composed herself and put her head around the sitting room door. 'Dinner's ready.'

* * *

'John, make sure everyone's got wine.' Penny gestured to the bottle on the table, then started dishing out the stew.

Martha put herself between her father, who sat at his usual place at the end of the table, and Jimmy on her other side – and as far from Toby as possible. She could still hear him above everyone else, his voice dominating the conversation, but at least he wasn't in her eyeline. She glanced across the table at Iris, who seemed to be hanging off Toby's every word.

Jimmy nudged Martha. 'I hear congratulations are in order. You got a promotion at work?'

'Ah, thanks, Jimmy, I've been offered the head of department.'

'That's fantastic news, well done you!' Jimmy raised his glass to his sister-in-law.

'Thanks. But to be honest I'm just looking forward to getting out of London for the summer. I'm thinking I might stay down here for a while – perhaps I can come and help you out at the B & B?'

Jimmy and Liv had renovated some old barns next to their cottage a few years before and now ran a flourishing holiday rental business.

'Actually that would be amazing, it's non-stop over the summer. I'm not sure we can pay you much but...'

'Oh no, I wouldn't expect anything really. It's just that if I am here for a few weeks, I'll need something to keep me busy otherwise I'll go mad.'

'Are you not going away this summer?'

'I wish. Can't afford it this year. Hopefully Mum and Dad don't mind me hanging around.'

'We'd love it if you were here.' Her father smiled and squeezed Martha's arm.

'Thanks, Dad.'

'You don't have to thank us.' He reached for the wine bottle and picked it up, shaking it as he did so to see how much was left. He'd filled everyone's glass but his own. 'Excuse me a moment, I'm just going to get another one of these.'

She turned back to Jimmy and lowered her voice. 'Can I ask you something?'

'Uh-oh.'

'What?'

'I think you're going to ask me what I think of Toby.'

'How did you know?'

'Because Liv's not keen and I can tell you don't like him either.'

Martha grimaced. 'Is it that obvious?'

Jimmy laughed quietly. 'I'm afraid so. But she's obviously mad about him.' As if on cue, Toby delivered yet another punchline only for Iris to fall about laughing.

'Fine, I'll leave it. But for the record you can tell Liv I agree with her. He's a moron.'

Jimmy winked. 'I'll tell her. God knows how I got through you two.'

'We weren't paying attention,' Martha teased.

'Jimmy, have you got room for more?' Penny called up from the other end of the table.

'I'm good, thanks. But I will have more of those potatoes, they were delicious.'

The wine flowed as steadily as the conversation and as they picked over the cheeseboard talk turned back to the impending wedding. Martha sat through it for five minutes, then decided to busy herself putting plates in the dishwasher. She headed to the back door with her glass in hand, then reached into her old coat pocket for the squashed packet of cigarettes and lighter. She grabbed them and wandered out to an old bench by the side of the house, partially hidden by a tangle of wisteria branches surrounding it. The blooms had been and gone, and Martha was sad to have missed them. Her mother had sent her photos, but it wasn't the same as standing underneath them and breathing in their scent. She lit up her cigarette and inhaled, blowing out the smoke gently. She didn't even really enjoy smoking any more but felt it a better option than sitting inside listening to wedding plans.

'Who are you hiding from?'

The voice made Martha jump. 'Toby... how did you know I was here?'

'Fancied one myself.' He held up his hand, a lit cigarette between his fingers. Even in the dusky light she could see his eyes were glazed.

Martha shifted on the bench, instantly feeling uncomfortable. She stubbed out her cigarette. 'Well, I've finished this now, so I'd better go in. I'll leave you to it.' She went to stand.

Toby took a step towards her, blocking her way. 'But you'd only just lit it.'

Martha stepped back. Once again, his face was now so close to hers she could smell the wine and smoke on his breath. 'I was just about to...' Martha tried to get past, but he grabbed her arm, making her spill the wine in her glass.

'Come on, don't you think we should at least get to know each other a bit better? We're about to be related after all.' He sat down on the bench and patted the space beside him, grinning. 'At least give me a chance.'

Martha looked at him, his face flushed with alcohol. All she wanted to do was go back into the house. 'No, really, I don't even smoke.'

'So I can see,' said Toby, picking up her hastily discarded cigarette butt from the ground and tossing it into the flower bed beside him. 'Come on, I don't bite.' He took a long drag.

Martha shifted from one foot to the other. As much as she wanted to go back in, she didn't want to appear rude. Maybe she was being too hard on him? He was trying at least. Perching on the arm at the other end of the bench, she crossed her legs, wrapping her arms in front of her. 'You must be excited?'

He fixed her with his eyes, a small smile on his face. 'Very.' He took another drag of his cigarette, his eyes not leaving hers.

Martha's stomach turned. Was he flirting with her? He

couldn't be, surely. She looked away, an awkward silence now between them.

'So come on, what's your type?'

'I beg your pardon?' Martha couldn't believe what she was hearing.

'I said, what's your type?'

'Of what, car?' Martha stared at him, determined to show she wasn't intimidated by him.

'I think you know exactly what I mean.' He moved towards her.

Martha stood up again. 'I really don't think it's any of your business, to be honest.'

'I think I know,' Toby said conspiratorially. He tapped the side of his nose.

She resisted the urge to slap him, wiping the awful self-satisfied smile off his face in the process. 'Don't be so ridiculous.' She turned to go inside, not wanting to spend another second anywhere near him. He was being deliberately provocative and Martha had had enough. Suddenly she felt that hand on her arm again. She turned to face him, now standing in front of her. 'Let go of my arm.' She spoke through gritted teeth.

'Come on, Martha. You've been looking at me across the table all evening.'

'Jesus, Toby, are you being serious? You're about to marry my sister!'

He grabbed her other arm, his fingers pushing hard into her skin. 'Literally couldn't take your eyes off me, could you?' He was still smiling but his eyes were cold.

Martha tried to shake herself free from his hold. 'Not because I fancy you, you idiot. Now, please, let me go!' She couldn't believe what was happening.

He leered back towards her, his wet lips landing on her neck.

Martha jerked her head away from him. 'What the hell do you think you're doing?'

Still he gripped her arms. 'Don't be like that. I thought you'd be grateful. I mean, it's not like you've got a queue of them waiting, is it?'

'Get off *me*!' Martha finally yanked an arm free from his grip. 'How dare you?' With an almighty tug she freed her other arm and pushed him as hard as she could.

He staggered back onto the bench. Before he was able to get himself back up, Martha kicked him hard in the shins.

'What the hell?'

'Don't you ever try anything like that again, do you understand?' Martha jabbed a finger in his face, then turned and walked quickly back towards the house, fearful tears in her eyes. She felt a tightness in her chest, her breath short.

'Martha, come back. I was just kidding.'

She left his words hanging in the still air. Standing by the back door for a few seconds, she tried to compose herself, not wanting to alert anyone to what had just happened. As she crept back into the house, all she knew was that she wanted to be anywhere but under the same roof as Toby. She went straight through the kitchen and carried on upstairs into her room, shoving her clothes back into her bag. But Martha knew she couldn't leave without getting a lift, which would mean having to explain her sudden departure. She lay on the bed face down, her hands trembling. Saliva collected in her mouth and before she knew it, vomit was in her mouth. She ran across to the small sink in the corner of her room and threw up.

Moments later, there was a gentle knock at the door. Her mother stood there, a worried look on her face. 'Martha, goodness me, what's happened?'

Martha hid her face, knowing that if her mother saw it she'd know something was seriously wrong. It already felt like a bad dream; telling her mother would make it a reality. One that they'd have to deal with, whether that meant keeping it a secret or telling Iris. Martha looked at her reflection in the mirror above the sink. She took a deep breath and hoped her voice wouldn't betray her current state. 'Nothing, Mum. It's just talking about the wedding, you know...' Her voice was small. She couldn't think what else to say.

'Oh, darling, I'm sure it's hard but think of your sister. It's her big day and she's so excited about it.'

Martha shook her head, fighting back the tears. 'I know. I'm sorry.' At least her mother seemed to believe she was upset because of the wedding. 'I hope you don't mind, but I think I'd better get back to London tomorrow.'

'I thought you were here until Sunday?'

Martha racked her brain for a suitable excuse. 'I've got so much prep to do before next week, it's our last week in before the summer break and with this new job and everything, it's... you know, I've got to get myself properly organised.' She hoped that sounded convincing.

'You could have brought it with you, got some work done in peace.'

'I know, I should have done but I'll just have to go back. I'm so sorry, Mum.'

'It's all right, darling. I know this can't be easy for you.'

Martha nodded. 'I think I'm just going to get into bed. Will you say goodnight to the others?'

Thankfully, her mother stayed by the door. 'I will. Try and get some sleep. I'll see you in the morning.'

'Night, Mum. And thank you.' She waited until the door closed, then went to the window and closed the curtains. The moon threw shadows on the sloping lawn in front of the house below her. She looked out across it and beyond to the glimpse of sea in the distance, light dancing on the water. Opening the old sash window to let the air in, she heard the familiar whisper of waves.

Then two voices. Iris and Toby.

At first, she couldn't make out what they were saying but as they got closer she could tell from the tone of Iris' voice her sister was angry. Martha caught a waft of cigarette smoke.

Iris said something but Martha still couldn't quite catch it. They stopped at the bench below the window, the one she'd been sitting at just moments before.

'I'm telling you she went for me.' Toby's voice was quite clear now.

'Like, an argument?'

'No, not an argument. I mean, Iris, and I'm sorry to say this, but she tried to bloody kiss me!'

'What? Are you being serious?'

'I'm telling you, I went to join her for a cigarette, and she literally pounced on me.'

Martha stopped herself from yelling down from where she sat, wanting to hear what else he might say. She held onto the window frame to stop the window from sliding back down, her knuckles white.

'I can't believe Martha would do that. Are you sure?' Iris sounded utterly bewildered.

'I know, I can't believe it either. She just doesn't look like the type... not to mention the fact that she's your bloody sister!'

'I know this has been tough for her after everything that happened but that's just...' Iris stood up. 'I'm going to have to say something.'

Martha leaned back behind the curtains, hoping her sister wouldn't look up and see the open window.

'No, don't. Leave it, Iris.'

'How can I leave it? My sister just tried to jump my fiancé, for God's sake!'

'Listen, I think all this wedding talk has sent her a bit mad. She was pretty drunk.'

'Really? She didn't seem drunk.'

Martha wanted to scream, call him out for the liar he was. But it was her word against his. And everyone would then know what had happened. Martha watched as they walked away from the house, a feeling of dread as she saw Toby wipe away her sister's tears and take her into an embrace. They kissed in the moonlight; Iris had obviously chosen to believe him.

Martha moved slowly away from the window and back towards the bed. She climbed under the duvet, pulling it over her head, still fully dressed. Tears of rage fell from her hot cheeks onto the pillow.

Moments later there was another knock at her door. It creaked as it opened a smidge.

'Martha, it's me, Liv. Can I come in?'

'Please, Liv, I'm so tired.'

Martha felt her sister sit down gently on the end of the bed.

'What is it, Martha? I feel like I've missed something. I know having to hear Iris bang on about that bloody wedding is enough to send anyone from the room, but you seemed fine one minute and then the next it was like, I don't know... you disappeared.' Liv spoke softly.

'Liv, I'm sorry. I just need to sleep.' Martha's voice was muffled by the duvet.

'Well, it's up to you. But you know you can talk to me, about anything.'

Martha so wanted to tell her but, by doing so, knew she'd be putting things in motion that, once started, couldn't be stopped.

She'd already blown her life up once. She wasn't prepared to do it again; she just wanted to close her eyes and for it all to go away.

Martha felt Liv get up from the bed and heard the door shut quietly. She reached out an arm and switched off the light, hoping that sleep would indeed come. Her head ached, her eyes were heavy. She slept in fits and starts and eventually, as soon as it was light enough, she crept downstairs with her bag, buying the dogs' silence with biscuits as she passed through the kitchen.

Martha put on her coat and scribbled a note to her parents to let them know she'd see them the following weekend. Closing the door behind her, she made her way down the track and met the road, walking through dawn all the way to the station in the hope of catching the first train back to London. Never had she been so desperate to get away from the place she called home. Once on the train, she watched through the window as the fields raced past, the dark uneven hedgerows set against the pale violet sky. Taking out her phone, she set her alarm to wake her before reaching London and, with her head resting against the glass, drifted into sleep, too tired for dreams.

4

Birdsong had woken Penny early, as it often did. She sat at the kitchen table, a steaming cup of black coffee in front of her. The table was unusually tidy, having been cleared up the night before. Penny would have happily left plates piled up by the sink but after Martha's sudden departure the evening had taken a slightly peculiar turn. Liv and Jimmy had insisted on doing the washing up; Penny suspected they offered simply to avoid sitting around the table any longer than they had to without being impolite.

Much as she wanted to like her middle daughter's future husband, Penny thought him verging on unbearable. The first few times they'd met him he'd obviously been on best behaviour but the last couple of occasions he'd been quite different. Loud and obnoxious were just two words that sprang to mind. Whatever Iris saw in him, Penny didn't.

She tugged at the cord on her dressing gown, pulling it tighter, then picked up her cup and sat back in the big chair at the end of the table, blowing gently before taking a sip. She looked at the cut flowers in the vase in the middle of the table, taking in their shapes and colours. Her eyes then fell to the notepad in front of it, a note written on the page. She must have missed it earlier, her eyesight not being what it used to be. Reaching for the glasses that hung around her neck, she popped them on. As she read Martha's familiar looped handwriting, Penny's heart sank.

She knew her daughter had gone; she'd heard the crunch of gravel as Martha headed down the track earlier that morning. But much as Penny had wanted to go after her, she knew Martha would want to leave without a fuss. She'd clearly underestimated just how upsetting her youngest daughter was finding all this – and there was still the wedding to get through. Penny reread the note, taking comfort in the fact that Martha promised she'd be back the following weekend at least. She traced Martha's name with her finger, thinking of her sweet girl. Penny sometimes felt sad that Martha had grown up almost entirely separately from her sisters given the age gap. And it wasn't as if, being the youngest, she'd been spoilt. Quite the opposite. She'd had to work hard to keep up with her sisters, constantly trying to show them that she could run as fast, climb as high, swim as far.

A memory came to the surface, one Penny usually kept buried deep. She closed her eyes, suddenly back on the beach on that unbearably hot summer's day thirty years ago. The three sisters had gone to swim, Liv and Iris under strict instructions to look after their sister in the water as Penny read her book on the beach. She'd watched them splashing in the water, shrieking with delight, going back to her book every few moments to read another page.

At first, Penny thought the shrieks were a game but then suddenly the older two were screaming Martha's name. Penny sprang to her feet; Martha was nowhere to be seen. She raced towards the water, stripping off her clothes as she ran. She remembered diving under repeatedly, forcing her eyes to open, desperately looking for Martha. The water was opaque; Penny could barely see her hand in front of her face. Again and again, she took a breath and swam underwater, arms sweeping around her in a frenzied manner. Then she heard Iris shout Martha's name.

Penny swam over to where Iris was treading water and reached down, bringing Martha to the surface. Her daughter's eyes were closed, her body limp. Penny swam on her back to the shore holding Martha out of the water and then carried her to the sand, laying her down gently. She'd never forget the way Martha's dark hair fanned out on the ground around her head, like seaweed. Penny sent Liv and Iris back to the house, telling them to call for an ambulance. Left on the beach, she set about breathing life back into her daughter. After what felt like forever, Martha choked, coughing up the water in her lungs. Penny held her daughter against her chest, talking to her softly until she heard the siren coming down the track to the beach. To this day, the sound was a constant reminder she nearly lost Martha to the sea.

For a while after, Penny barely let her youngest daughter out of her sight, wanting to know where she was at all times. And she felt such terrible guilt for having taken her eyes off them, no matter how many times John tried to reassure her that it was simply an accident. Although Martha was young, barely seven at the time, she'd been a confident swimmer. She'd swum out to keep up with her sisters, got out of her depth and gone under. It wasn't a place known for rip tides, but they'd never known exactly what had happened.

Penny always said the universe had been on their side that day. If it hadn't been for Iris spotting bubbles on the surface and Martha's bright red costume in the water, Penny might not have been able to save her. Just a few weeks later, Martha was back in the water as if nothing had happened. She was determined not to be left out, wanting to swim with her sisters. But from that day on she never went far from the shore, certainly not beyond where her feet could safely touch the bottom.

Martha remembered little of that day; her sisters carried the memory in far more detail having observed their mother on the beach, bent close over Martha's body. In fact, Martha would make them retell the tale growing up, delighted to be at the centre of the story for once. As the years passed, the drama was all but forgotten by the girls. Not by Penny, though. Knowing Martha was hurting in any way was almost unbearable. But this time she knew couldn't save her daughter. This time, Martha had to do it herself.

* * *

London looked beautiful bathed in Saturday morning sunshine as Martha walked across the common from the Tube station back to her flat. People were out and about, enjoying the chance to get outside. Groups played football, the muted cheers reaching her over the sound of the traffic. Parents called out names of children as they raced past her. She walked along the path, dragging her small suitcase behind her. It kept tipping slightly to one side thanks to a dodgy wheel. Hitching her handbag up higher onto her shoulder, she picked up the case by its handle and continued, resolving to get it fixed properly. Just then her phone rang. She plonked herself onto a bench at the side of the path and rifled in her jacket pocket for her phone. She looked at the screen, Joanie's face lighting it up.

'Hey,' said Martha.

'How come you're back in London?'

'How d'you know? Are you spying on me?' Martha smiled.

'Find My.'

'Have we still got that on?'

'Obviously.' Joanie laughed. They'd added each other months ago when they'd been struggling to find cabs home having both missed the last trains. 'To be honest I only went on to stalk Ian, who still hasn't figured out I can track his every move.'

'You really shouldn't do that. Nothing good will come of it.' Martha sighed.

Joanie and Ian had been together for six months or so before it all came to a predictably horrible end, given that Ian was Joanie's boss at school. And married, even though Joanie had insisted on pointing out that he was separated whenever Martha had dared to bring it up.

'I know, but he's so stupid, I don't think he even knows I can see where he is. Which, by the way, you won't believe when I tell you.'

Martha gasped. 'Where?'

'What road does Mr Bentley live in again? The one just off Honeywell Road, isn't it?'

'Shut up! He's not...'

'I think he is.'

'With Mr Bentley?'

'No, with his wife. At least I think so, although knowing Ian it could be either. Or both. He wasn't exactly fussy.'

'Joanie, please. It's too early for me to be thinking about that. Can we change the subject?'

'Sure. Let's start with why you're back here. I thought you'd gone for the weekend.'

Martha shut her eyes for a moment, the memory of the previous evening coming back to her. 'Are you free for lunch? I really can't face hanging around in the flat all day.' Martha didn't want to start explaining what had happened with Toby on the phone. She wanted to say it once, then hope that whatever she should do next would magically present itself. The problem was, she didn't know what to do. Talking it through with Joanie might just help.

'Well, as you know, I am a very busy woman but, luckily for you, I've had lots of last-minute cancellations today according to my PA so, yes, I do have a window for you. What time and where?'

Martha laughed. 'Thank you for fitting me in. Shall we say one o'clock at The Queen's Head?'

'Does that mean you're going to make me walk up Primrose Hill afterwards?'

'Yes, it does, and don't sound like that, you always say how much you love it when we get to the top.'

'Do I?'

'Yes, you do. See you at one-ish.'

Martha made her way back to her flat, dumped her bag just inside the door and immediately turned round and headed back to the Tube. Putting her earphones back in, she turned up the volume, hoping the sound of Fleetwood Mac would keep the image of a sweaty-faced Toby lurching towards her out of her head. For now, at least.

* * *

Iris wandered into the kitchen wearing her old silk kimono she'd had since she was a teenager. It still lived on the back of her old bedroom door. Her father sat at the other end of the table reading the paper. 'Morning. Where's Mum?'

'In the garden, I should think. She's gone into overdrive trying to get all these flowers ready for next weekend.'

Iris went to the range behind her father and picked up the old tin kettle, shaking it gently. She let out a heavy sigh.

'Sorry, I had the last of the coffee. I didn't make another as I wasn't sure what time you two might surface.'

'It's fine, I'll make it.' She filled the kettle with water, then busied herself washing out the dregs from the now empty cafetiere. 'Dad, did Martha say anything to you before she left?'

John put the paper down. 'No, I missed her. She left very early this morning.'

'Do you know why?'

He shifted in his seat. 'I don't, no.' He paused. 'But I think it's probably not that easy for her, you know, after what happened.'

Iris sat down next to him. Much as Iris wanted to tell her father what had happened the night before, Toby had persuaded her not to say anything for now, not least to spare Martha's blushes given she was obviously already in a state about the wedding. She sighed heavily. 'I know it was a horrible time for her but it's my turn now. And she shouldn't be trying to ruin it.'

John looked at his daughter, putting his hand over hers. 'I'm sure she's not planning on ruining anything. She'll be here next weekend and it'll all be fine. Stop worrying.'

'What will be fine?' Penny walked in from the back door, shaking off her gardening boots onto the back doorstep and slipping on her shoes before joining them at the table. 'Ooh, are you making more coffee, Iris?'

Iris got up. 'Yes, I was just doing it. I was saying to Dad I think it's a bit unfair that Martha's making a thing about this.'

'You needn't worry. Look,' she said, gesturing to the notebook on the table. 'She says she'll be back next weekend.'

Iris peered at the note. 'I hope she's not all dramatic about it.'

John folded up his paper and put it on the table. 'How about you go and get Toby up? Then we can walk down to the church together. What time are you meeting the vicar?'

Iris glanced at the clock on the kitchen wall. 'Eleven o'clock.

Loads of time. I'll just take a coffee up; he needs a bit of time to get going in the morning.' She picked up two steaming cups and headed out of the kitchen, her kimono swishing behind her as she went.

* * *

Martha found a table outside and sat waiting for Joanie, two glasses of pale rosé and a separate glass filled with ice in front of her. She dropped a couple of cubes into her own glass and took a sip of the cool, crisp liquid. Putting her sunglasses on, she turned to face the sun, enjoying the warmth against her skin.

'Ooh, how delicious!' Joanie cried, hugging Martha from behind. 'Don't get up but I am going to have to get crisps. We can't have pink wine and not have snacks, it's just not how the world works.'

Martha watched as her friend disappeared into the pub, waving as she went. She took another sip of her wine and absent-mindedly checked her phone. Two missed calls from her mother but nothing on her answerphone, so she quickly tapped out a message to let her know she was back in London and would call later. She put her phone back in her pocket and looked out across Primrose Hill in front of her, watching pockets of people as they walked through the park. How many of them were carrying a secret? she wondered. She shuddered at the thought of Toby, his lips stained with red wine, the smell of stale cigarettes on his breath.

Joanie dropped three crisp packets on the table, all different colours. 'One is never enough.' She grinned at Martha as she climbed over the bench and took a seat opposite her. 'Cheers.' They clinked glasses. 'Right, Ms Martha. What the hell is going on with you?'

Martha looked surprised. 'What do you mean?'

'You go all the way to Devon, only to race back the next morning. Was it really that bad?' Joanie fixed Martha with her huge brown eyes.

Martha took a deep breath. 'Something happened and I don't know what to do about it.'

Joanie opened a packet of crisps and put it between them, taking a handful. 'I'm listening.'

'It's Toby.' Martha looked at her glass, unable to meet Joanie's gaze. 'He... er, I'm not really sure, nothing happened but he definitely tried to kiss me last night.'

'What the...? Where?'

'In my parents' garden.'

'Where was Iris?'

'Inside.'

'Does she know?'

Martha shook her head. 'No, she doesn't know. I went to bed straight after and got out of there as soon as I could.'

'Okay, that's heavy,' said Joanie, lighting up one of her thin cigarettes and blowing a straight line of smoke up into the air.

'Yes, you're telling me. What do I do? Tell Iris?'

'What do you mean what do you do? You must tell Iris!' Joanie laughed. 'Were you seriously thinking you weren't going to tell her?'

'I don't know, I thought... if I tell her what happened, it's going to all kick off.'

'Too bloody right, it will. She has to know, Martha. Before she marries him.'

'But it's his word against mine and I know he'll deny it. In fact, he already has. I heard him talking to her in the garden afterwards. He said I went for him.'

'This is your sister you're talking about; she's not going to believe him over you surely?'

Martha shrugged. 'I think she already does.' The fact that her sister had been so quick to believe Toby had upset Martha far more than she was letting on. Did Iris really think she was capable of doing such an awful thing? Every time she thought about it, her stomach turned.

'Yes, but when you tell her the truth she'll be livid with him, not you. You didn't do anything wrong!' Joanie's voice rose.

'Maybe. But I can't help but feel she'll think I'm doing this because, you know...' Martha tailed off, not wanting to say what she was thinking out loud.

Joanie knew exactly what she was thinking. 'Listen to me. You have done nothing wrong. He made a pass at you. And if you'd said yes, he would have been straight in there. Iris must know.'

'But with everything that happened—'

Joanie interrupted her friend. 'No, I'm not having that. I know what you're going to say, and I won't have it.'

'What?'

'That she'll think you're trying to break up her wedding because you didn't have one blah blah blah.'

Martha couldn't help but smile at Joanie's delivery.

'Bull. Shit.' With each syllable Joanie slapped the table with the palm of her hand for emphasis. 'That's not how it is and if Iris really thinks that then... well, I don't know what to say. Sorry, I know she's your sister and I know you love her but that's not right. Tell her.'

Martha picked up her wine and took a long sip. She nodded. 'I know. I knew as soon as it happened. But this is going to lead to the almightiest shit show and, given my track record at wrecking weddings...'

'You didn't wreck a wedding. You saved yourself and Joe from what would have been – and sorry for saying this out loud but you know I love you – a marriage of convenience. One day he will thank you for it. Well, maybe not to your face but he really will.'

Martha thought for a moment, picked up a crisp. 'I know you're right. But I honestly don't know how I'm going to tell her.'

'Face to face.'

'I thought you might say that.' Martha could picture Iris' face, tears streaming, screaming at her. They'd had enough fights over the years for Martha to be wary of her sister's temper. 'And I have to do it sooner rather than later.'

'Correct.'

'She's coming back to London tomorrow night.'

'Then you need to message her and tell her you need to see her. On her own.'

Martha felt sick at the thought.

'Do it tomorrow when they're on their way back up, otherwise she'll ring, and you'll have to tell her on the phone.' Joanie sighed and reached across for Martha's hand. 'I'm so sorry but this isn't your fault, Martha. You do realise that, don't you?'

Martha nodded. 'I do.'

'Right, then you don't need to worry about it. And imagine if you don't say anything and then she does marry him and then he does it to you again, or to someone else. You are basically doing womanhood a massive favour by calling him out. In fact, you deserve a bloody medal.' Joanie stubbed her cigarette out furiously. 'Now, do we really have to walk up that bloody hill or shall we have another glass of wine and a bowl of chips in the sunshine first?'

Martha laughed. 'Okay, but you're not getting out of it.'

'Might as well get a bottle, no?' Joanie winked and headed to the bar.

5

Martha woke up and opened one eye, barely able to lift her head from the pillow. 'Ow.' She reached for her phone on the bedside table, the light from the screen physically hurting her eyes. Dropping it to the floor, she carefully moved her body until she was sitting up, then made her way tentatively to the sitting room. Rubbing her head, she took in the scene in front of her; empty silver food containers covered the coffee table along with two wine-stained glasses and an empty bottle.

Slowly, she pieced the night before back together. The walk to the top of Primrose Hill. The tinned cocktails Joanie had produced at the top as they sat on a bench overlooking the London skyline. The bus ride into town, trying and failing to contain their laughter on the bus. The noisy pub in Soho. The dingy tequila bar with a pink chihuahua painted on the door complete with sticky dance floor inside. More cocktails, more laughing, then dancing.

A man with blue eyes and longish dark hair. Very handsome. Said he was an artist. Saying goodbye to Joanie. The cab ride home. Kissing the man in the cab. Coming up the stairs to her flat, barely able to contain themselves. Having sex on the sofa. Feeling hungry. Ordering takeaway. Arguing over who was going to pay. Laughing. More sex. Eating takeaway. Talking until it was light outside. Heading to bed and falling asleep.

So, did that mean he was still here? Martha's skin felt clammy. This was not like her at all. She walked quietly back towards the bedroom, hardly daring to look in the bed. There, with his back to her, was a body of a man. She could see his broad shoulders moving gently as he breathed, took in his mop of dark hair. For a moment she wondered if she should leave, not being able to face having a conversation with someone she'd only just met, despite what they'd done the night before.

'Shit.' Martha hadn't meant to say it out loud.

The body in the bed stirred. He turned over and looked at her.

She stood there, completely naked, stock-still like a deer caught in headlights.

'Wow.' The body spoke again.

'Um, hello.' Martha waved and attempted to smile, despite the wave of nausea currently threatening to engulf her.

'It's Art, remember?' The voice was gravelly with sleep.

Martha nodded. 'Yes, art. You're an artist.'

'Sorry?'

'An artist, I remember you telling me last night.'

The body shifted himself until he was sitting up in bed. He smiled back at her. 'Almost. My name's Art. I'm the barman from last night.'

Martha felt her cheeks flush red. 'Yes, exactly.' Suddenly the room seemed to tilt. She steadied herself with a hand on the doorframe. Then she felt her mouth fill with saliva. 'I'm really sorry, I think I'm going to...' Martha turned and raced to the bathroom, holding her hand over her mouth.

A few moments later, she stood in the bathroom looking at her reflection in the mirror. She looked awful; tired and drawn with bloodshot eyes. The dark circles underneath were almost comical. Not wanting to face anyone, let alone Art, she locked the door and turned on the shower. Standing under the jets, she wished she could wash away the feeling of shame. Not just about the relative stranger in her bed but about everything she felt in that moment. Maybe sleeping with strangers was the way forward? That way she wouldn't hurt anyone. Perhaps that was the price she had to pay for ruining Joe's life and now probably her sister's too. She closed her eyes and turned up the heat until the water was almost unbearably hot. She then turned it to cold, the jets feeling like a thousand needles on her skin.

She heard a knock at the door. 'Is everything okay? Can I get you anything?'

She turned off the shower and wrapped a towel around her body. 'No, don't worry. I'm fine,' she lied, shaking her head at the irony. She was a long way from fine.

'I can go and get us some breakfast if you like?' He spoke from the other side of the door, his voice disarmingly kind.

'No, please don't worry. You go. I'm not feeling great, to be honest.'

'Really? Food might help. Coffee definitely will.'

Martha screwed up her eyes. She knew he was only trying to be nice, but she wanted him gone. 'No, honestly. I've got to be somewhere soon, anyway.' Another lie.

There was a pause. 'I'll let myself out, then.'

'Thank you.' A fresh wave of guilt washed over her. 'It was... nice meeting you.' She cringed at her own words. She waited in the bathroom for a few moments until she heard the door of her flat shut softly. She put on her dressing gown, wrapped her hair in a towel and went out into the sitting room. She started clearing the debris, moving as slowly as she could so as not to disturb the rocks residing in her head.

Just then her phone started ringing. Martha went into the bedroom and picked it up from the floor where she'd dropped it earlier. It was Joanie.

'Please don't say anything about the barman,' pleaded Martha.

'Are you kidding? He was gorgeous! A little young, maybe, but my God, Martha, you are such a dark horse sometimes. I didn't even see you talking to him!'

Martha sat down on the bed. 'There wasn't much conversation, to be honest.'

'Is he still there?'

'No, he's gone, thank goodness. I'm so embarrassed.'

'Why?'

'Joanie, you are very sweet but he was at least a good ten years younger than me. I don't know why I thought a one-night stand was the answer.'

'Tequila?' Joanie laughed.

'Yes, probably. But that's it. No more. I swear I'm done.'

'Don't be ridiculous, Martha. You've just got The Fear. Trust me, he won't be feeling it. In fact, he's probably skipping down the street as we speak. Probably can't believe his luck. Have you messaged Iris yet?'

'Not yet. I'll do it later.'

'Remember what we talked about. You're literally saving Iris by doing this. She might not see it like that straight away but, trust me, she will in time.'

'I'm not so sure.' Martha sighed. The thought of having to tell her sister what had happened with Toby made her physically shiver. Her phone screen told her that she had a call from home.

'I've got to go, Joanie. I think Mum's calling. I'll let you know how it goes, I promise.'

'Speak later.'

'Bye.' Martha took a deep breath and accepted the other call. 'Hi, Mum.'

'It's Iris, actually.'

'Iris! Hi!' Her sister's voice took Martha by complete surprise. She tried to sound calm. 'Is everything okay?'

'You tell me, Martha.' Iris' voice was flat.

'Oh God, what has he told you?' The words were out before Martha could stop them.

'That you tried to kiss him the other night, Martha, that's what he's told me.'

'Iris, that's not what happened... I would never do something like that.'

'I know your wedding didn't work out, but you don't have to ruin mine.' Iris was seething.

'Please, I—'

'Shut up, Martha. I don't want to hear your pathetic excuses. You just couldn't bear seeing me happy, so you had to go and ruin it, didn't you? Had to have what's mine because you can't find your own.'

Martha felt hot tears sting her eyes. 'Iris, I promise you it wasn't like that. He tried to kiss me, not the other way round.'

'Well, you would say that, wouldn't you?' Iris let out a small sarcastic laugh.

Martha tried desperately to keep her voice steady. 'It's the truth, Iris. He was quite drunk.'

'Don't patronise me, please.'

'I'm sorry. I was going to tell you later today, when you got back to London. I was going to come and tell you face to face because... I think you should know before you marry someone like that.'

Iris gasped. 'I can't believe you're trying to turn this on me. Actually, I can. Classic Martha move, deflecting all the blame.'

'You don't have to believe me but I'm telling you the truth. And I think the reason he's told you is because he knew I'd tell you sooner or later. He couldn't keep it from you.'

'Why are you talking like you know him better than me?'

'I don't. But I know he was drunk and perhaps he thought he would get away with it. Why would I make something like this up?'

'So that you're not the only sister who's a total disaster!' Iris screamed.

Martha felt winded. She wiped the tears away from her face. 'I'm not a disaster,' she whispered.

'Grow up, Martha. That's exactly what you are.' With that, the line went dead.

Martha looked about her bedroom. How had everything gone so horribly wrong? One minute she'd been at home with her family, determined to put on a brave face for the sake of her sister. The next, that same sister had cut her off with words sharp as knives over something that simply wasn't true. But it was her word against his. Iris had clearly picked her side and there was nothing more Martha could do about it.

Just then she saw a scribbled note by her bedside, in writing she didn't recognise.

Tequila on me next time. Art x

Martha ripped up the note. 'There won't be a next time,' she whispered, dropping the torn pieces of paper onto the floor.

* * *

The rest of the day was a write-off. Martha stayed in her dressing gown with the blinds in the sitting room pulled down, drank endless cups of sweet tea and eventually, when the pounding in her head started to subside, opened her laptop, sat on the sofa and tried to work. With a potential new job on the horizon, Martha knew she had to go into school the next day well prepared for the end-of-year staff meeting. But as much as she tried to put the drama of the last two days out of her head, she couldn't stop thinking about that moment in the garden. That face, that smell. She wished she could wipe it from her memory.

Martha replied to a worried message from her mother saying she'd call later even though she had no intention of doing so. The thought of having to face her family after what had happened was almost too much to bear. What if her parents now believed Toby too? She imagined them all discussing her behaviour over breakfast that morning, shaking their heads in pity as Toby recounted how he had been taken by total surprise by the sister clearly desperate to sabotage Iris' happiness. Maybe leaving so quickly made her look more like the guilty party? It was an awful, sorry mess and she couldn't see a way out of it.

It was late in the afternoon when Martha, still in her dressing gown, one eye on her laptop screen watching an episode of a suitably dark Netflix drama series, heard her doorbell go. She went to the door and pressed the button.

'Hello?'

'It's me, Liv.'

'Liv! What are you doing here? Come on up.'

Martha took a quick look at her reflection in the mirror, wiping at her blotchy face with her free hand. She opened the door to her flat and waited at the top of the stairs for her sister to appear.

'How come you're here?' Martha repeated the question.

'I was worried about you.' Liv hugged her hard.

'Me? Why?' Martha braced herself, not knowing what Liv might say next.

'Let me come in and put this bag down.' Liv gestured to the holdall in her hand.

'Are you here for the night? There's only a sofa...'

'I know, it's fine. I'll just stay tonight if that's all right with you. I'll go back first thing tomorrow.'

Martha went into the kitchen. 'Do you want a cup of tea?'

'Yes, please.' Liv followed her into the tiny galley kitchen. 'Actually, you nearly had Dad here, but I insisted on coming.'

Martha's heart lurched. 'What did Iris tell you?'

Liv tugged at her sleeves, pulling them over her hands. 'The wedding's been called off.'

'Why?' Martha kept her gaze on the kettle.

'She said that Toby tried to kiss you on Friday night.'

'She said that?'

'Is that not what happened?'

Martha sighed with relief. 'Yes, it's exactly what happened. It's just that I told her that and she said she didn't believe me. I spoke to her this morning. She said that Toby had said I tried to kiss him, and I swear, Liv, on my life I didn't.'

'Martha, I know you didn't. And I think, really, deep down Iris knew that too.'

'So then why did she say to me that she didn't believe me?'

Liv sighed. 'She obviously didn't want to have to believe you.'

'Did she tell you she called?'

'Mum heard her on the phone to you. She rang me and asked me to go over and talk to Iris. She'd tried but Iris was having none of it. There was an almighty row between Iris and Toby in the garden, apparently. Mum said she and Dad stayed in the kitchen until it was all over, then Toby stormed back in and told them Iris had called the wedding off. He went and got his stuff and disappeared off in his car. I got there about half an hour after he'd left to find Iris in floods of tears at the kitchen table. She told us she'd spoken to you. She was in a terrible state, to be honest. I think she just feels so humiliated. I'm afraid you took the brunt of it.'

'What made her change her mind?'

'I think she knows you wouldn't do something like that but she obviously didn't want to believe Toby would either.' Liv put her hand on Martha's arm. 'She said those things because if she could blame you, then she wouldn't have to face the truth.'

'She said I'd done it so that I wasn't the only one who was a disaster.'

'I know, she told me. But I promise you, she was just angry. After Toby left, we walked down to the beach. She said when Toby told her she knew deep down you wouldn't have instigated anything, she just didn't want to admit it. Anyway, all that matters now is that we help her get through this next bit because it's not going to be easy.'

'I can't tell you how relieved I am, Liv. Honestly, I thought she'd never want to speak to me again. I've been imagining you all practically disowning me.'

'As if.' Liv gently wiped away the tears of relief now rolling down Martha's face.

'And she's really decided to call off the wedding?'

Liv laughed. 'Yes, it's most definitely off. And if Toby has any sense he won't even try and persuade her otherwise. Anyway, if he comes anywhere near the house, I reckon Dad will throttle him. I don't think we'll be mentioning his name in Dad's company again.'

'Were you surprised? At Toby, I mean. Like, I know you weren't a huge fan.'

'Was it that obvious?'

'Jimmy more or less said so.'

'What did you think of him?'

'The first few times, he was all right. Not exactly Iris' usual type and a bit – actually, really quite – annoying but at least he seemed to make her happy.' Martha shivered at the thought of him. 'I think she's had a lucky escape. If it wasn't me, I'm sure it would have been someone else in time.'

'I'm pretty sure Iris realises that too.'

'What's she going to do now?'

'Stay down with Mum and Dad this week. She'd taken the week off anyway so she's just going to work from there. But she does want you to come down next weekend.'

'Really?'

'Obviously there's no wedding but she still wants us all to have a party.'

'Are you serious?'

'That's what she wants. We thought it was a crazy idea at first, but she said she doesn't want the weekend to go to waste. She's going to tell people that the wedding is cancelled but then ask them if they'd still like to come.'

Martha laughed. 'Only Iris could turn this situation into an excuse for a party. Is she really going to be all right with me?'

Liv took Martha's hands in hers. 'What's happened can't be undone. But none of this is your fault.'

Martha smiled. 'That's what Joanie said.'

'Does she know?'

'About Toby? Yes, I told her. When I came up yesterday, I honestly didn't know what to do with myself. I felt so awful, Liv. That's why I left so early. I knew I'd have to tell her what had happened. I was going to when she came back to London but then she called.'

'Sometimes life has a funny way of sorting itself out. Maybe getting dressed up and having a great big party will do us all some good. Talking of which, are you really going to stay in your dressing gown all day or do you think you might be up for putting some clothes on? I fancy going to get something to eat. Can we go to that lovely wine bar on the corner? The one that does all the little snacks.'

Martha winced. 'I might not manage any wine but I'm definitely up for snacks.'

'Come on, hair of the dog will do you good.'

'Hair of the dog might make me throw up.'

'Go and get dressed. My treat.' Liv shooed Martha away.

'I won't be long.' Martha turned back to her sister. 'Thank you, Liv. I really appreciate you coming.'

'Bar the family drama, it's practically a mini break for me.' Liv winked at her little sister. 'Now go, otherwise it'll get too late.'

6

Martha couldn't help but feel nervous as she boarded the train on her way down to her parents' house that Saturday morning. She'd immersed herself in work but every night she'd found herself lying awake until the early hours, the memory of Toby lunging at her in the garden and the disappointment in Iris' voice playing over and over in her mind.

Martha's father was there to collect her from the station as usual, greeting her with his customary hug. 'How was your trip?'

'Fine, thanks. Dad, is Iris really okay with me?'

Her father chuckled. 'She seems pretty good. To be honest, I think you might have done her a favour.'

Martha looked at him. 'I'm just sorry it happened like it did.'

Iris was indeed pretty good, greeting Martha on the drive with open arms when they arrived at the house.

'How are you?' Martha whispered to Iris, hugging her back.

Iris took Martha by the shoulders. 'I'm good. And I'm sorry I was such a cow, I really am. But I was so angry. Not with you, with him. With myself. I really thought he was different. Turns out he was one in a long line of arseholes. One day I'll get better at picking them, hopefully. But for now, I want to celebrate my near miss.'

'Hello, darling.' Martha's mother appeared at the back door.

'Hi, Mum.' Martha kissed her mother on the cheek.

'Iris, show Martha what you've done with the tent. I'll bring some drinks down in a minute.'

Iris grabbed Martha's hand, her eyes sparkling. 'Come and see.'

They walked around the corner of the house to the front lawn and there, in the middle, was a huge red and white striped tent.

'It's like a circus!' Martha couldn't believe what she was seeing.

'Exactly.' Iris laughed. 'I started to call everyone to cancel everything. The marquee, caterers. And we weren't going to get our deposit back on the marquee so I asked them if we could change it. The last thing I wanted was a bloody wedding marquee, so I changed it to this one instead. The caterers were brilliant. They took pity on me, I think, so they're only charging a small cancellation fee. Instead, everyone's bringing a plate of something, and Jimmy and a few of the boys are doing a big barbecue.'

'Are the band still coming?'

'Of course! No way was I going to cancel them. And I've got a karaoke machine for later. If I'm not going to have a wedding, I'll just have a bloody great party instead. And you just wait until you see my dress.' Iris grinned.

Martha looked at her, one eyebrow raised. 'You're not wearing your wedding dress, are you?'

'Yes, but I've customised it.'

'You what?' As far as Martha knew, Iris had never threaded a needle in her life.

'Turns out vodka really gets the creative juices flowing. It's a bit shorter than it was. Oh, and a different colour. But you'll have to wait until later to see it. Some traditions are worth keeping, even if it isn't a husband that I'm keeping the dress a secret from.' She laughed.

'What did you tell everyone?'

'I just emailed and said the wedding was off but there would still be a party and that I'd love everyone to come if they can. The only ones not coming are anyone to do with Toby, obviously.'

'So did he tell his family?'

'No idea, I haven't spoken to him. And to be honest, I don't intend to either. Not if I can help it. I hope I never lay eyes on him again.' Iris' voice hardened. 'Unless it's so I can punch him in the face, obviously.'

Martha swallowed. She'd been dreading asking her next question but she knew she had to. 'Have you told people what happened? I'd understand if you wanted to, by way of explanation, I mean.'

Iris took Martha's hand. 'Listen, no one needs to know what happened. I can just say I changed my mind.'

'But won't you want people to know?'

'Martha, I really don't care what people think. Honestly, I'm happy just saying I've changed my mind.' Her sister shrugged her shoulders. 'The awful thing is how many friends emailed me back saying they were quite relieved I wasn't marrying him after all. Turns out most of them were pretty underwhelmed by him anyway. I've made them all promise to tell me next time.' Iris winked at her sister.

Martha laughed. 'I love that you're already talking about next time.' She thought of Joe, briefly.

Iris squeezed her sister's hands. 'I'm sure this garden will host a family wedding one day. Just not today.'

'Anyone hungry?' Their father appeared behind them holding

a tray laden with food. 'Go up to the house, your mother's got another tray with plates. And bring down a bottle of white from the fridge, will you?'

Martha walked back to the house with Iris, happy to be home.

* * *

As it turned out, the party was an excellent idea. Iris had instructed everyone to come wearing clothes absolutely not fit for a wedding and soon the lawn in front of the circus tent was covered with people dressed in all manner of outfits, not a muted pastel among them. Once everyone was gathered, glass in hand, Jimmy made an announcement.

'Everyone, if I can just have your attention for a moment, can we please give a warm welcome to the person we're here to cele-brate?' He looked beyond the crowd into the circus tent. The sound of ABBA's 'Dancing Queen' filled the air. Everyone looked around and there, in the tent, standing where the band was set up to play, stood Iris, microphone in hand, wearing the most beau-tiful red silk dress slashed to the thigh on one side, her long blonde hair loose and tousled. Her voice rang out across the lawn, belting out the opening lines.

The crowd joined in and soon the tent was filled with people, dancing and singing at the tops of their voices. Martha watched as Iris sang her heart out, her own almost bursting with pride. If there was one thing about Iris, she always got stuck in. Martha wished she could live as fearlessly.

The evening went in a glorious flash, full of music and laugh-ter, food and litres of local cider. Iris made a speech that had everyone in stitches and the room was full of love. The party continued long into the night and later, well after midnight, Martha found herself sitting on a hay bale around a firepit in the garden, alone for a moment. She watched the flames in front of her. A few of their old family friends had asked her about Joe that evening, wondering if they kept in touch. Martha couldn't help but feel a little sad, not to mention awkward, as she told them that no, they didn't. Apparently, he and his wife had a baby now, a little girl. 'Ah, that's lovely. I'm happy for them,' she'd said to one particular old neighbour of theirs – and she'd meant it. But it was still hard to know that and feel completely comfortable with it, wondering if she'd really done the right thing. Perhaps she and Joe would have been fine after all. They might now be happily married with kids. She shook her head and took a sip from her paper cup.

'Penny for them?'

Martha turned to see Iris standing, still in her dress but now barefoot, her heavily kohled eye make-up smeared after hours spent on the dance floor. Iris lifted a leg over the hay bale and sat down beside Martha.

'Oh, Iris, what an amazing evening. There's no way I could have done what you've done tonight.'

She thought for a moment, then took the cup from Martha and had a sip, handing it back afterwards.

'That's because you don't dare let go.'

Martha looked at her sister. 'What do you mean?'

'Just that. I love you, Martha, so much. But ever since Joe I think you've been punishing yourself. Or rather, protecting yourself. I get that you don't want to get hurt, or maybe it's that you don't want to hurt anyone else, but love is messy and sometimes you've just got to pile in.'

'I piled in with a barman last weekend, actually.' Martha made a face, making Iris laugh.

'That's not piling in. That's playing at something you know isn't ever going to be anything else. I know you haven't asked me for an opinion but I'm going to give it to you anyway. As someone who's definitely had too much to drink at her own not-wedding party I'm allowed to say anything, I reckon.'

'Okay but please don't be too brutal.' Martha shifted on the hay bale, taking another slug.

'I won't. And I wouldn't be saying it if I didn't think it needed to be said. But since Joe you just play everything so safe. You work, you come down here, but you need to get back out there. Have a change of scene.' Iris paused for a moment. She looked at the fire, then back at her sister. 'There's something I do want you to do for me. Well, it's for you but it would make me really happy.'

'Go on.' Martha wasn't sure she was going to like whatever she was about to hear.

'I'd booked a honeymoon. To Greece, actually. I'd hoped Toby might book something but when it became clear he had no plans, I went ahead and found the house, nothing fancy but right on the beach, in Paxos. Booked it for two weeks. Got flights and everything. Anyway, I went to cancel it all when I was trying to sort out this mess and I just couldn't bring myself to. I'd thought that after this party I might just feel like getting on a plane and disappearing to a remote island for a bit and not seeing anyone. But I know myself well enough to know that's my ultimate nightmare. Having to spend a whole day by myself is bad enough, let alone two weeks. I need company. So, then I thought I'd make you come with me, by way of paying me back for Toby kissing you.'

'But that...' Martha interrupted.

Iris laughed. 'I know, I'm teasing. Seriously though, I thought we could go together. I know you're off now for the summer. Mum said you were planning on staying here for a couple of weeks so don't pretend you've got plans.'

'You and me, go together? I'd absolutely love that!' Martha

couldn't believe it. A holiday with her sister! It was just what she needed.

'Well, not exactly.' Iris looked at Martha. 'The thing is, I'd love to come but, honestly, I think my best policy for now is to hang here for a few days, help clear up and then get back to London.' She glanced over her shoulder into the still heaving tent, everyone dancing with their arms in the air. 'I think hanging out in the place I was supposed to be on honeymoon might just tip me over the edge. I'd rather get back to work and possibly numb the pain with alcohol in familiar surroundings for a while longer if that's all right with you.'

Martha couldn't hide the panic in her voice. 'You mean you want me to go on my own?'

Iris nodded. 'Yes, I want you to go on your own because, darling Martha, I think it would be good for you.'

'And you know I can't say no because I feel so guilty even if you say it wasn't my fault.'

'Exactly.' Iris laughed.

'God, you're annoying.'

Iris shook her head, her long hair moving gently as she did. She touched Martha's face with her hand. 'I think it'll do you the world of good. And it's a free holiday, for God's sake!'

Martha tried to think of reasons to say no but knew her protests would fall on deaf ears. 'Leaving when?'

'Monday morning.'

'Have you told Mum and Dad?'

'They think it's a brilliant idea.'

Martha nodded slowly, realising this had all been discussed without her. 'So, you all think I'm hiding.'

Iris smiled gently. 'It's my idea and I really want you to say yes.'

Martha knew there was only one thing she could do. She took Iris' hands in hers. 'Okay, then. My answer is yes.'

'It's not a bloody proposal, Martha.'

'Very funny.' Martha gave Iris a playful shove.

Iris stood up and held out her hand. 'Good, that's sorted then. Time to join the party.'

* * *

'You're doing what?'

Martha had to hold her phone away from her ear to stop Joanie's voice perforating her eardrum. 'I said I'm going to Greece.'

'When?'

'Tomorrow.'

'Who with?'

'On my own.'

'Is this Martha I'm speaking to? I mean, you never go away.'

'Well, I'm not paying for it, which kind of swayed me a little.'

'Even so, this is last minute. And you don't do last minute, remember?'

'Iris asked me to go in her place. At first, I thought she meant with her, but she says I have to do it on my own.'

'Why?'

'I'll explain when I see you but basically she thinks it'll do me good.'

'Are you sure you don't need a companion? I think you need a companion. Preferably a funny fellow teacher who's already got the time off.'

'I'd love you to come more than anything, Joanie, but Iris has stipulated the conditions and I don't feel I can go against them.'

'You still feel guilty, don't you? We talked about this. It's not—'

'I know, it's not my fault. Everyone keeps telling me that. But whatever, I've said yes. I'm packing now.' She looked down at the bed in her flat, currently covered in a sorry selection of vaguely summery clothes from her cupboard.

'Where is it again?'

'Paxos.'

'Where's that?'

'An island just off Corfu. I fly there and then get a ferry to the island. Iris has given me all the details. I just need to get myself there.' She looked around the room, trying not to stare too long at the ever-increasing patch of damp on the wall in the corner. 'I'm actually really looking forward to it.'

'I bet. Promise to message when you get there? And at least one beach shot.'

'I promise.'

'Love you.'

'Love you too.'

Martha picked up an old sarong bought on a holiday many years ago and stuffed it into her small suitcase. Thinking about it, she hadn't been abroad for years. Maybe it really was time to broaden her horizons. She threw in her cut-off denim shorts along with a few old T-shirts and a pair of cotton trousers. Rummaging through her knicker drawer she found the top half of her bikini but not the bottoms. They were nowhere to be seen of course. Just when she needed them. Half an hour later, she was packed and ready, the fridge emptied, and a note written to pop under her opposite neighbours' door so they knew she was away.

That night she hardly slept, worrying about her alarm not going off. A small knot formed in her stomach. This would be the first time she'd travelled abroad on her own, ever. And to an unfamiliar place. How hard could it be? Martha rechecked her passport to make sure it was in date, despite having done so at least twice already, then closed her eyes tightly and told herself it would be an adventure. She was a woman in her thirties with no reason to be afraid of the unknown. And yet she was.

The alarm went off at five o'clock, not that she was asleep. She gulped down a cup of tea, showered and had one last look round the flat before she left, closing the door gently behind her. Climbing into the taxi in the grey morning light, Martha suddenly felt a jolt in her stomach. But this time it wasn't a knot. It was more like butterflies. Could that be excitement she was feeling?

'Heathrow, please.'

As she sped away from London out on the M4, one of the few cars to be leaving the city at this time in the morning, she rested her head against the window watching as the empty concrete offices and brightly lit billboards flashed by.

'Where you headed?' the taxi driver called over his shoulder.

Martha smiled. 'Greece.'

'Me and the wife went there on our honeymoon. It was years ago now, but it was lovely.'

'Actually, this was supposed to be a honeymoon.'

The taxi driver looked at her in the mirror, his eyebrows raised. 'Yours?'

'My sister's, but now I'm going in her place. Long story.'

'Oh, I didn't mean to...'

Martha smiled. 'No, it's fine, really. Shame to waste it.'

'And you'll have a lovely time.'

'I know, but I've never been on holiday on my own before.'

'You get used to it after a while, don't you worry.'

'Oh, I thought you said you were married.'

'Widowed. She died four years ago now.'

Martha's face fell. 'I'm so sorry.'

'Thank you for saying so. Cancer. But I still go back to the places we went as a couple; it helps me remember the times we had together if I'm honest. I didn't want to go anywhere familiar at first. Even being in the house was almost unbearable. But now I find it quite nice, reassuring even. The thing is, you realise you can't stop because they're not here any more. In fact, it's even more reason to carry on, but you need to let go a bit to do that.'

'I think you're right.' She remembered her sister's words in that moment shared by the fire a few days before. It had been such a happy night, despite the circumstances leading up to it. Now it was up to Martha to make this a not-honeymoon to remember.

7

As she stepped from the plane, the heat hit Martha with force. She stood in the queue for passport control, looking around at her travelling companions. A few older couples, already sporting deep tans, stood silently with an air of having done this a thousand times before. Children ran excitedly under the temporary ropes, ignoring the pleas of their knackered-looking parents to not mess about. Younger couples stood close together speaking to each other quietly with smiles on their faces and knowing looks in their eyes. Martha scanned the hands of the women to see if she could spot any telltale wedding manicures belonging to newly-weds. She counted three, then stopped.

Eventually she got to the front of the queue. The man behind the glass silently took her passport without acknowledging her cheery attempt at hello in Greek. He scanned the page with her photo on it, looking from it to her and back to the photo for what felt like an unnecessary number of times. He slowly flicked through the pages.

Eventually he looked up and spoke. 'You not been anywhere?' He gestured to her passport. 'No stamps?'

Martha tried her best not to look affronted. 'Erm, no. I think yours will be my first.' She gave him what she hoped was a winning smile.

He duly stamped her passport with a flourish and handed it back to her, stony-faced. 'Have a nice stay.'

She took it before he changed his mind, and headed for the exit, past the crowds now forming around the luggage carousel. At least her micro summer wardrobe meant her bag had been so small, she'd been able to carry it onto the plane.

Looking up, Martha searched for a sign for the taxi rank, having been instructed by Iris to get a taxi to the ferry terminal. She joined the queue for the waiting taxis and was soon heading towards the port. She smiled as she looked out of the window, taking in the sights as they whizzed through the streets. It was all much easier than she'd imagined.

However, when she got to the ferry terminal, it was chaos. There were crowds of people waiting outside the building, taxis queueing to get near the doors. One couple tried to climb into hers before she'd even paid.

'What's going on?' Martha asked her driver.

He called out of his window to another driver and they exchanged a few sentences. Then he turned to look at Martha in the back seat. 'No ferry.'

'Why?' Martha felt the panic rising.

Her driver shrugged. 'Maybe the wind is too strong. You need to ask in there.' He pointed towards the ferry terminal.

'Okay. Thank you.' She handed him some notes to cover the fare and got out of the taxi. Despite the bright blue sky and searing heat, the wind was indeed much stronger than when she'd left the airport. She weaved her way through the crowds into the building and joined the queue snaking back from the information desk.

In front of her, she overheard an English accent, an older couple. Tapping the woman on the shoulder, she smiled. 'Excuse me, have they cancelled the next ferry?'

'Not just the next ferry, love.' The woman rolled her eyes.

'They've cancelled them for the rest of the day,' added her companion.

'Do you know when they'll start again?'

The man shrugged. 'You never really know.'

'So, what do we do?' Martha tried her best to sound calm, despite feeling quite the opposite.

The woman laughed. 'We do what we always do here. We go and have a drink and hope there'll be another one soon.'

Martha forced a small laugh. 'Right, thank you.'

Just then, the man sitting behind the information desk closed the window. The queue surged sideways to merge with another even longer queue and soon people were jostling for space. Martha tried to join but was bundled to the side by a family of tourists, all seemingly more familiar at navigating chaotic Greek ferry terminals.

She glanced back to see the couple she'd spoken to in the first queue making their way out of the building. 'Excuse me?' She went after them, calling until they stopped and turned. 'Sorry to chase you but were you serious, when you said before there's nothing to do other than wait?'

The woman nodded. 'I'm afraid so, love. You can check the website but it's better to just stay nearby and keep checking with them in there in our experience.'

'But there's no one to check with!' Martha shrugged.

'I know,' said the man. 'But you'll know when there's a ferry ready. Just stay nearby and get in that queue as quick as you can. It's a bit of a bunfight.'

'Thank you.' She managed a smile but, really, she was starting to panic. It had all been going so well. Too well, she thought. Martha fished for her phone in her pocket and started to look up ferries but the website was impossible to navigate. She started to feel light-headed. Looking for somewhere to sit, she spied a low wall and went to perch on it. Holding her head in her hands, she suddenly felt very much on her own.

Racking her brains for what to do next and failing to come up with options, she finally decided to take the couple's advice and walked to a small bar on the waterfront at the quieter end of the harbour. Taking a seat at an empty table, she rested her feet on her bag and looked out across the bay. Maybe she should take this as a sign and cut her losses, turn back and head home to familiar surroundings. Now she thought about it, this whole idea had been rather forced upon her. She was only doing this to make Iris happy, after all. A waiter appeared at the table and asked what she would like. In English, which annoyed her. Clearly, she didn't look like a mysterious, sophisticated traveller of the world.

'A beer, please.'

He nodded and went to fetch it.

She looked at the website for the ferries but it still showed everything as running as normal. For all she knew, she might be stuck here for hours. The temptation to call the whole thing off and book a flight home instead was gathering momentum. The waiter soon returned with an enormous beer in a tall glass. If she'd realised it was going to be so big, she would have asked for a small one. Still, it was too late to do anything about it, so Martha simply smiled and said thank you.

For a while, she sat at the table gazing out at the view. The wind was still strong but the air warm. The fishing boats in front of her bobbed on the now slightly choppy water as if vying for her attention. Scooters zipped along the road behind her. She looked out across to the mainland on the other side. It was vast, the mountains much higher than she'd expected. The blue-black sea between moved urgently, white horses forming on the tops of the waves.

As she sat and sipped her drink, Martha tried to relax, give in to the uncertainty. But much as she wished she were a go-with-the-flow kind of person, that simply wasn't her. This whole situation was making her feel very on edge. She reached for her book, hoping to get lost in the pages of her old, dog-eared paperback copy of *Jane Eyre*, a story she'd read countless times before but still an absolute favourite.

She was a few pages in, about to meet Mr Rochester for the first time, when she suddenly realised someone was speaking to her. Martha looked up to the waiter standing there. 'Would you like something to eat?'

She smiled at him. 'I won't, thank you. I'm hoping to catch a ferry soon.'

'No more ferries today.' The waiter shook his head.

Martha's face fell. 'Really?' This was turning into the holiday from hell and she hadn't even made it to the island.

The waiter smiled. 'You haven't been here before, have you?'

'No, I haven't. Any ideas how I get to Paxos, then?'

'My cousin might be able to take you. He has a taxi boat. He's on his way back from there now but he'll be going back over later. The wind will drop soon. He lives on the island. You want me to call him and ask?'

Martha couldn't believe her luck. There must be a catch. 'How much does he charge?' She braced herself for an astronomical figure. He told her but she couldn't do the conversion in her head. 'Hang on.' She reached for her phone and put the amount into the search bar. It was more than double the cost of the ferry, but she figured she'd save herself an unexpected night's accommodation in Corfu, not to mention the cost of a panic-bought flight home. 'How long does it take?'

'An hour. It's much quicker than the ferry.'

Martha decided to take a chance. 'Would you mind asking him?'

The waiter nodded. 'I call him now. Wait a moment.' He walked towards the harbour wall and Martha watched as he spoke quickly on his mobile phone. He was smiling as he walked back. 'No problem, he will take you.' He looked at his watch. 'You will be there around 6 p.m. You need to pay cash, is that okay?'

'Yes, of course, I'll go and get some out now. So, what time do we leave?'

'My cousin says in about an hour. Be ready then.'

Martha put a note on the table for the beer. 'Thank you so much.' She made her way back to the ferry terminal, having spotted a cash machine there earlier. It was now almost deserted, the ticket office closed, the information desk still firmly shut. She headed for the cash machine and started to rummage through her bag for her wallet. She busied herself punching numbers into the machine, making sure she hit the right buttons. She took her money and folded it carefully, tucking it into her purse. Just then she noticed a boy sitting quietly on the floor underneath a large clock that hung on the wall just above the entrance. He was looking around, rather desperately, she thought. Walking towards him, she realised from the look on his face he was trying hard not to cry. His cheeks were flushed red, his dark curly hair hanging almost to his eyes. She guessed he must be no more than ten years old.

Martha went over to the boy. 'Hi, I'm Martha. Are you okay?' She gave him what she hoped was a reassuring smile.

He looked at the floor, then met her gaze. He tried to smile but tears gave him away. 'I'm supposed to be getting the ferry home and I can't reach my grandmother to tell her there isn't one. She normally comes to meet me but she's not here. I called her but now my battery has died.' He held up his phone in his hand.

'Where are you trying to get to?'

'Paxos. I live there. Not all the time but in the summer I do. With my father too. I came over this morning to see my best friend who used to live there but he moved back here last year. When his mum dropped me off, the ferries were running but I missed it. I thought I'd get the next one but then everything was suddenly cancelled.'

Martha knelt beside him. 'I have a boat coming to take me to Paxos in about an hour. How about we ring your grandmother from my phone and you can tell her I can bring you across?'

'But I don't know her number.'

'Is there anyone else we can try?'

'I don't know my dad's number off by heart either.' The boy thought about it for a moment. 'We could call the restaurant near my grandmother's shop. They can tell her I'm coming.'

'What's it called?'

'It's called Connie's, after my grandmother. It's in Loggos.'

'Is it hers?'

'It used to be. Not now but they still call it that.'

'Will there be someone there, do you think?'

'I think so.'

Martha looked it up on her phone and showed the boy the image on her screen. 'Is it that one?'

He nodded.

Martha hit the number on the screen. 'I hope they speak English. My Greek isn't quite yet up to speed. Do you speak it?'

'My grandmother usually speaks to me in Greek so I have to.'

Martha listened as the phone started ringing. 'I don't know your name.'

'Milo.'

Martha smiled. 'Hi, Milo.' She held up a finger as someone answered the phone. 'Hello? I'm hoping you might speak English. You do? Oh, thank goodness. Anyway, sorry... my name is Martha and I'm here with Milo in Corfu. He says he's trying to get to Paxos but the ferries have all been cancelled. I have a boat taxi coming in about an hour and I can bring him with me, but I just want to check that's okay with his grandmother. Her name is Connie. Do you know Connie?'

Martha nodded whilst listening to the response then held the phone out to Milo, smiling with relief. 'Apparently your grandmother is there. You can speak to her, explain what's happened.'

He took the phone from her and waited for a moment. When he heard his grandmother's familiar voice, his eyes lit up. 'Yia-yia! It's me.'

Martha could hear the woman speaking fast to the boy. She sounded ecstatic. Milo listened to her, then started speaking to her in Greek. Martha couldn't understand a word he was saying but his face was a picture of relief. After a few minutes, he held the phone out to Martha.

'She'd like to speak to you.'

'Oh, okay.' She took the phone. 'Hello, this is Martha.'

'I cannot thank you enough.' The voice was soft now, calm. 'He's done this trip back to the mainland before on his own to see friends, but this has never happened. Are you coming on a boat taxi from the Old Town?'

'Yes, we'll get to Gaios around six o'clock, apparently.'

'I'll be there to meet you. What's the name of your driver?'

'I'm not sure, actually.' Martha suddenly felt foolish. She really should have taken a name at least.

'Don't worry, I can find out. Just make sure you don't pay more than twice the fare of the ferry.'

Martha grimaced. 'Too late, I've agreed a price.'

'Then I will pay half.'

'Oh no, you don't have to. I'd be coming anyway.'

'Please, I insist.'

Martha knew from the sound of her voice there was no point in arguing. 'That's very kind. Thank you. We'll see you there.' She turned to Milo. 'I don't know about you but I'm thinking ice cream. What do you think?'

He nodded enthusiastically.

'Favourite flavour?'

He didn't even have to think about it. 'Chocolate.'

'Me too. Let's go.'

* * *

Connie walked back from the restaurant and took her usual seat in the shade just outside her shop, overlooking the small harbour, the deep blue sea lolling gently in front of her. The sun was still high in the sky. She watched as the tourist boats came back in from their days out, depositing tourists as red as freshly cooked lobsters on the dock. She waved at the various captains as they saw their small boats in, a few coming over to chat.

Connie had lived in the village of Loggos as a little girl but had moved to the mainland in her late teens, determined to forge a career for herself away from the tiny island her parents had called home. Spotted in Athens by a photographer, she'd worked as a fashion model for a few years. The money was good, but before long, she found herself wanting to help make the clothes rather than just get paid to wear them. Against the odds, she managed to talk her way into a job working as an assistant in a Paris fashion house, sourcing fabrics and working as a cutter for some of the smartest names in couture. But every summer, without fail, she'd always returned to run a small shop in her childhood village, selling scarves, bags, jewellery and a small selection of clothes, most of them made by her. Over the years she developed a devout following, with people coming from all over the island to the shop, like a pilgrimage of sorts. They left with their newly purchased bags stuffed with sarongs, their tanned arms sporting new bangles and bracelets. Now retired and living on the island full time, she always swore each summer would be her last for the shop but when it came to it, she couldn't quite bring herself to close it permanently.

Connie loved the island, particularly the corner that she called home. Over the years she'd seen the place change as it became more popular as a tourist destination, but this little village had never lost its heart. There was the original bakery she'd gone to as a child. The village grocery shop still had the same feel as it had always done, with seemingly no order to where things were placed on the shelves and a selection of fresh produce to rival any in nearby towns. Bars and restaurants lined the front and, even though the road didn't look like a road, everyone drove their cars along the front as if it were a boulevard. When the bus went through the village, the look of total bemusement on the faces of the onlooking tourists never failed to amuse the locals.

Then there was Milo, her beloved grandson. She'd spent every summer with him since he was two years old. He barely knew life without her, and she certainly couldn't imagine hers without him. From the moment she'd first laid eyes on him, that tiny baby with his beautiful olive skin and enormous blue eyes that seemed to look right through her, she felt as though her whole life made sense. She was a mother herself, but her relationship with her daughter had not been straightforward. When it came to Milo, she'd sworn to herself she would not make the same mistakes she'd made with her own child all those years ago. Milo was her second chance and she was determined to get it right.

Connie sipped the last of her water and glanced at her watch. It was nearly time to head to Gaios to meet Milo and the mysterious Englishwoman off the boat. Closing up the shop, she grabbed her keys and made her way along the front to her car at the other end. She called out to the owners of the taverna as she passed, telling them she'd be back in time to eat with Milo. They both clapped their hands with joy at the mention of the boy.

Soon she was winding back down towards the coast road that would take her to the port, unable to keep the smile from her face. She parked and wandered down to the harbour, past the larger ferries and up towards the smaller boats. A couple of phone calls was all it had taken for one of her skipper friends from Loggos to find out who was bringing them over, and sure enough, as she sat on a bench watching for theirs to come in, she soon spotted the small navy hull of the *Island Express*, as it was optimistically called. She saw Milo and the woman she presumed must be Martha, and as soon as he saw her he called out, the wind carrying his greeting to her.

'Hello, darling!' Connie stood and walked towards the harbour wall. She smiled at the skipper and he nodded back, throwing her a line from the bow. She knew from the sheepish look on his face that he'd overcharged Martha.

Milo jumped ashore and ran to his grandmother.

'My lovely Milo, what happened?' said Connie, before kissing the top of his head and ruffling his mop of hair. She looked up and saw the Englishwoman climbing unsteadily onto the harbour wall. She had on a loose black linen sundress and battered trainers, an old green bag slung over her shoulder and a bright orange cotton scarf shielding her shoulders from the sun. Connie liked the look of her instantly, taking in the woman's bright eyes and dark hair.

Martha extended her hand. 'Hello, I'm Martha.'

Connie smiled and reached out her arms, her silver bangles jingling as she took Martha into an unexpected hug. 'I can't thank you enough.'

Martha smiled. Connie was obviously mortified. 'It was just lucky, really. I went to get some money out to pay for this and there he was. I couldn't leave him. Calling you seemed like the best idea.'

'Yia-yia, can Martha come and eat with us tonight? Please?'

'Oh no, Milo, you go and spend time with your grandmother tonight. I'm here for the next two weeks, I'm sure I will be coming to Loggos to eat at some point so we can meet up then, yes?'

Connie turned to Martha, fixing her with her pale green eyes. 'Where are you staying?' Her skin was deeply tanned with lines crossing her face.

'At a house not far from Kipos Beach. I can't remember the name of it for the life of me, but I do have an address somewhere.' Martha started rifling through her bag.

'Can we give you a lift there, then? We go right past the road down to Kipos on our way home.' Connie looked at her hopefully. 'Please, it's the least we can do.'

'As long as you are sure, that would be amazing. I'd planned to get the bus.'

Connie laughed. 'Then we're definitely giving you a lift! You could be here for a while, otherwise.'

'Thank you.' Martha was grateful. After hours of travelling, she was looking forward to getting to her house and standing under a cool shower.

'I assume you've paid him already?' Connie gestured to the skipper.

Martha nodded. 'I have but, honestly, you don't need to pay half. I was coming anyway.'

'Well, knowing how much you've probably had to pay, I insist. You can tell me in the car.'

The skipper sloped off into the cabin, avoiding Connie's gaze.

Connie looked at Martha's bag. 'Is that all you've got with you?'

Martha shrugged. 'I figured I'd travel light.'

Connie laughed. 'The best way. Welcome to Paxos.'

8

Connie's old yellow Beetle made surprisingly light work of the steep hills and sharp turns as they headed north towards the top of the island. The only air-conditioning was having the windows down; Martha couldn't remember the last time she'd been so hot. It was almost half past six in the evening but the heat was still heavy. The island was rugged, the steep hills carpeted with trees. Martha marvelled at the size of the olive trees they passed, their trunks as thick as the old oak trees in the garden back home. Black nets lay on the ground, ready for the olive harvest, and every now and again the green was broken up by the brightest of flowers with bougainvillea and hibiscus in abundance. As changes of scene went, this took some beating. Martha felt as if she'd arrived in paradise.

Milo and Connie pointed out places to Martha as they passed through small hilltop villages, from restaurants to shops to the nearest pharmacy on the island. Martha didn't have the heart to tell them that she planned to get to the house and not leave it unless absolutely necessary. She didn't drive anyway. Having failed her driving test five times as a teenager, she'd long ago decided that driving wasn't for her. But she was still embarrassed to admit it, so was relieved that Connie hadn't even asked.

'It's this little turning here, quite easy to miss, but just remember it's the one opposite the rust-red gates with number fourteen painted on it.'

Connie turned the car into the narrow road and they slowly made their way down towards what Martha presumed was the coast, bumping along and swerving to avoid the enormous potholes.

Martha spotted a sign to Kipos Beach. 'Is that the footpath down?'

'The footpath? No, it's the road.' Connie laughed.

'Ah, right.' She looked at the directions Iris had sent her on her phone. 'It says just go to the end of this lane until you get to a white gate and that's it.'

Moments later they came to the end of the track and in front of them was a large white gate, just as Iris had said. Before Martha could offer, Milo had jumped out of the car and walked up to open it. It took both hands for him to heave the metal rod keeping the gate closed out of the ground.

Martha watched as Milo moved it back to reveal an olive-tree-lined drive leading down to a small garden. Beyond, Martha caught a glimpse of turquoise. Until that moment, she hadn't dared believe the house would really be a stone's throw from the beach.

As Connie edged the car forward and down the drive, the pale stone house came into view on the left, small but perfectly formed with a red tiled roof and shutters painted to match the blue of the sea. She could see a table and chairs shaded by a bamboo roof on the terrace and an empty hammock sat slung between two more olive trees further down the garden. Wild-flowers mingled with the tall grass beyond.

Connie pointed at a small gate at the end of the garden. 'Go through there and you're on the beach. You can only get here by that little road we've come down or by boat so it's one of the quietest spots on the island. It will still be busy at this time of year but if you get there in the early morning or evening, you'll practically have it to yourself.'

Martha tried to take it all in. 'It's so beautiful,' she whispered. She really couldn't quite believe she was here and this slice of island paradise was all hers for the next two weeks.

Milo appeared from the side of the house. 'Martha, come and look through the window. It's so cool!' He'd already done a full recce from the outside, clearly. He grabbed her hand and pulled her from where she stood, taking it all in.

'Milo, I think we leave her here. I'm sure she'll be fine,' said Connie.

'But I want to have a look inside.' He looked at Martha, pleadingly.

'Please do, come and have a look.'

They followed Milo to the door at the back of the house.

Connie looked up at the building. 'This used to be an old farm building. I remember it. Much smarter now.' She winked at Martha.

Martha fished under a pot with some lavender in, again as instructed by Iris, and found the key to the front door. She opened it, revealing a large room with a cool, dark concrete floor and enormous glass sliding doors on the far side looking straight out onto the garden and down to the sea. A countertop ran along two walls with a cooker, sink and open shelves above and, to one side, a small table with four chairs around it. A long sofa sat in the middle of the main room and to the right lay a huge open fireplace stacked with wood. A selection of sizeable oil paintings hung on the wall, mostly landscape pictures.

'These are local,' said Connie, pointing at one of them, then another. 'That's the harbour in our village and that one's painted looking back at the land from the beach.' She squinted at the initials in the corner. 'I don't know who did them but they're very good.'

Martha looked around. 'I can't believe it.' She laughed. 'Thank you, Iris.'

'Who's Iris?' asked Milo.

'Long story.' Martha quickly changed the subject, not wanting to answer any questions on why she was here on her own. At least, not yet. 'I think the bedroom must be down here.' She walked through the large room to the other end and opened the door. An enormous timber four-poster bed took up most of the room with a dressing table on one side. Another door led onto the bathroom, dominated by a huge free-standing roll-top bath.

'There's a shower outside too,' said Milo, appearing just behind her.

Connie joined them. 'So beautiful! I can't believe I didn't know they'd done this with the place. What a well-kept secret.' She looked at Martha and tapped her nose. 'We won't tell anyone, we promise.'

'I definitely can't, given that I don't even know what it's called.'

'It's called The Hideaway,' said Milo.

'How do you know that?' asked Connie.

'That's what it says on the front of the book by the door.' He walked over and picked up a small black visitors' book, turning the front to show them. There, in gold letters, it spelt out the name. 'See?'

'Well, I'm glad I found it.' Martha gazed around her. 'I'm thinking I'm going to be quite happy here for a while.'

'You must promise to walk into the village. It's just over the hill. Tomorrow or the day after, come and find me. I have a shop, it's the last one at the far end of the harbour. You can't miss it. See you then?' Connie fixed her with those bright eyes of hers.

Martha nodded. 'I'll need to come and find food tomorrow; I haven't brought anything with me.'

'What will you eat tonight?'

'Apparently they've left some food for tonight.' Martha opened the fridge. 'There's some milk and butter in here, and some eggs. I'll be fine, honestly. I think I'll just have a quiet night and I'll come and find you tomorrow.' She looked at Milo and smiled. 'I promise.'

He held his little finger up and she hooked hers into his so they could shake on it. 'See you soon.'

'See you soon.' As she waved them off, she knew luck really had been on her side, first with the ferry situation, then meeting Milo and Connie. But for now, she was very happy to be alone. She walked back into the house and crossed the large open living space, enjoying the coolness of the concrete on the soles of her feet. Tipping her clothes out onto the bed, she decided to head straight to the beach. She pulled on her new swimming costume, bought at the airport, and grabbed a sarong, tying it loosely around her waist. She put her sunglasses on her head, took a beach towel from the pile in her room and shoved her feet into her flip-flops. Opening the glass doors, she stepped out into the still warm air and slid them shut behind her.

A path had been cut through the long grass leading straight to the gate Connie had pointed out. She went through it and walked on down a narrow path, barely wide enough to pass another person. The sound of the sea was familiar and strange all at once. It was a different sea, bluer than the familiar green of the sea at home and much calmer, too. She stepped onto the small beach, just a handful of people still on it. She dropped her towel and slipped off her flip-flops, untying her sarong and dropping her sunglasses on top. She hobbled over the stones towards the edge of the sea, the heat and shape of them throwing her off balance. She watched as an older lady walked out, noticing the wetsuit-like shoes on her feet. Martha made a mental note to put a pair on her shopping list for the following morning as she gingerly made her way across the last stony bit before reaching the sand.

She walked into the water, launching herself in as soon as she could, wanting to feel salt water on her skin. She put her head under and came back up for air, instantly revitalised. With one foot, she reached down to check she wasn't out of her depth, just as she always did. Looking back at the shore, she realised the house was almost hidden from view. Higher up on either side sat several much bigger houses, with tree-lined gardens and terraces. But apart from the stragglers on the beach, the bay was all hers. She lay on her back and floated for a while, closing her eyes and listening to the sound of the water around her. Martha let her mind empty for just the briefest moment.

Suddenly, she felt as if her skin were being cut with a thousand razors. She shrieked and grabbed at her shoulder where the pain was coming from. She started swimming towards the shore, trying not to panic. All she knew was that she wanted to get out of that water as fast as she could. She stumbled across the stones, swearing loudly. She sat down heavily on her sarong and tried to look back at her shoulder. It felt as if her skin were melting; the pain was excruciating.

'You've been stung by a jellyfish.'

She turned to look at the face peering down at her. He looked old enough to be her father. Well, not quite, but not far off, she thought. His hair was grey, his skin tanned by the sun. His deep blue eyes practically matched the colour of his crumped linen shirt.

'You think?' She couldn't keep the sarcastic note out of her voice and immediately regretted it. He was clearly trying to help. 'Sorry... can you have a look and see if there's something still there? It feels like there are actual needles in my skin.'

He crouched down next to her and gently turned her other shoulder towards him. 'Definitely a jellyfish sting, I'm afraid. There's been a spate of them here recently. It'll blister but try and leave it alone and it'll go down before long. Some people swear by putting bicarbonate of soda on the sting and scraping it off but I've tried that and it didn't seem to make much difference, to be honest.'

'And I'd been having such a lucky day, too. Guess I had it coming.' Martha sighed and turned to look at him properly for the first time. 'Thank you.' Maybe he wasn't quite as old as she'd first thought.

'Okay, well, I think you'll live. Just maybe put some cream on there tomorrow if it's still sore. Ask in the pharmacy perhaps.'

'Thanks,' said Martha, trying to smile through the stinging feeling, which, she was relieved to notice, was definitely fading.

'No problem.' He stood up and waved a little half-wave, slightly awkwardly, before turning and heading back along the beach.

Martha sat for a while, watching as he left. The pain was slowly subsiding. She lay back gently on the stones, using the towel as a cushion behind her. Listening to the sound of the waves on the shore, she gave in to the tiredness from her early start and closed her eyes.

Martha woke with a start. Her skin was suddenly cold and, sitting up, she realised she must have slept through her first Greek sunset. It was so unlike her to fall asleep like that. She'd never mastered the art of napping and felt as if she was always chasing sleep rather than the other way round. Her body ached all over from lying in one position on the stones and, as she sat up, a dull ache in her shoulder reminded her what had happened. She reached round to touch it, the tips of her fingers lightly brushing the blisters on her skin. Slowly she got up and gathered her things. The beach was now almost completely empty apart from a youngish-looking couple at the far end, sitting closely together and talking, their faces glowing over the flames of a small fire. The dusky light made the water look much darker, more menacing. Martha shivered a little, then took one last look around before heading back up to the house.

Just before she opened the door, Martha went to hang up her swimming costume and still-damp sarong on a line casually strung up between two trees just by the house. As she got closer, she noticed a cool box on the table along with a note propped up against it, held in place with a smooth pebble. She walked over and picked up the note. It was from Connie.

Just a few things to keep you going tonight (we didn't want you going hungry)! Here's my number below, call if you need anything.

Connie x

Martha put the note down, opened the lid of the box and looked inside. On top was a fresh loaf of bread wrapped in a thick tea towel. She took out the first paper box and carefully opened the lid. It was filled with light pink taramasalata. Dipping her finger in, she savoured the tang. The next box was filled equally generously with houmous and after that came a jar of fat green olives. There were a couple of different cheeses carefully wrapped in wax paper and a bottle of perfectly chilled white wine. Martha took it out and turned it to look at the label. She scanned it to see if there was a word she recognised. In black italics was the word *Assyrtiko*. She seemed to remember that might be a grape, having seen something similar in her local wine shop recently, but she had no idea what it might taste like.

She carried the box back to the house and put it on the table, then quickly showered and threw on a light cotton shirt and long trousers to keep the mosquitoes away. Rummaging through the drawers in the kitchen, she found some tealights and took them outside along with a glass of the white wine. The sky was clear of cloud, the stars numerous and impossibly beautiful. Martha piled a plate with bits from all the boxes: the bread and dips, olives, some cheese and a saucer of olive oil. Sitting under the bamboo roof, her current favourite playlist playing from her phone, she took her time over the spread in front of her, savouring all the different flavours in each mouthful. It had been so long since she'd eaten like this, relaxed and unhurried.

Martha mopped up one last bit of dip with her bread, the saltiness of the taramasalata making the cool, crisp white wine taste even more perfect. She then put her feet up and sat back in her chair, the dim light overhead casting just enough for her to read her book. But much as she tried to lose herself in the pages, her mind kept going back to the man on the beach. He'd seemed familiar, somehow. She reached under her shirt and touched her shoulder gently. She remembered the feel of his hands on her skin, goosebumps appearing at the thought of it.

Shaking her head, she laughed quietly to herself. It had been one of the most unexpected days she'd had in a very long time – and she'd enjoyed almost every minute of it. She could have done without the stress of the ferry, but then she wouldn't have met Milo and Connie. Everything happened for a reason, as

Martha's mother often liked to remind her. Thinking once more
of that touch, she decided the jellyfish sting had been worth
it, too.

The sound of drilling reached Martha through her dreams and
her heart sank. She stretched out her limbs, making full use of
the size of the bed, then swung her legs around and padded
across the room to pull back the thin white cotton curtains and
opened the glass door. The noise grew louder. She peered round,
squinting as she did. The sun was up and the light so bright, she
couldn't open her eyes properly. She put on her sunglasses, threw
on a long T-shirt and stepped out into the garden to see where the
noise was coming from. Looking up, she presumed there must be
another house being built further up the hill. She could see the
yellow of what she thought must be a digger and heard men's
voices calling out to each other.

'Great,' she said under her breath. Here she was in the most
beautiful place she'd ever been, and it was right next to a building
site. Well, not right next to it but near enough for the sounds
coming from it to wake her up in the morning. She looked
around, once again taking in the beauty of the garden, the sea just
beyond. Okay, the noise was annoying, but she wasn't going to let
it ruin her slice of paradise. She'd just have to stick in her
earphones and drown it out.

Going back to her room, she left the door open to let in the
fresh air and picked up her phone from the bedside table.
Switching it on, she looked at the time, surprised to see it was
already after nine o'clock in the morning. Having slept on the
beach the previous evening for over an hour, Martha had been
fully expecting a fitful night's sleep. Back home, she was always

awake by six-something, even when she wasn't working. But after nine? This was some kind of record.

The home screen on her phone filled with notifications. One from her mother, one from Joanie and three from Iris. Martha suddenly realised that, with all the events of the previous day, she'd completely forgotten to let anyone know she'd arrived safely. She tapped out a few messages letting everyone know all was well. She took a quick photo of the view and sent it to Joanie, deciding it might be better to call Iris later and let her ask rather than send look-what-you're-missing photos.

She made a cup of tea and took it to the table outside to drink it. The sounds from the building site were at least sporadic, not continuous, and for a while she sat and soaked up the peace whilst sipping her tea. It tasted different, as tea with milk anywhere but home always did. She liked it. In fact, everything felt good. The breeze on her body and the sun on her face. The noise of the insects on the grass, the smell of the flowers around her. It was as if her senses were waking up after a long spell in the dark.

Finishing her tea, she checked around quickly to make sure no one could see before slipping off her T-shirt and putting on her swimming costume straight from the line so she could go for a morning swim. She put on her shoes and grabbed her sarong before making her way down to the beach. It was still relatively quiet with just a few people in the water.

As she stood at the shoreline, watching the waves trickle in and cover her toes, she focused on the feeling of her feet sinking into the sand a little more with each new wave. The water was so clear she was able to check for jellyfish from where she stood and when she was quite sure it was safe, she walked slowly into the water. She took a breath and glided into the sea, opening her eyes once she was under the surface. She looked around her as she swam parallel to the beach from one end of the bay to the other, constantly dipping a leg down to feel for the bottom. Much as she wanted to lie on her back and float as she had done the day before, the previous day's jellyfish experience had put her off. Instead, after swimming the length of the beach and back, she walked back to the shore and sat for a while, drying off in the sun. Martha picked up one of the smooth stones from the beach and held it in her hand, turning it over gently whilst looking out to sea. She sighed happily. The next couple of weeks really promised to be the perfect not-honeymoon.

Just then the drilling started again.

Well, almost perfect.

9

The walk into the village was a little more challenging than Martha had anticipated. It took only about fifteen minutes but by the time she got there, having first done the steep climb to the main road and then back down into Loggos, she was out of breath. She walked along the road, sticking close to the edge as various cars and buses sped by. As she rounded the corner at the top of a hill, the curve of the bay below came into view, buildings lining the road that hugged the shore. There were a few larger boats moored further out and along the harbour wall fishing boats bobbed gently. She watched as tourist boats sped out towards the open water, carrying visitors off for a day of sun and sea.

Martha walked on, a small bag over her shoulder. She stopped to take a few photos further down the hill into the village. The smell of the bakery on the corner practically pulled her in but she decided to have a look around first before buying anything. Besides, her first purchase would have to be a bigger basket to carry everything home. There had been one at the house by the door, but she didn't feel quite right taking it, thinking she could do with one anyway.

She carried on along the narrow road, the sea wall to her right and a line of buildings to her left. There were houses and shops, tavernas and more shops, painted in a variety of different colours that somehow all worked together perfectly, from rustic red to deep blue, pale yellow to orange and the brightest white. The walls outside the bars and tavernas were lined with painted tables and chairs, most of them set but still empty other than a few already hot-looking tourists sipping cold drinks.

A handful of locals sat in the shade on benches outside their shops and restaurants enjoying their morning coffees. A few looked up to glance at her as she passed by, but no one stared. For some reason she'd thought travelling on her own would draw attention, but it wasn't the case, not here anyway. Everyone seemed happy enough doing what they were doing. She carried on along the front and passed a shop with some baskets and hats hanging around the door, and a rail hung with brightly coloured, stripy cotton scarves to one side and, on the other, a rack with flip-flops and shoes. She browsed outside for a moment, then headed for the door. As she did so, a man sitting at a table at the next-door restaurant stood up, leaving his coffee on the table and lit cigarette in the ashtray. He was tanned and bald, with a wide smile. His eyes were hidden by his aviator sunglasses but from the creases around them she could tell he smiled with them too.

'Hello, please go in and have a look.' The man gestured to the door. 'I'll be right here if you need to ask me anything.'

Martha returned the smile. 'Thank you.' She stepped inside, the cool air a relief from the heat of the morning sun outside. She looked around the small shop, shelves from floor to ceiling piled with baskets, bags, scarves and shoes. Before coming in she'd noticed a biggish basket with woven straps hanging on the end of the rail. Having scoured the shelves to see if there was anything she liked better, she went back to the basket outside. Pointing to it, she asked the man how much it was. She smiled broadly, hoping that might make up in some small way for not being able to speak a word of Greek.

'That one is twenty euros. Good price.'

'I'll take it.' She went to get a note out of her wallet and realised to her horror she'd left it back at the house. She felt the prickle of embarrassment, her cheeks reddening on the spot. 'I'm so sorry, I've left my wallet. I'll have to go back.' She cringed as she said the words, thinking it sounded decidedly dodgy.

'It's okay, you take it. Bring the money later.' He took the bag off the rail and handed it to her.

'No, I really can't do that. Honestly, I'll come back.' Martha was mortified, cross with herself at her own stupidity.

He continued to hold it out. 'Take it, please. I think you must be Martha, no?' He lifted his glasses and looked at her, still smiling.

'How do you know?' Martha couldn't hide the surprise from her voice.

The man turned and called over towards the door of the taverna. 'Hey, Milo, look who's here!'

Milo appeared at the door. 'Martha!' He ran over and hugged her.

'Hello, you! What are you doing here?'

'I was helping run boxes to the storeroom. This is Spyros.' Milo pointed at the man. 'He's funny.'

Spyros ruffled Milo's hair. 'And so are you.'

'Come with me to see Yia-yia.' Milo grabbed Martha's hand. 'Did you get the box of food we left you?'

'I did, thank you so much. You didn't have to do that but, honestly, it was so delicious, I'm so glad you did.'

'Let's go.' Milo pointed and started towards his grandmother's shop.

Spyros held out the basket once more. 'Here, take it. Pay me later. Anyway, if you don't you might spend your money in her shop and not mine.' He laughed.

Martha took the basket and put it over her shoulder, slipping her smaller bag inside. 'Thank you, Spyros, I will.'

Martha followed Milo down the street, watching as he waved to people as they passed. Everyone seemed to know him – and now her, judging by the smiles and waves she was getting from the locals too. At the other end of the harbour, on the far side, sat a small shop with a tiny window and a simply painted sign above the door saying 'Connie's' in faded blue paint.

'Is she open yet?' Martha looked at the closed door.

Milo shrugged. 'She opens the shop when she feels like it but she's there now.' He walked in ahead of Martha and called out for his grandmother.

It took a moment for Martha's eyes to adjust from the bright light outside. It was like a tiny dark cave stuffed with treasures. The walls were covered with hanging clothes and beautiful scarves, the shelves below holding rolls of fabric. In the middle of the room was a table covered with baskets full of silver jewellery and beads. A strong scent of earthy incense filled the room. For a moment, Martha couldn't see anyone but Milo. Just then, the jangle of bracelets came from the corner, then Connie's voice. 'Martha, how are you?' Connie stood up from behind an old desk on which sat a sewing machine and a crumpled pile of fabric.

Martha laughed. 'I didn't even see you there! How do you work in here? It's so dark.'

Connie shrugged and smiled. 'Years of practice. Always so bright outside. I like hiding in the dark. I have my little light here—'

she pointed at a small desk lamp '—and that's enough for me.' She pulled her small glasses from her nose and let them hang loose around her neck. 'Now, you got your supper last night, I hope?'

'I did, thank you. I said to Milo, you didn't have to do that but I'm so grateful that you did. I've never had houmous or tara-masalata like it. Or olives, to be honest.'

'And how's the house?' Connie came out from behind the desk and kissed Martha on both cheeks.

'So lovely, I honestly can't believe my luck. First the thing with the ferry, then the food from you last night. There is one thing, though.' Martha pointed at her shoulder. 'I got stung by a jellyfish.'

Milo's eyes widened. 'Oh, cool! Can I see? Has it blistered? You must leave it alone or...'

'Yes, someone told me on the beach. Luckily, they also made me not panic too much about it. I mean, it hurt but they're not poisonous or anything like that.'

Milo pointed to his forearm. 'I got stung here once, it got stuck to my arm. But you can't tell. I didn't even cry.'

'Well, you are obviously far braver than me. I shrieked and cried, the whole lot.'

Connie put a hand on Martha's arm. 'Not a nice way to start your Greek holiday. Now, have you had coffee yet?'

Martha shook her head.

'Before you do anything else, that is what we must do.'

'I'm so sorry but I left my wallet at the house. I can't pay.'

Connie waved a hand. 'Don't worry, I have some money for you. I know how much you paid yesterday. Which was too much, by the way.' She reached into her bag hanging on the back of her chair and took out her purse.

'I know, but I wasn't really in a position to argue.'

'I insist, here.' Connie held out some notes for Martha. 'Take it, please.'

Martha did as she was told. 'Thank you. I already owe money for this.' She pointed at her basket.

'Milo, please can you watch the shop for fifteen minutes? You know where I am if anyone comes.'

Milo nodded and settled in the seat behind the desk. 'See you in a bit.'

As the two women walked back towards the taverna, Connie slipped her arm through Martha's as if they were old friends. There was something about this woman that made Martha feel so comfortable, even though they were practically strangers.

'Does Milo always look after the shop for you so willingly?' Martha couldn't believe how happily he'd agreed to sit and do it.

'It means he gets fifteen minutes in peace on his phone, which is basically his idea of heaven.' Connie laughed. 'He's a good boy but his father doesn't approve of the phone. He doesn't even answer his own phone half the time. But I think if you ban something completely it only makes them want it more. They must learn to self-regulate, don't you think?'

Martha thought about it. In her experience, most of the children she taught were given very few boundaries – and most of them were set by the school, not at home. 'I agree, but it's hard for children when they don't have a good role model in their lives.'

Connie looked at her. 'You're obviously used to children. Are you a teacher?'

Martha laughed. 'Is it that obvious? Yes, I am.'

'I just watched you with Milo. You were so good with him, made him feel at ease yesterday. He's normally very quiet with people he doesn't know, but not with you.'

'You mentioned his father just now. He did too, a few times yesterday. He obviously adores him.'

Connie's face hardened just a little. 'He does – and I do.' She sighed. 'But it's complicated. Here we are.' She walked towards the dark pink taverna next to the shop Martha had been into earlier and gestured to a table at the back, with a bench seat against the wall. 'After you.'

Martha slipped in first and tucked her legs under the table, leaning her back against the wall. They were shaded from the sun, with an uninterrupted view over the bay and across to the mainland far on the other side. Connie ordered two coffees from the waiter, who greeted her with a friendly wave. Martha thought about asking for her usual cappuccino, but decided it was best to go along with whatever Connie had ordered.

Martha waited for a moment. The last thing she wanted to do was pry but at the same time, she was curious. 'So how long is Milo's father here in the summer?'

'He's normally here for about a month. For years he had a small house on the other side of the island, but he's finally decided to move to this side. It was supposed to be finished by now, but of course it's taken longer than expected. So, for this summer at least, I've got them both.' Connie smiled, taking the coffee from the waiter.

Martha wondered how far to go with the questioning. Milo had talked about his father as they'd chatted on the trip over the previous day, but not his mother. And Martha hadn't wanted to ask, despite really wanting to know.

'So, what are your plans whilst you're here?' As if sensing the questions running through Martha's mind, Connie closed the line of questioning down and changed the subject.

Martha laughed. 'It was so last minute I haven't even really thought about it.'

'I didn't ask yesterday. I think I was so relieved to have Milo here. What brings you to Paxos?'

Martha wondered for a second whether to use a cover story but then decided it would be simpler to tell the truth. It wasn't as if Connie knew any of the players in this particular drama. She took a sip of coffee, the strong bitter taste hitting the back of her throat. She choked a little.

'You're not used to Greek coffee?' Connie looked apologetic. 'I'm sorry, I should have warned you. Put a bit of sugar in there.'

Martha picked up the brown sugar cube on her saucer and dropped it in, stirring it as she began to speak. 'This was supposed to be my sister's honeymoon.'

Connie's cup stopped halfway to her mouth. She put it back on the saucer. 'What happened?'

'Long story short, she was about to marry someone. It had all been quite quick but Iris, my sister, is, well... it was a surprise and not a surprise all at the same time. She's quite...'

'Impulsive?'

'Yes, I guess so. All in if you know what I mean. Anyway, I'd met him a few times and to be honest I wasn't a massive fan. Cocky.'

'Cocky?' Connie raised an eyebrow.

Martha laughed. 'Oh no, I don't mean... basically he was just not my type of person. Not that it mattered, it wasn't me getting married. Not this time, anyway. So, my parents asked us all down for a big family dinner the weekend before the wedding. They live in a small village on the south coast.' Martha knew she was padding out the story to avoid saying what happened next. 'We were all there, me, Iris and Toby, that's his name. And my sister Liv and her husband, Jimmy and everything was fine but then I, he...' Martha stopped and shut her eyes for a few seconds. 'He tried to kiss me in the garden. He was drunk.'

Connie nodded. 'Ah, I see. What did you do?'

'That's the awful thing. I had to go back inside and join

everyone and I was just sitting there thinking I've got to say something but I knew it was throwing a hand grenade into the whole situation. To be honest, it was a little more complicated because...' Martha took a breath '...I'd called off my own wedding just a few years before. I know that should have nothing to do with it, but I knew my sister would be angry with me, even though what happened with Toby wasn't my fault, and, well...'

Connie took Martha's hands. 'Go on.'

'The last thing I ever wanted to do was hurt my sister, but I had no choice but to tell her. However – and I think this definitely didn't help – he told her before I did. He must have known I'd have to say something, and it would just be his word against mine, so he got his story in there first. I think Iris wanted to believe him. I'd gone back to London by then, where I live, and she called and said some really awful things.' Before she could stop them, tears fell from Martha's cheeks.

Connie passed her a napkin. 'It's okay, really. You did the right thing.'

Martha sniffed and held her hands to her face. 'Honestly, I felt horrible. Not for me, but about how she felt, that she thought I'd do such a thing. Anyway, Liv – that's my older sister – came to see me and reassure me that everything would be okay. Which it was, in the end. We went down to my parents' house and instead of cancelling the whole wedding Iris wanted to have a huge party instead. Honestly, it was incredible. Iris had cut up and dyed her dress, she looked like a brilliant, crazy queen. I don't know how she did it. She's much stronger than me. When I called my wedding off, I hid from everyone for months. I just couldn't face anyone, felt like I'd let so many people down.'

'What about you?' Connie fixed Martha with her pale eyes.

'What do you mean?'

'You keep talking about how everyone else is, but what about you? How did you feel?'

Martha sat back. 'I felt enormous relief. I just didn't feel like I could say that out loud. It felt too cruel.'

'Well, this I think is the problem. You worry too much about other people and not enough about yourself.'

'But I don't want to be selfish.'

'Putting yourself first sometimes is not selfish, Martha. Trust me, you need to look after yourself. Only then you can look after others.'

Martha twisted her hair around her finger. 'My life is usually quite... uneventful. I know I'm lucky, really.'

Connie slapped the table with her hand. 'There you go again! Stop apologising. A bad thing happened, and you're allowed to feel whatever you want to feel about it. But you did the right thing. You know that don't you?'

Martha sipped her coffee. She shrugged her shoulders. 'The ridiculous thing is I hate drama.'

'Well then, you've come to the right place.' Connie smiled. 'So, Iris asked you to take her place here, I assume?'

Martha nodded. 'At first, she wanted to come too but then she insisted I come alone. She said it would do me good.' Martha looked out across the bay, watching as a tourist boat quietly backed away from its mooring, carrying another small group off for the day. She could hear them chatting and laughing excitedly. 'Funnily enough, she was kind of saying what you're saying. Not to be selfish, exactly. More to just stop making excuses.'

'What's holding you back?' Connie spoke softly.

Martha looked at Connie. Her eyes were kind. Even though she barely knew this person, she felt in that moment she only had one option. It was as if Connie could see into her soul. 'I'm scared.'

'Of what?'

'Of everything. Of being hurt, of hurting someone again. I'm scared to be on my own. I'm scared to be with someone. I don't think...' Martha looked about, as if hoping the words would come to her.

'You don't think what, Martha? Just say what you're thinking.'

'I don't trust myself. I don't trust...' Martha picked up her coffee cup. 'I don't know what I'm trying to say.'

'Life?' said Connie.

'Maybe. I'm sorry, I don't know where all that came from.'

'I thought I told you to stop apologising.'

'You did, sorry... I mean...' Martha laughed. 'I'm not sure what Paxos has done to me but I'm feeling better already.'

10

'You have to be kidding me!' Harry looked at the newly laid concrete, a set of paw prints running right across the middle of the pegged-off area. He'd turned his back for a moment to speak with the foreman and the next minute a dog had appeared from nowhere and gone straight through the middle of it.

Just then, one of the builders came up to Harry. 'Mr Ford, we have a problem.'

This whole house is a problem, Harry thought. 'What is it this time?'

The builder pointed to a trench in the ground, a pipe running alongside that was presumably to go in it. 'We dug here to put in this—' the builder looked at the pipe '—and I think we hit another one.' Harry followed the builder's gaze to a spot in the ground where water was bubbling up through the soil.

'Oh, great. Perfect. So, we've managed to take out next door's water pipe?'

The builder shrugged. 'I think so. We'll turn it off here but that might cut their water next door...'

Harry looked at the builder's crumpled face. 'And you want

me to go and tell them we're turning their water off, is that what you're saying?'

The builder wiped at his forehead, sweat dripping off it. 'I think better for you.'

Harry shrugged. 'Fine, I'll go down there in a minute. How long will we need to turn if off for?'

'A few hours, maybe more?'

Harry didn't have the energy to get cross. Building this house had seemed like such a good idea all those months ago. Now he wished he'd never started. It had just been one problem after another. But he was too far down the road and had no choice but to see it through. Besides, he'd lose money on it if he gave up now. 'How much longer are you here for?' He glanced at his watch. It was almost four o'clock in the afternoon. He knew they'd be gone by now if he weren't here.

The builder shrugged again.

'Just sort that pipe for now and I'll see you tomorrow.' He waved the builder off and went to his car to get his sunglasses. Then he set off down the path to the house below. He didn't know what it was called, just that someone had done it up years ago and now presumably charged a fortune to rent it out to tourists who seemed very happy to stay in what obviously used to be an old animal barn.

Harry had been coming to the island every summer for years and had seen it change a fair bit in that time. He loved it but, in the summer, when it got busy – and nowadays it got really busy – he stayed away from the towns as much as possible. Instead, he holed himself up in his house and wrote. He'd been a reporter for newspapers since his early twenties and now, as a man on the wrong side of fifty as far as newspaper editors were concerned, he wrote articles about anything they wanted him to. It was a far cry from his early career as a political pundit for the newspaper back in Washington DC, but it kept him just about busy enough. He subsidised it by writing historical crime novels under a pseudonym whenever he could, which he did to keep his agent happy more than anything. His agent was forever telling Harry he could be a better writer if only he allowed himself to be, but Harry couldn't quite let the journalism go. It was part of who he was and he liked it that way. His masterpiece would have to wait.

Harry walked on towards the house and opened the gate. He knew someone was there. In fact, he'd planned to go there after he'd finished at the house because the woman staying there had brought Milo over from Corfu the day before. He'd heard all about her from his son the night before, who'd not stopped talking about her since. The problem was, he was now having to tell her that she might not have any running water in her house for a while.

Harry knocked on the door gently but there was no answer, so he walked around the side of the house, calling as he went. The last thing he wanted to do was give her a fright. As he reached the garden, he could see from the shape of the hammock that someone was in it. He called out again. The shape in the hammock didn't move. He went wide so that he could approach whoever it was from the front and not scare her but, as he got closer, he realised she had earphones in. Not only that, from the way her book had fallen onto her bare chest, she might possibly be asleep. Deciding now was not the time to wake her, he turned to leave. Maybe he'd just write her a note and leave it on the door.

'Can I help you?'

He looked back to see a woman's face, flushed, her dark hair piled up on her head. She held the hammock in place just high enough to cover her body, leaving just one shoulder exposed.

Harry concentrated on meeting her gaze. She looked beautiful. And familiar.

'I said can I help you?'

Harry realised it was his turn to speak. 'Yes, sorry, hello. I'm Harry.'

She continued looking at him. 'You helped me on the beach yesterday.'

He smiled. 'So I did! How is the sting?'

She reached back, feeling the spot he'd so gently touched the previous evening. 'It's fine, thank you.'

'And I didn't know it at the time obviously, but you brought my son over yesterday. I've come to say thank you.'

The woman's face broke into a smile. 'Oh, hi, nice to meet you properly. I'm Martha. I would get up but...' Martha reached for her sarong and held it to her chest, then turned to face him again. 'Was I snoring?'

Harry laughed. 'No, you weren't snoring.'

'I'm surprised I wasn't. I had two glasses of wine at lunchtime, and I'm not used to it.'

'All right, maybe just a little but nothing to scare the neighbours. Talking of which...'

'Can I just say, your boy is gorgeous. He was the best travelling companion. We had quite the adventure.'

Harry shifted on his feet. 'Yes, I heard all about your journey last night. I'm just sorry I haven't come to say thank you before now, but I have been... look, I have some kind of annoying news too.'

'Oh, really?' Martha's eyes narrowed.

Harry struggled for his words. What the hell was wrong with him? 'I'm working on the house just up there.' He pointed over his shoulder.

'So, it's you I need to ask not to start drilling first thing in the morning.' She raised an eyebrow. 'Well, at least that makes it easier. I thought I was going to have to try and explain this in Greek.'

'Yes, the thing is, we've hit a bit of a problem. Well, a pipe to be exact, and it might just mean you won't have running water until we manage to fix it.'

'Oh.'

'I'm sorry. We'll get it done as soon as possible.'

Martha thought about it for a moment. 'Well, I'm happy to manage without but I might need your help.'

Harry looked relieved. 'Anything. I certainly owe you.'

'Hang on.' Martha turned her back to Harry and slipped on her T-shirt. She swung round in the hammock and sat with her legs dangling down. 'I've got a bit of food to keep me going tonight, thanks to your... mother-in-law?'

'Connie? Yes, she said she'd dropped some food down for you last night.'

'But I could do with some more bottled water if I haven't got any running water. And I don't have a car.'

'You don't have a car? How are you going to get around?'

'I don't plan to go very far while I'm here. Maybe a trip to Gaios? Connie said I must visit there.' Martha clocked the confused look on his face. 'We had coffee this morning. She's given me a rundown of places I need to visit.'

Harry smiled. 'She is a force.'

'She certainly is. Anyway, if you could do a water run for me, perhaps some more bread and cheese and another bottle of wine, then we'll call it quits. How about it?'

'I think I owe you more than that. You saved the day with Milo, not to mention clearly winning Connie over. I've never known her to have a coffee with a tourist.' Harry chuckled.

'I'm flattered.'

Harry ran his hand through his hair. 'How about I take you to

Gaios, with Milo, tonight? We'll go and get something to eat, my treat. It's the least I can do.'

Martha swung her legs gently. 'I'd love to, thank you.'

'Great!' He looked relieved. 'We'll pick you up at, say, seven? We can have a drink and walk around; we can show you Gaios and go to a restaurant that belongs to a friend of mine. His place is one of my favourites on the island.'

'Sounds good. See you then. I'll wait by the gate.'

'See you then.' He turned and headed back to the car.

Martha waited until she was sure Harry had gone. Then she scrunched up her sarong and screamed into it. When he'd asked her for dinner, her mind had gone straight to all the reasons to say no. But when she'd looked at him waiting for her to speak, something about him had made her want to say yes. Before she could change her mind, she'd blurted out her answer. Now she couldn't quite tell if she was more excited or terrified. Whichever it was, Martha was relieved Milo would be there too. It was just a thank-you dinner from a father and son, she told herself. Nothing to get excited about.

She went straight to her room and took out her entire wardrobe, suddenly wishing she'd packed more than just the pitiful pile of clothes in front of her. But then again, it wasn't a date so why was she worried? Martha took off her T-shirt and placed it on the pile, then went to the bathroom and turned on the taps. Nothing but a slow trickle of water came out. She rolled her eyes and collapsed onto the bed, smiling to herself.

* * *

A few hours later Martha took a quick look at her reflection in the mirror. She'd tried to tame her hair but a late afternoon swim and not being able to wash the salt water out afterwards meant that her hairstyle was best described as full volume. She gave up the fight, pulling it back and forcing it into a ponytail in an effort not to look quite so messy.

Falling asleep in the hammock in part shade also meant one shoulder was a little – okay, looking at it now in the cold light of the house, a lot – pinker than the other. Thankfully she'd plastered the SPF on her face so sported, for her, an impressive glow. Picking through the clothes on the bed, Martha had gone with the smartest option. The old band T-shirt was out and instead she'd chosen a cream linen blouse with tiny red flowers embroidered down the front and a pair of dark blue cotton wide-legged trousers.

Martha hadn't brought any make-up with her, a decision she now slightly regretted. Again, she reminded herself this wasn't a date, just dinner with new friends. She told her reflection to get a grip, grabbed her new basket – which she still owed Spyros for – double-checking she did have her wallet this time, and made for the door.

As she opened the gate, she heard a car bumping its way slowly down the road. An old open-top light blue Land Rover appeared round the corner and Martha silently congratulated herself on tying her hair up. She waved as they came towards her, Milo standing and waving back, holding onto the roll bar with one hand as he did so. She couldn't quite see Harry's face, just the top half of his head, sunglasses firmly in place, his hair ruffled. She quickly reached into her basket and put her sunglasses on too. Watching them come towards her, she felt a wave of something – what was that? – sweep over her. Excitement? Terror? Happiness? Before she could figure it out, the door swung open and Milo motioned for her to get in.

Martha climbed up and said hello to them both. She suddenly felt self-conscious, grateful to have Milo sitting between her and Harry. He waved back, telling Milo to help her with the door, saying there was a knack to closing it. Milo reached across her and slammed it shut. Harry swiftly reversed the car, and they swept back up along the track towards the main road.

'Thank you for doing this,' Martha shouted over the noise of the engine.

'Our pleasure,' said Harry. 'I hope you're hungry. I called ahead and told my friend we're coming. He's got fresh lobster, prawns, mussels, tuna, dorade, bass, whatever you want. His parents still cook in the kitchen during the season, so you'll meet them. They're legendary for their food on the island.'

Milo looked at Martha. 'Do you like seafood?'

'Love it. I live not far from the sea at home. Well, my parents do. I was brought up by the sea. My favourite sandwich in the world is a fresh crab sandwich.'

'My favourite thing is their seafood spaghetti, that's what I'm having,' said Milo. 'What about you, Dad?'

'I'll have whatever Spyros' father tells me to have, then you know you're getting the best thing on the menu.'

'Is everyone called Spyros on this island?' Martha laughed.

'Quite a few,' shouted Harry.

'We call him "Singing Spyros" because he always gets his guitar out after he's finished cooking and sings songs to us. Then there's "Grumpy Spyros" – you met him yesterday.'

Martha looked at Milo quizzically. 'I don't think I've met a grumpy one.'

'You did,' said Milo. 'He runs the shop next to the taverna.'

'He wasn't grumpy, he was lovely!'

Milo laughed. 'That's because he liked you.' Milo puckered his lips as if he were kissing someone.

Harry nudged Milo. 'Hey, don't tease.' He looked across at Martha. 'He's not grumpy really, he just plays up to it sometimes.'

'Well, he was very kind to me.'

She took in the view as they whizzed along the coast road, high above the treetops, looking out across the sea. The sun had started to dip towards the horizon, casting a golden glow beneath the still blue sky above. Sheer white cliffs dropped down to a calm sea below. She almost had to pinch herself. Here she was, speeding along with two people she'd only just met, going out for dinner on an idyllic Greek island.

There had to be a catch. Martha tried to push the thought away and just enjoy the moment. As they wound their way further south, Milo chatted away, pointing out places to Martha as they went. People waved as they passed; everyone seemed to know Harry and Milo. Soon they turned down a sharp road heading down into the town below. Martha caught a glimpse of the sheltered bay dotted with tiny forested islands, the turquoise water glistening.

'Welcome to Gaios,' said Harry. They left the car by the road-side and started walking into town. It was a harbour town, much bigger – and busier – than Loggos with a square lined with buildings, all ochres and pale pastel-coloured walls. Bougainvillea spilled out of windows, trailing lazily down to the ground. The bars and restaurants were starting to fill up. Couples sat with their drinks as children ran through the square clutching ice creams. The air was still warm, the intense heat of the day now cooled by a gentle sea breeze.

Harry walked slightly ahead, Martha and Milo a step behind as they weaved their way through the crowds towards the harbour front. Large motorboats sat with their sterns to the town, the people on board sitting with their evening drinks self-consciously as the crowds snaked past them.

'We're going this way.' Harry reached back and put his hand

gently on Martha's back, guiding her in front of him. 'Milo, you run ahead. Tell Spyros we'll be there in a moment.'

Milo nodded. 'Please can I have a Coke?' He looked hopeful.

'Just one, go on,' said Harry, shooing his son away with mock anger.

Martha watched as Milo made his way through the people ahead, his skinny brown legs moving fast. Harry moved his hand from her back. Martha couldn't help but wish he hadn't. She spoke to break the silence. 'He is a lovely boy. You must be very proud of him.'

Harry smiled but kept his gaze ahead. 'I am. But, Martha, I just wanted a moment with you before we sit down to eat. I feel I should tell you a bit more about us now; I'd rather not say it in front of Milo. I don't know what he told you on your boat journey...'

'He didn't really. I mean, we talked the whole way over and he told me about you and Connie, but I didn't ask any questions about...'

'His mother?'

To Martha's relief, Harry finished her sentence. 'Yes, I didn't ask because he didn't mention her and I didn't want him to feel like he had to explain anything. Which, by the way, you don't have to, either. Unless you're married, in which case that's a different matter.' Martha stopped and looked at him. 'Hang on a minute. Are you married?'

Harry shook his head. 'No, not married.' He started walking again, slowly. 'But I was with Milo's mother for a few years before he was born.'

'Oh.' Martha waited for him to carry on. The crowds were thinning out as they walked on towards the quieter end of the harbour wall. Shops and restaurants were replaced with houses, some derelict yet still grand, almost Venetian in appearance. 'Where is she now?'

'She disappeared just before Milo was two years old. He barely remembers her, sadly.'

Martha swallowed hard. 'I'm so sorry. What was her name?'

'Asya.' It was clearly still painful for Harry to say her name out loud.

'Can I ask what happened?'

There was a brief silence, then Harry spoke softly. 'It happened about eight years ago. Here, on the island.'

Martha stopped again and looked at Harry. 'Oh God, I'm so sorry.'

Harry shrugged. He went to say something, then stopped.

'How... what...?' Martha struggled for words too. 'I'm sorry, I don't know what to say.'

'It's okay, most people don't. It's perhaps why we don't talk about it much. Asya was a very beautiful person, she loved Milo so much. We weren't together when it happened. Well, I was here on the island but we'd...' Harry looked out over the water and sighed. 'Anyway, I've carried on coming every summer with Milo so that he can spend time with his family here. He loves his grandmother, of course.'

'So, he lives with you in... where do you live?' Martha realised she had no idea.

'In the States. Washington.'

'And you get on with Connie?'

He didn't answer straight away. Martha wondered whether she'd gone too far.

'We do, but it's complicated.'

Martha remembered Connie's words when they'd had coffee earlier that day. Things were starting to make sense. 'But you still come?'

'It's important for Milo. He needs to know his roots here. Given he doesn't have a mother, his relationship with Connie is so good for him, I think.'

'When you say she disappeared... what do you mean? Did she leave?'

Harry looked at her. 'She was last seen heading to a beach where she loved to swim, as she often did at sunset. She'd left Milo with Connie. Asya's house was on the other side of the island. I was staying not far away, here for a few weeks to see Milo. It was my first time here since Asya and I had separated.' He looked up and pointed ahead at the restaurant sign. 'It's that one at the end.' He faced Martha. 'That's why I wanted you to know. It's not an easy situation but there it is. If Milo brings it up, at least you know.'

Martha had so many questions, but now clearly wasn't the time to ask them. Milo called over to them from the table where he'd taken a seat. A large man stood beside him, a hand on Milo's shoulder. He looked part man, part bear, with a kind face and eyes that practically disappeared when he smiled.

'Harry, my friend!' The man came towards Harry, his arms out ready to receive a hug.

'Hello, Spyros, good to see you.' They embraced warmly. Beside them, Milo beamed. 'How have you been? Have you had a good summer? I'm sorry we haven't been over before now.'

The man waved Harry's words away. 'Don't come here with your excuses. What is it this time? Too busy writing another bestseller?' He slapped Harry on the shoulder.

Harry looked embarrassed. 'I'd hardly call my books bestsellers, Spyros. But I love your enthusiasm.' He tried to laugh it off.

Martha looked at Harry and raised an eyebrow, making a

mental note to come back to that particular subject. There was no way she was going to let that one go.

'Dad, come and see Papa Spyros!' Milo got up and tugged Harry's arm.

'I'll wait here,' Martha said, taking a seat at the table. 'You go.'

'You're sure? We won't be a moment.' Harry picked up the wine list and gave it to her. 'Choose something from here.' He headed into the restaurant following Spyros and Milo. Martha watched as an older couple sitting quietly at a table at the back got up as Harry approached, hugging him in turn. The old woman's face lit up as she talked to Harry, holding his face in her hands. They chatted animatedly, Milo looking up and laughing as they spoke.

Opening the wine list, Martha scanned it to see if there was anything she recognised. It was all in Greek, and none of the names were familiar. A waiter came over with a jug of water and greeted her warmly. 'Would you like some wine?'

Martha looked at the list again, then looked back at him. 'I don't really know what I'm looking for, I'm so sorry.'

He smiled. 'What sort of thing do you like normally?'

'I had one before.' She scanned the page, hoping to spot it. 'I think it was called Ah-something.'

'Assyrtiko?'

'That's it!' Martha practically sighed with relief. 'Please can we have a small carafe of that?' She resolved to have just a glass, a couple at the most, given she'd already had lunchtime wine. Too much and she might start asking questions again. She didn't want to do that, not with Milo here.

'No problem. And just so you know, everything that's come in today is up there on the board.' He nodded at the sign above the open kitchen. 'Anything with a line through it means that it's all gone already. We only cook what we catch today.'

'Thank you, I'll be quick in that case.' Martha smiled at him and, when he'd gone, turned to look out at the view. Behind them, she could still hear Harry and Milo chatting to Spyros and his parents. The tables around them were still empty but she noticed that every single one was reserved. Lights on the boats out in the bay began to glow as the sky turned a deeper blue, the moon soon to take centre stage.

'Sorry about that.' Harry reappeared and took a seat opposite her, Milo next to him.

'Please don't apologise, they were obviously very happy to see you.' Martha took an olive from the bowl on the table, slick with oil, and popped it into her mouth, the sharp nutty tang hitting her taste buds. She felt her shoulders drop as she sat back in her chair.

The waiter came back with the carafe and poured out two glasses.

'Cheers,' said Milo, holding up his, full to brim with Coke and ice.

Harry and Martha raised theirs. 'Cheers,' they said, in unison. Their eyes met and, for a moment, neither knew what to say next.

'I think the first one was a better colour on you. It looked divine.' Connie sat behind her desk, a small fan blowing wisps of her dark-grey hair that had escaped from the bun at the back of her head.

'You think so?' The woman Connie was speaking to stood in front of the mirror at the back of the shop, turning this way and that. 'I'm not sure...'

In fact, Connie was hoping the woman wouldn't buy either dress because what she really wanted to do was shut up the shop.

It had been a busy evening with a seemingly continuous line of women with varying degrees of sunburn coming in search of something new. As ever, she'd sold armfuls of bracelets, one of her most lucrative lines. She picked them up by the basketful from a supplier on the mainland every winter and sold them with an almost embarrassing mark-up in her shop in the summer. It meant that she didn't have to rely on selling the clothes so much and, given they cost a lot more to make, not to mention the time it took, she was happy enough.

'I'm going to have a think about it, if that's all right?' The woman smiled apologetically.

'Of course, please do,' said Connie. 'You must only buy it if you really love it.'

Standing back to look at her reflection once more, the woman pulled a series of new poses. 'Oh, I just don't know...'

Connie tried not to show her impatience. 'In which case, don't buy it. Really. You must be sure.'

The woman looked quite surprised. 'Oh... okay, then. Maybe you're right.'

Connie came out from behind the desk and started lifting the scarves and bags draped on hooks around the door, gathering them in her arms and moving around the woman, still sizing up her reflection. She put them on a table in the middle of the shop. 'Don't let me rush you but I am closing soon.'

A few minutes later, the woman left empty-handed, thanking Connie as she went. Connie knew from experience that she'd be back. The way the woman had looked at herself in the mirror, Connie knew it wasn't just about the dress. It was never just about the dress. It was having something new on holiday, something that put distance between who you were at home and who you wanted to be in a different setting. And this woman wanted to be the version of her that wore a floaty holiday dress.

Once everything was inside, Connie collected the day's takings and put them in her purse. She locked up the shop and made her way across to the taverna. Normally she'd walk straight home but this evening she needed some company, if anything to take her mind off what was happening elsewhere on the island.

She took a seat at her usual table and waited for someone to join her. There was usually someone ready to sit and talk for a while. Spyros spied her and came to join her, sitting at the end of the table so he could keep an eye on his shop. Some of the tourists were finishing dinner and this was often a lucrative hour for him, the wine having loosened the inhibitions, not to mention the wallets, of potential customers.

'How was your day?' asked Connie, pouring him a glass of red wine from the jug on the table.

Spyros took a sip and smacked his lips. 'Good, thank you. How was yours?'

'Good. You know Harry has taken Martha for dinner this evening?'

Spyros lit a cigarette and looked at her. 'Yes? And what do you think?'

Connie looked out to the sea and sighed. 'I knew it would happen at some point. It's just... well, you know. It makes me think of her, how she'd be if she were here.'

'Of course, it must. I miss her too.' He raised his glass to hers. 'Asya.'

Connie looked at him, her eyes sparkling with tears as she whispered her daughter's name.

11

Martha opened one eye. The light streaming in through the window was enough to wake her. She looked about, relieved to see she was in her own bed. And alone.

Harry had been in her dreams, only.

She turned and lay on her back, feeling the light breeze come in through the open door – she hadn't even closed them last night, so unlike her – and ran through the events of the previous evening in her mind. Dinner had been delicious, the setting just perfect. After they had finished the seemingly never-ending platefuls of food, Singing Spyros had lived up to his name, pulling up a chair by their table and playing a couple of beautiful Greek folk songs on his guitar as Harry, Milo, Martha and all the diners around them had listened and applauded in turn. Martha had loved every second.

After that initial moment of awkwardness, conversation had been surprisingly easy. Martha had asked them all about island life and their life at home in the States, careful to avoid any questions that might involve explaining their situation. She'd wondered whether Harry or Milo might mention Asya at some point, but neither had said her name. She'd known it wasn't her place to do so but she couldn't help but think it strange not hearing it at all.

Martha went to sit up, her head pounding as she moved. Despite her intentions not to have more than a couple of glasses, she suddenly remembered the evening had ended with ouzo. She'd been asked to dance by Spyros' father, which she duly had, as Spyros had played his guitar. It had all felt quite magical. Not so much now.

Martha got up and gingerly made her way across the room to the door, looking out to the sea. There was only one way to shift this hangover and that was with a swim. She walked to the line outside, naked, and took down her bikini, slipping it on. She grabbed a sarong, her new sea shoes purchased the previous evening in Gaios along with a well-worn straw hat from the house and headed for the beach.

It was quiet. The early morning swimmers had obviously been and gone. A few groups were busy setting up their camps for the day, some walking the length of the beach before picking their spot, others heading straight to wherever they were the day before. Martha walked straight into the sea, thankful not to have to pick her way across the stones at last. She dived under the water, the coolness enveloping her body, making her senses seemingly snap back into action. She looked around underwater and came up to the surface, taking a huge gulp of air before disappearing under again. She checked again for jellyfish, now a habit, and once she was satisfied the area was clear she reached one foot to the seafloor then turned and lay on her back. With each swim, she was getting a little braver.

As she floated with her eyes closed, Martha recalled the plan they'd made the night before. According to Harry and Milo, a day's boat trip was enough time to go round the whole island and it was, they said, the best way to see it. Only by boat could you get to the hidden caves and coves. Harry had suggested she book one of the boats via Grumpy Spyros and when she'd agreed to it, Milo had begged to come too. She remembered Harry saying Martha mustn't feel obliged, but she'd said he must come, she'd love the company. Harry then had insisted on sorting it out, telling her to get to the village around ten the following morning. Martha realised she had absolutely no idea what time it was.

She swam back to shore quickly and, after drying herself hurriedly, made her way back up to the house. She ran into her bedroom and picked up her phone. It was flat; she'd obviously forgotten to plug it in before falling asleep. She looked around for her watch, finding it on the dressing table. It was already half past nine.

She quickly packed her straw bag with a dry towel, her sun cream, sunglasses and wallet, threw on her old black sundress over her still damp bikini and headed into the village. When she arrived, Milo was already waiting at the taverna with Spyros, who was, as usual, smoking a cigarette and drinking a small, strong coffee. They waved as Martha neared them and she waved back, realising she was so out of breath she couldn't speak.

'Martha, look! That's our boat for the day.' Milo pointed at a small boat with a canvas canopy. A shirtless man was loading a cool box onto it. He was young, Martha reckoned in his early twenties, in denim shorts and with a very toned, tanned body. Dark curls tried their best to escape from the faded baseball cap on his head.

Spyros nodded in the direction of the boat. 'Morning, Martha, that's Nico. He's your skipper today and he's got everything you need: water, beer if you want it.'

Martha shuddered slightly, the taste of ouzo still in her mouth despite brushing her teeth. Twice. 'Thank you, Spyros. Hey, Milo.' She grinned at Milo. 'Sorry to keep you waiting. I didn't realise it was so late.'

Spyros laughed. 'You're fine, no hurry. You want a coffee before you go?'

'Do we have time?' Martha was desperate for a coffee.

Spyros nudged Milo. 'Go and ask for a coffee for your friend.'

Milo sprang up and disappeared inside.

'So, how was your dinner last night?' Spyros' sunglasses stayed firmly in place, no trace of a smile on his face.

She felt momentarily awkward. 'It was lovely, thank you. Delicious food.'

Spyros took a long drag of cigarette, careful to blow the smoke away from her when he exhaled. 'You know, it's none of my business but I think you need to talk to Connie. She needs to tell you about her daughter.'

'What do you mean?' She didn't want to let on what she already knew.

Spyros lifted his sunglasses onto his head. He fixed Martha with his deep brown eyes. 'Asya...' he whispered the name '... broke everybody's heart and he...' Spyros looked in the direction of the door where Milo had gone '...is too young to remember. One day he will need to know. I think you need to understand what you are... you know...' He struggled to find the words.

'But I'm not...' Martha stopped and sat down next to him. 'If you mean understand what I am getting into, I can assure you I'm not intending to get into anything.' She knew she wasn't being entirely truthful. 'But whatever happens, I will look after him.' She said the words quietly as Milo slowly approached the table carefully carrying her coffee on a tray along with a glass of water. He put it down next to her. 'Thank you, Milo.'

Nico whistled from the bow of the boat.

Spyros nodded and held up his hand. 'Just coming. Right, Milo, you know what to show Martha. You must do the caves and don't forget the cove where you can catch fish with your hands, you know the one?'

'Of course, I'll bring back your supper!' Milo laughed.

'Good, well, you two have a good day. Lunch is sorted, Martha; Harry has organised something for you. Nico knows the details.'

Martha went to protest, but Spyros was having none of it. She thanked him, drained her coffee cup and followed Milo to the boat, taking a seat at the back as instructed. As the boat backed out from the harbour wall, she and Milo waved Spyros goodbye. Just before the boat turned, Martha saw a familiar figure come out from the door of the shop at the far end of the harbour. It was Connie, watching as they left the bay.

* * *

The day was perfect, a cloudless sky above them and a calm sea below. As they ventured out further from the shore the wind picked up, cooling the heat of the morning sun. The boat bounced gently over the waves and soon they were zipping along, running parallel to the shore. The stark white cliffs looked far more imposing from the sea, rising higher than Martha had realised. The land was carpeted with trees, houses nestling in among them. She sat at the back of the boat and Milo joined Nico by the wheel. She watched as they chatted easily, in Greek, and after a while closed her eyes and turned her face to the sun.

After about twenty minutes, Nico took the boat back in towards the base of the cliffs, navigating with ease under arches carved into the rocks by the sea. They rounded a corner and a beautiful empty cove revealed itself, not a single other boat in sight. The water had changed from a deep blue to a turquoise colour so bright, Martha could barely look at it without her sunglasses on. The boat slowed and Nico asked Milo to take the wheel whilst he looked around, checking, Martha presumed, for rocks.

'Do you want to swim here?' Nico called back to them.

'Yes!' Milo shouted. 'Are you coming in, Martha?'

'I just put the anchor down,' said Nico. 'Milo, put the engine in neutral.'

Milo did as he was asked and Nico watched as the anchor settled on the bottom. Once happy it was holding, he signalled for Milo to cut the engine.

Milo did so, then stripped off his T-shirt and, with a loud whoop, jumped off the side of the boat and into the water.

Martha watched as he came back up to the surface, his face breaking into a huge smile as he looked up at her. 'Martha, you must come in! It's so cool!'

Nico laughed. 'Hey, make yourself useful and catch something, will you?'

Milo kicked up his feet, sending water splashing into Nico's face. 'You come and catch them!' He laughed. 'Come on, please!' He looked at Martha, clearly desperate for her to join him.

Martha moved to the edge of the boat and put her hand over the side to touch the water, mercifully cool to the touch. But as she watched Milo's feet below the surface, kicking as he trod water, she knew it was too deep for her to stand. She felt her chest tightening, her hands started to feel light. It was as if her mind was transmitting its fear to her limbs. She felt sick – and embarrassed. How could she tell this boy, so fearless and full of fun, that she was too scared to go in because she couldn't touch the bottom? Her whole life she'd managed to avoid situations like this, finding a way to excuse herself so she wouldn't have to face her biggest fear. But this one had come out of nowhere.

It had all been so last minute. Martha had been so focused on the boat, on the landscape, she hadn't thought ahead to having to jump off it into the sea. And yet here she was, looking at this beautiful boy begging her to join him. Just the thought of being out of her depth was enough to make her hands tremble.

Nico seemed to sense something wasn't quite right and stepped up. 'Move, you little shrimp. I'm coming in!' He threw his cap into the boat, slipped off his shoes, winked at Martha and jumped in making a huge splash, much to Milo's obvious delight.

She watched as they swam and dived, calling to each other as they raced around the boat. Milo tried to persuade her once more as he trod water, but Martha smiled and shook her head.

'I'll come in later, I promise. Anyway, it's fun watching you from here,' she said, laughing. How could she possibly explain it to him? In fact, she struggled to rationalise it to herself. A swimming accident so long ago she didn't even remember it, yet she'd never dared venture out of her depth again.

Once, on a summer holiday with Joe, they'd been staying in a small apartment in Spain. It had been advertised as being not far from the beach but when they'd got there, not far had turned out to be a good twenty-minute walk, which, in the heat of the Spanish sun in high season, had been no fun at all. There had been a shared swimming pool for people staying in the apartment block, but it was always crowded so every day they'd walked down to the beach until, one particularly hot day, Joe had suggested swimming in the pool instead. They had made their way down and, as usual, Martha had headed for the steps at the shallow end. Joe had jumped straight in at the deep end.

She'd walked into the water until it was up to her shoulders, then started swimming towards him. But when she'd put her feet down to find the bottom, there had been nothing there. The bottom of the pool had dropped away steeply, and she'd been left for a few seconds – although to her it had felt like minutes – trying to get her feet back on the ground. Surrounded by bodies, she'd panicked and lost her bearings, moving into deeper water. The next thing she'd known Joe had been supporting her in the water, swimming on his back, reassuring her that everything was okay.

Later that day, as they'd sat having a drink on the tiny balcony of their apartment overlooking the now quiet swimming pool, he'd asked her what had happened. She'd told him the story, about her fear of being out of her depth. Joe had, of course, been kind and understanding. He always was.

'Here, take this.' Nico's voice shook Martha from her thoughts. He stood in front of her, his body glistening with water. He was holding out a tin of lager.

Martha took it, holding the cold tin to the side of her face for a second. 'Thank you.'

'You don't like swimming?' Nico looked at her, his head to one side.

Martha shook her head. 'Too deep for me here.'

'We can go to another cove just around the corner, it's beautiful. White sand, no rocks. I can get us much closer in.'

'I'd love that, thanks, Nico.' She was grateful to him for not making it a big deal. 'But no hurry.'

'We're never in a hurry here.' He smiled and shook his head, the drops of water from his hair catching the sunlight. He was, Martha thought, quite beautiful.

'Can we go to the bay with the beach?' Milo appeared behind Nico, almost breathless and dripping with water.

'That's the plan,' said Nico. 'Let's get the anchor up.'

They made their way along the coastline, zipping along over

the waves further out then slowing as they came in towards shore to explore. As Nico had promised, they dropped anchor in another bay further along, white sand below them and not a rock – or jellyfish – in sight. Nico nosed the boat slowly towards the beach, keeping an eye on the depth gauge until they were as close to the shore as they could safely get. This time, all three of them went into the water, Nico and Milo jumping off the bow of the boat whilst Martha launched herself gently off the steps at the back. And just as Nico had promised, she was able to stand, just. She swam through the crystal-clear water towards the deserted beach, then walked along the sand before making her way back to the boat.

By the time she got there, Nico and Milo had set up lunch on a little fold-out table at the back under the shade of the small bimini. Martha wrapped a fresh cotton towel around her and sat down. She took in the spread before her: a crisp green salad, cheese, dips and a plate piled high with sandwiches.

Milo pointed to them, grinning. 'Dad said you liked crab sandwiches.'

Martha laughed. 'I do! How on earth did he manage that so quickly? I only told him last night.'

Nico pulled out a bottle of rosé from the cool box. 'He said you might like a glass of this with them?'

For a moment, Martha wondered if she might be dreaming. What had she done to deserve such treatment? 'I'd love some, thank you.' Nico opened the bottle and poured her a glass. 'Am I the only one?'

Nico nodded. 'I don't drink when I'm on duty.'

'Fair enough. Well, cheers.' Martha held up her glass and they joined her in a toast.

They feasted on the sandwiches, easily as good as the ones she'd loved so much from home when she was a child and even better with a glass of pale Greek rosé. By the time she'd finished her sandwiches, she'd had two glasses. Then when they'd mopped up the dips and finished the salad, Milo and Martha cleared up whilst Nico pulled up the anchor.

'Now we go catch some fish, yes?' Nico said, beaming.

'Yes!' Milo shouted. 'Martha, you are not going to believe this place.'

They motored on along the coast, in and out of bays until they went right up to the base of some steep cliffs. Moving gently through the arches of the caves, Nico steered the boat through a low tunnel, the water changing from light to midnight blue without the sun on it. They emerged from the other side into a near-perfect circular pool, surrounded by steep cliffs on either side.

Martha peered over the side. 'I can't see any fish.'

'Just wait,' said Nico knowingly. 'Milo, put some bits of bread over the side.'

Milo grabbed the paper bag with the leftover bread and tore a piece off, scattering the large crumbs into the water. Suddenly, a whole shoal of fish appeared, mouths gaping open to grab the bread. In a lightning move, Nico swept his hand through the water and pulled out a fish, scales gleaming in the light.

'Woah!' Milo stared in disbelief. 'How do you do that?'

'Practice,' said Nico, winking at the boy. He dropped the fish into a bucket on the floor of the boat. 'Your dinner tonight.' He turned and looked at Martha. 'I can fillet it for you if you like.'

'I could get used to this.' She laughed.

They carried on fishing for a while, Nico with his bare hands and Milo with a rod. Martha was determined to try and catch something by hand but soon realised there was a real knack to it – one she clearly didn't have.

'Fancy one last swim on the way home?' Nico asked as he carefully dismantled the fishing rod once they were done.

'Yes, please!' Milo nodded enthusiastically.

Martha nodded, hoping she looked keener to Nico than she felt.

They sped along back towards the harbour, stopping off at another small hidden beach just around the corner from where she was staying. Milo was in the water as soon as Nico was happy the anchor was holding, then Nico set about cleaning and preparing the fish for Martha, using a small knife from his bag.

Martha stretched out on the seat at the back, watching as he did so. 'Have you known Milo for a long time?'

'All his life. I knew his mother.' Nico didn't take his eyes off the task in hand, working the knife quickly. 'Asya was like an older sister to me.'

'What was she like?' The rosé at lunchtime had rather loosened Martha's tongue.

Nico thought about it for a few seconds. 'Like a beautiful nightmare.' He laughed then called over to Milo on the shore, waving to him and waiting for him to wave back. The boy was busy peering at something in the sand. 'Harry doesn't talk about it in front of him—' Nico gestured to Milo '—but I think it's tough for him. He doesn't really remember her.'

'What were they like, Harry and Asya? Together, I mean.'

Nico looked up at her.

'I'm sorry, I don't mean to pry,' said Martha. Maybe she'd gone too far.

'No, it's okay. It's nice to say her name, to be honest. We don't say it enough. When she disappeared it was a tragedy, you know? No one really knows what happened. People blamed Harry, even. But I always felt like Asya was only here for a while. I'm not sure how to explain it.' Nico shrugged, wiping at his face with the back of his hand. 'It's him I feel sorry for.' Nico looked over at Milo again, now standing at the water's edge.

Martha sat up and turned to watch Milo as he made his way back towards them, gliding through the water. He was a strong swimmer, despite those skinny limbs of his. She smiled. 'He's a beautiful boy.'

'Yes, he really is.' Nico lit up a cigarette, offering one to Martha. She shook her head. 'He looks like her, too.' Nico fixed her with his gaze. 'You like Harry?'

Martha took a moment to realise what he was saying. 'Oh no, Nico. I'm not... God, no.' She laughed awkwardly.

'Why?'

'Because...' She was about to say Harry was clearly too old for her but changed her mind. 'Nico, let's not forget, I only met him a couple of days ago. And anyway, I might already have a boyfriend.'

'Whatever you say.' Nico shrugged, a half-smile on his face.

Martha changed the subject. 'Tell me how to cook that tonight.'

Nico wrapped the filleted fish in paper and put it in the cool box. 'Just grill it on the barbecue. You have one at the house?'

'Yes, I think so.' After all that sun she was already looking forward to an evening in the hammock with her book for company.

'Great, there's enough for two.'

'Nico, are you trying to set me up?' She looked at him over her sunglasses. She laughed. 'I'm just here to have a little holiday. Nothing more.'

Nico winked at her. 'Whatever you say.'

* * *

From his position on the far edge of the terrace overlooking the bay, Harry could see the boat with Nico and Martha aboard, Milo swimming around it. He watched as they chatted and laughed, hearing whoops of joy from his boy as Milo climbed up the ladder at the back of the boat, walked to the front and dived off into the water over and over again. He could hear Martha shouting encouragement, holding up her hands to score each dive. Harry thought about the previous evening, remembering how beautiful Martha had looked. She was funny and kind, interested and interesting. He loved how she'd been curious about his life, wanting to know about his writing. She'd even got him talking about the book he one day hoped to write – and he'd never told anyone about that before. But when he'd asked her about her life back home, she'd been quick to change the subject, not wanting to talk about her own situation. The more he'd tried, the more she'd closed the conversation down, quickly moving it on to something else.

As they'd driven back along the road in the darkness, Milo asleep between them with his head on Martha's shoulder, a song had come on the radio.

'I love this one,' Martha had whispered.

'Me too,' Harry had said, turning it up a little. They'd driven on, Jackson Browne singing 'Late for the Sky', that soft voice filling the space between them.

'I think that might be one of the most beautiful sad songs ever written,' Martha had said as the last haunting chords had played.

'It is, but there's something hopeful about it too,' Harry had said.

'How do you mean?'

'Well, it's like he knows there's something else waiting. It's the end of one particular relationship, but it's not the end.'

Martha had thought for a moment. 'The need for human connection,' she'd said.

'The most important thing in the world,' Harry had said.

Instinctively, Harry had reached across and gently touched her knee. Martha had placed her hand on his. It had felt both new and natural, a matter of seconds but enough for Harry to know he was in trouble.

12

As the boat headed back into the harbour, Martha savoured the feeling of sun and salt water on her skin. Milo stood on the fore-deck with the bow line in his hand and as they got closer Spyros appeared from his shop, waving them in. Milo threw him the rope and jumped ashore. Connie was seated at her usual table at the front of the taverna, tucked in the shade.

'Yia-yia, we caught fish!'

Connie clapped her hands.

'Here.' Spyros extended his arm to Martha. She grabbed his hand and stepped onto the shore.

'Thank you.'

'You caught the sun today.' Spyros pointed at her face.

'I know, I can feel it. Think I'd better go and get some after sun before I go back to the house.'

Connie appeared behind him, smiling. 'How was it?'

'You were right, the perfect way to see the island. And I had the best tour guides.' Martha looked at Milo.

'I caught her a fish too,' said Milo, trying not to look too pleased with himself.

'You did, thank you.' Martha put her bag over her shoulder. 'In fact, I'd better get it back and into the fridge before the ice melts.'

'Come and have a drink in the shade with me first. Nico can run you back up there in a bit.' Connie looked at Nico, who nodded and carried on unloading the boat. 'I heard you went to Gaios last night; did you enjoy it?'

Martha wondered what Harry, or perhaps Milo, had told Connie about the previous evening. She felt slightly uncomfortable. Was this Connie's way of letting Martha know she had her eye on what was happening? But nothing was happening, Martha reminded herself. She'd just been taken for dinner by Harry as a thank-you gesture for bringing Milo to the island. And the boat trip hadn't been her idea; Harry had insisted. Martha suddenly realised Connie was still waiting for an answer.

'Yes, it was lovely, thank you. The restaurant was gorgeous. Such a pretty town, too.'

Connie nodded. 'Come, let's get into the shade.'

Martha followed Connie as she made her way back to the table, calling over an order for drinks as she did. A moment later a waiter appeared with a tray with a jug of water, two small beers and a bowl of crisps.

'Please can I get an ice cream, Yia-yia?' Milo appeared at the table.

'Yes, go and put it on my account.' She watched as he disappeared around the corner towards the ice-cream shop.

Martha picked up the jug of water and poured them each a glass, gulping hers down straight away. 'Sorry, so thirsty.'

Connie picked up her beer and took a sip. 'Martha, can I ask you something?'

Martha's heart jumped. She tried to keep her tone light. 'Yes, of course.'

'Did Harry tell you about my daughter last night?'

Martha nodded slowly. 'Yes. He told me she... disappeared. And, Connie, I'm so sorry. I can't imagine how hard that must have been.'

'Well, it was a while ago now but yes, it's still hard. Missing, presumed...' Connie couldn't finish the sentence. 'I wondered if Milo mentioned it at all?'

'No, he hasn't.'

'I thought as much.' Connie sighed. 'It breaks my heart almost as much as losing her. Harry doesn't talk about her, barely mentions her name. And I worry that Milo is growing up afraid to talk about her too.'

'Do you talk about her with Milo?'

'As often as I can. And at home I have photos everywhere. I want her face to stay familiar for Milo. But as soon as Harry's around, the subject of Milo's mother is closed.' Connie took another slow sip of her beer. She put her glass down and looked at Martha. 'This really isn't your problem so forgive me, but I think Harry needs to talk about her to Milo. It's not right to just pretend someone doesn't exist any more.'

Martha put her hand on Connie's, not knowing what to say. 'I'm so sorry.'

'I think Harry still feels guilty and it was very hard, for all of us, for years. The truth is we'll never really know but, whatever happened, I don't blame Harry for it. The problem is, he blames himself. It's why he can't talk about her. And that's going to affect Milo. It already is.'

'Do you ever try and talk to Harry about it?'

Connie shook her head. 'Impossible. He just shuts down. Won't even have the conversation.'

'That must be hard for you too.'

Connie nodded her head gently. 'I have wonderful memories

and they keep me going. But I want Milo to be able to talk freely about her and I think he doesn't because he's worried about upsetting his father.'

Milo appeared, an ice cream in each hand. 'I got you one too, Martha.' He held out a rapidly melting one.

'Chocolate?' Martha took it from him, licking the side of the cone to stop it dripping.

'The best flavour.' Milo grinned and continued eating.

'Thank you,' said Martha through a mouthful.

'Do you need anything for tonight?' asked Connie.

'I thought I'd just get a few things from the shop on the way back, some tomatoes to have with my fish later.'

'Will you come and have dinner with me here tomorrow night, in that case?'

'I'd love that, thank you. I'll walk in, let me know what time.'

'Any time you like. If I'm not here, I'll be in the shop.'

'Can I come?' Milo spoke through a mouthful of ice cream.

'Let's see if your father has any plans first.' Connie wiped at his face gently with a paper napkin. 'Talking of which, where is he?' She called over to Spyros and Nico, both sitting outside Spyros' shop. 'Do you know where Harry is?'

'He's at the house. I just spoke to him. They've managed to fix that water pipe,' said Spyros. He drew heavily on his cigarette then blew two thick streams of smoke from his nostrils.

'Hey, Martha,' called Nico, 'do you want a lift back? I'm going up to help Harry with a few things in a bit.'

'Yes, please, that would be brilliant. I think I'm too exhausted to walk, even though I've done nothing except sit and enjoy the view today.'

Connie laughed. 'It's the heat and all that sea air. It really takes it out of you if you're not used to it.'

'I'll just walk up to the corner when I've finished this—'

Martha gestured to her drink '—and get a few things from the shop. Meet you there in ten minutes?'

Nico nodded. 'See you there.'

She turned to Connie and lifted her glass. 'I'll get these.'

'Absolutely not. Now go and have a lovely evening. I'll see you tomorrow.'

Martha drained the last of the beer from her glass and stood up. 'Thank you, Connie. See you tomorrow. You too, Milo.'

'Enjoy your fish!' Milo beamed at her.

'I will, thank you.' She waved, thinking how alike they looked, a beautiful light in their eyes.

Nico dropped Martha back and once she'd showered and washed the salt water from her hair, she slathered herself in after sun, practically sighing with relief as it cooled the sunburn on her shoulders. Peering at her reflection in the mirror, she tugged at her hair and now, with colour in her cheeks, she felt better than she had in a while. Gone were the bags under her eyes, normally a permanent feature.

Still naked, Martha opened the doors from her bedroom, leaving the mosquito screen in place, and let the cool sea breeze blow in. She threw a white cotton shift dress over her head and sat back on the bed, checking her phone and replying, in turn, to her mother, Liv, Iris and Joanie, all of whom had left messages of varying lengths. Her mother's message was short and sweet, asking if she was all right and to let them know when she had a moment, signing off with two kisses as usual. Liv's message was similarly unfussy but she did insist Martha send a picture of the house so she could envisage exactly where her sister was.

Iris' message was typically hilarious, instructing Martha to tell her it was rubbish even if it wasn't so she wouldn't be sad about not being there herself. There was no mention of Toby or what had happened. Instead, Iris just wished Martha a lovely holiday and said she'd better bring her back a nice present seeing as she'd gifted her a free honeymoon. Joanie's message made Martha laugh out loud. This one detailed a particularly disastrous Tinder date from the previous evening and was littered with swear words and emojis. Martha tapped out a reply, sent Joanie some pictures she'd taken that day on the boat then lay back on the white sheets, listening to the sound of the sea below. She closed her eyes and was asleep within seconds.

* * *

'Hello? Are you all right?'

Martha heard the voice in her dream. Harry's voice, asking if she was all right.

'Martha?'

His voice was louder this time. And not in her dream.

Martha opened her eyes and sat up. Her dress had fallen off one shoulder, exposing a breast.

'Oh God, I'm sorry!' He looked away hurriedly, towards the garden.

She hoicked up the dress, then rubbed at her eyes, pushing her hair out of her face. She focused her gaze, realising it was Harry and he was standing outside her bedroom on the other side of the mosquito screen.

'I didn't mean to scare you. It's just I was finishing up next door and Nico messaged asking me to check that you had charcoal.'

'Did he?' said Martha.

'Yes, for the barbecue, you need it tonight apparently.'

She had to admire Nico's determination. 'Your son caught me a fish for my supper.' Martha gathered herself together and stood up, making her way to the screen. She fiddled with the catch, trying to open it. 'I can't work this thing out...'

'Push that bit down, then slide it along.' Harry pointed at a catch on the floor.

Martha did as Harry instructed, and the screen began to retract to the ceiling. She held onto it as it went up. They stood opposite each other, so close she could feel his breath on her cheek, the smell of his skin reaching her. Neither moved for a few seconds.

Martha looked at the darkening sky. 'What time is it?'

'Almost eight o'clock. Here.' Harry held up a bag of charcoal. 'I was just going to leave it by the barbecue.' He looked around. 'I can't see one.'

'Maybe there isn't one. It doesn't matter, I can just pan fry it.' All she wanted to do was kiss the man in front of her. It was all she'd wanted to do since that moment in the car the night before. Instead, they were talking about cooking fish. She'd hardly dared to think about him since he'd dropped her off, knowing she was in danger of finding herself in a situation if she wasn't careful. And that would just be too complicated. He was a good deal older than her, lived in America and had a son. Three very good reasons not to let anything happen.

'So, we could just do that?'

Martha realised he'd been speaking, and she hadn't heard a word. 'Sorry, say that again.' She rubbed her eyes and grinned. 'Still half asleep, obviously.'

'I said we could take this down to the beach and cook them there instead.' He looked at her, his eyes an impossible blue in the evening light.

Martha tried to focus. More than anything in the world she wanted to go to the beach at the end of the garden with this man and cook food over fire and eat and swim and make love in the moonlight...

'I'm so sorry, I can't.' Martha looked at the ground.

'Oh, right.' Harry was clearly taken aback. 'I didn't... I thought...' He trailed off.

'I'm so sorry.' Martha's voice shook. 'I want to, but I just can't.'

'Why?' Harry's voice was soft.

'Because I think it might be easier if I don't.' She raised her eyes to meet his.

He held his hand to her face, stroking her cheek softly.

Martha put her hand over his and brought it down to her neck, then to her chest, and guided it beneath her cotton dress. She took his other hand and pulled him towards her, stepping back into the room. With his arm behind her back, their faces so close their lips were almost touching, he laid her gently back on the bed. Their eyes didn't leave one another's gaze for a second. The connection was so strong, resisting it was pointless.

As he moved his hand across her skin, she couldn't control the shivers that seemed to course through her body. It felt so new and yet so familiar and Martha let her body respond to this man's touch without thought. In turn, she wanted to explore his. He started to unbutton his shirt and she lifted it up, raising her head to brush her lips across his stomach. He let out a small groan, then lifted his shirt as she undid his belt. With increasing urgency, they removed each other's clothes as if the only thing that mattered in the world was being as close as they could possibly get. As they moved together, Martha felt her body take the lead. Her mind was clear. Nothing mattered other than what was happening right there and then.

Later, as they lay naked side by side, their limbs intertwined, the sea breeze blowing in gently, brushing their skin, Harry told Martha that he'd wanted to kiss her the moment he first saw her.

'At the beach when I got stung?'

'Promise you won't be mad, but I saw you before then. Naked, in fact.'

Martha sat up suddenly, her eyes wide. 'You what? When?'

Harry looked sheepish. 'I was working on the house, up there.' He gestured behind him. 'I didn't mean to but you came out and, with no warning, took off your clothes.'

'Oh my God, you saw me?' Martha was gobsmacked.

'Couldn't take my eyes off you.' Harry tried to look serious.

'I can't believe you did that.'

'I could say the same to you!'

Martha rolled on top of him. 'You know what we just did?'

Harry nodded.

'Can we do it all over again?'

Martha woke to the sound of the kettle boiling. The bedroom door was open and from the bed she could hear Harry pottering in the kitchen, opening cupboards, then the fridge. Judging from the dull light outside it was still early, the sun not yet up.

'Milk, no sugar, please,' she called out to him.

A moment later he appeared with a white towel wrapped around his waist, a steaming cup for her and a glass of water in his other hand. He looked, Martha thought, quite beautiful.

'Tea? Although I feel I should tell you I'm terrible at making tea. We don't really do tea in America.'

The words hit Martha with a jolt. 'Can we just pretend, for now, that you don't live in America and that this isn't going to be complicated?'

'Well, for a start, I live in America and here.'

'And you're much older than me.'

Harry put her mug of tea down by her bed and lay back down next to her, smiling. 'I'll pretend I didn't hear that.'

'And you have a son.'

'Who thinks you're wonderful.'

'Harry, I'm being serious. This is what I meant last night. I'm over complicated situations. I just want an easy life.'

'Well then, let's make it easy. How about you drink your tea and then we'll go and watch the sun come up?'

She propped herself up and picked up the mug, blowing on it.

'Well?' Harry looked at her, one eyebrow raised, a half-smile on his face.

'Fine. We'll do easy. Like, holiday-fling easy. And at the end, I'll leave, and you'll promise to keep in touch but after a few failed attempts at meeting up we'll just accept it's not going to work and go back to our normal lives.'

Harry laughed. 'Are you always this positive?'

Martha nodded and took a sip of her tea. 'Always.'

'Right, good to know. What about that sunrise?'

'Definitely. This tea is awful.' She put her cup down on the table and, with her glass empty, reached for the rest of his water instead.

Harry shook his head. 'So ungrateful.' He watched her drain the glass and put it back down, then gently rolled her onto her back and lifted her head with one arm, placing a pillow behind it with the other. 'If my tea is so awful, I'd better make up for it another way.' With that, he lowered his mouth to her stomach, parted her legs with his hands and slowly kissed his way down her body. Suddenly, the very last thing on Martha's mind was tea.

13

Harry had left just after sunrise. Martha fell back into a deep sleep and awoke to the sound of knocking at the door. She checked the time; it was after nine o'clock in the morning. She threw on the cotton dress from the night before and went to the door.

Opening it, she found a small dark-haired woman smiling at her. 'Hello, I'm the housekeeper. I come to clean, check if you need anything?'

Martha couldn't hide her surprise. 'Oh, right. I didn't know.' She opened the door fully. 'Please, come on in.'

'My name is Eleni, nice to meet you.' The woman held out her hand, still smiling.

Martha took it. 'Hi, I'm Martha.'

Eleni looked confused. 'Not Ms Iris?'

'Oh no, that's my sister. Change of plan. I came instead at the last minute. Long story.'

Eleni shrugged. 'It's okay. Is anyone else here?'

'No, just me.' Martha suddenly remembered the state of the

bedroom, the tangled sheets, the two water glasses. 'In fact, I'm just going to go and get changed before I go for a swim. I'll be back in a moment.'

Eleni smiled. 'I start here.' She pointed at the kitchen.

'Great, thank you. See you in a moment.' Retreating into the bedroom, Martha closed the door behind her and leant against it, letting out a long breath. She looked at the bed and, with an involuntary shiver, recalled the events of the hours before. She had loved every single second of it, wanted to do it all over again and again. For once, there was no feeling of shame or guilt. It had all felt so natural and familiar, yet new and different at the same time. Maybe it was because Harry was older, but Martha had to admit he was possibly the most generous lover she'd ever known. She'd lost herself in the lovemaking in a way she'd never experienced before.

The knock at the door made Martha jump.

'Are you all right? Can I get you anything?' It was Eleni.

'Just a minute!' Martha called back, reaching for her swimming costume and picking up the discarded towel from the floor. She opened the door a fraction. 'I'm just going to head down to the beach for a quick swim. How long will you be here so I don't miss you?'

Eleni glanced at her watch. 'An hour.'

'Great, I'll be back. See you in a bit.'

Martha grabbed her basket, shoved in her sun cream and a bottle of water and headed down to the beach. There were a few groups already settled in their spots for the day – a family of four, a small group of teenagers and a few older couples – and Martha's usual spot at the back was waiting for her. She put her bag down, slipped on her beach shoes and headed into the water. The sensation of the seawater on her now sun-kissed skin was blissful and, after a cursory glance around to ensure the water was clear, she launched herself in and under. The quietness wrapped itself around her and she swam out, eyes open. As she came up for air, she reached down with feet to find the bottom and rested her toes on the round stones below, letting the water sway her body like human seaweed. With the water up to her neck, this was deeper than she usually dared to go but here, on this now familiar beach, she felt brave.

With her face to the sun, Martha glided onto her back and moved her hands gently, her body floating back towards the shore. As she did so, she went back over the night before. The conversations, the closeness, the sheer pleasure of it all. It felt like a dream.

Before Harry had left that morning, he'd asked what her plans were that evening. She'd told him she'd already agreed to meet Connie for dinner, and he'd put her number in his phone, promising to message later so they could arrange to see each other afterwards. Martha had happily agreed.

By the time she got back up to the house, Eleni was watering the plants in the pots outside the main sitting room doors. She waved as she approached, and Eleni called out.

'How was your swim?'

'Gorgeous, thank you. It's so lovely having the beach at the end of the garden. This really is the most beautiful spot.'

Just then the sound of drilling started up from the house next door.

Eleni pointed towards it. 'Except for that.'

Martha smiled. 'I met the man building that house actually. I can tell him to keep it down.'

Eleni's face darkened. 'Harry?'

'Yes, do you know him?'

'Everyone does.' Eleni shrugged and went back to watering the pot in front of her.

'Really?'

'You know his wife disappeared? Everyone knows he was messing around, drove her to it.' Eleni said it so casually, not taking her eyes off the stream of water in front of her.

Martha felt herself catch her breath. 'Sorry?'

'Yes, terrible story. Years ago, but still, so sad.'

Martha felt her nails digging into her palms. 'Why would they say that?'

'He broke her heart. Then she swam out to sea and was never seen again.' Eleni turned the tap off and casually recoiled the hose, placing it back on the wall at the side of the house. 'Right, I am finished here. I'll be back next week, okay?'

Martha looked up at Eleni and tried to sound as casual as she could. 'Great, see you then.' She felt suddenly nauseous.

Eleni disappeared up the track. Martha waited until she couldn't hear her car, then made her way to the table in the garden and sat, looking out towards the sea. In the space of twenty minutes, she'd gone from feeling as if she were in a dream to realising it might, in fact, be the start of a nightmare.

Before anything went any further with Harry, Martha needed to know the truth. The question was, would he tell her?

* * *

The rest of the morning passed slowly as Martha kept trying to take her mind off what Eleni had said. Every time she tried to lose herself in her book, the words swam in front of her eyes. Thoughts of the night before had been replaced with questions about Harry and what had happened with Asya. She thought about fixing something to eat despite not having an appetite, then tried to distract her mind by stretching out in the hammock and listening to some music, but it was no use.

Martha looked out across the garden, hearing voices in the distance. She watched as the occasional boat passed, out in the bay beyond. Thinking about the previous few days, Martha was furious with herself for believing there wasn't a catch. Of course it was all too good to be true. How could she have possibly thought that life would let her rock up unexpectedly on an island miles away from home and meet a man she felt she'd known for a life-time? This wasn't a bloody fairy tale.

Harry had told her himself what had happened, but a seed of doubt had been planted and Martha knew she had to know more. But if she asked him about what Eleni had said, it would be obvious she didn't believe him. If that was the case, she decided the best thing she could do was extract herself from the situation completely, before it went any further. It was just too messy and the one thing she knew she didn't want was any more complica-tion in her life. Much as she had loved every second of the previous days, particularly the night before, not to mention the early hours of the morning, she knew getting involved with Harry was going to be anything but simple. And this was definitely a sign to pull the cord. Much easier to get out now than fall for someone who was probably, and quite understandably given his looks and charm, a playboy. She'd been so stupid not to see it before now.

Martha thought about making her excuses to Connie and not going to meet her that evening. She got her phone and started typing out a message saying she wasn't feeling well. But Martha couldn't bring herself to lie to the woman who'd been so kind to her since she'd arrived on the island. She deleted the message, instead resolving to keep the conversation light that evening, try to avoid the topic of Harry altogether, at least as far as she was able without being rude. Connie was only being kind. It wasn't her fault that Martha hadn't been able to see what was blindingly obvious now she thought about it.

She whiled away the afternoon on the beach, swimming and reading, dozing off occasionally only to be woken by the sound of children as they rushed past, their footsteps heavy on the sand. Martha knew she should be revelling in the solitude. She'd always been quite happy in her own company; she'd got used to it growing up. She was usually more than happy to be left alone with a book, but her mind kept wandering back to Harry and it irritated her. If she'd never met him, she'd be lying here now thinking of nothing but what she might be eating that night or which bit of the island she might explore tomorrow. Instead, she was wondering what he was doing, whether he was thinking of her. How had she allowed him under her skin? But as much as she tried to tell herself it was nothing, she knew she hadn't felt like this about anyone for a very long time. Perhaps ever. It was infuriating.

As the sun began to sink slowly behind the island, Martha knew it was time to head back up to the house to shower and get ready for the evening. She planned to walk into the village and spend half an hour or so looking in some of the small shops that lined the harbour front, hoping to pick up a few postcards to send, perhaps even treat herself to a new summer dress. She'd passed one in the window of a small boutique the day before, off-white linen with blue embroidered sleeves. She'd noted, happily, that it had pockets.

By the time she walked down the hill into Loggos, Martha was starving. The air was still warm, the sun casting a golden glow across the bay. Holidaymakers lined the cafés and restaurants along the front, the hum of chatter filling the air. Glancing at her watch, Martha checked if she still had time to pop into the shop before heading to the taverna to meet Connie. She walked up the steps into the small boutique to be greeted by a tall woman with long black hair and an enviable suntan.

'Hi there,' said the woman.

Martha had assumed she'd be Greek so was a little surprised by the very English accent.

'Hello.' Martha smiled. She pointed to the dress in the window. 'I spotted this yesterday and was hoping to try it on.'

'Of course, let me just get one for you. What size?' The woman looked at her.

'Medium, I guess?'

The woman nodded. 'I'll get you a small and a medium. They do come up quite large, these ones.' She went to a rail at the back of the shop and started sorting through the dresses. 'Here for the week?'

Martha nodded. 'Two, actually. You have very beautiful things in your shop.' Martha glanced around.

'Thank you. The one you've picked is one of my favourites, made by a Greek designer on the island.'

Martha suddenly wished she'd asked how much it was before trying it on.

'The changing room is a bit small, I'm afraid.' The woman hung the dresses on the hanger and drew a curtain around Martha. 'There's a mirror out here when you're ready.'

'Thanks,' said Martha. She put her bag on the small stool in the corner and peeled her old black dress over her head. 'How long have you lived here?'

'I don't live here; this is my mum's shop. I just come for the summer. She's getting on a bit so it's too much for her to manage on her own. I live in London most of the time.'

'Me too,' said Martha, slipping the new dress over her head as she did so. She smoothed it down over her body, feeling the soft fabric with her fingers. She pulled back the curtain and stepped out to see what it looked like in the mirror.

'Gorgeous,' said the woman.

Martha looked at her reflection, plunging her hands into the deep pockets. The material felt deliciously cool against her skin, moving gently as she turned her body. 'I love it. But I'm so sorry, I didn't even ask how much it was.' She prayed the price wasn't too high; she'd already fallen in love with the dress.

The woman stepped towards Martha and picked up the label at the back, turning it to read the price. 'It's eighty euros.'

Martha couldn't bring herself to say it was more than double what she'd thought she might pay for it. 'That's a bit above my budget, I'm so sorry. I really should have asked before.'

'Don't worry.' The woman smiled.

Martha took one last look at the dress – it really was gorgeous – then made her way back towards the dressing room.

Martha changed back into her old dress and came out of the makeshift changing room, holding out the other dress on the hanger in her hand. 'I'm so embarrassed.'

'Please don't be, it doesn't matter at all. And if you change your mind, you know it's here.'

Martha felt her cheeks reddening. 'Thanks.'

'Are you here for dinner?'

'Yes, I'm meeting a friend. Well, we've only just met but, long story short, I brought her grandchild with me when I came from Corfu.'

'Oh, you're Martha!'

Martha couldn't hide her surprise. 'Yes! How did you know?'

'We've all heard about Milo's great adventure. You were quite the heroine.' She held out her hand to shake Martha's. 'I'm Janie. I'm an old friend of Harry's.'

Of course you are, thought Martha. 'Anyone would have done the same.'

'Well, it's all he's talked about. You've obviously made quite the impression.'

There was something about the way she said it that made Martha feel suddenly self-conscious. 'He's a very lovely boy. Well, I'd better go, Connie will be waiting. Nice to meet you.'

'And you,' said Janie. 'And don't forget, if you change your mind...' She pointed at the dress in the window.

'I won't,' said Martha, secretly a little grateful to get out of there.

Walking along the front, she passed full tables lining the street. Moored fishing boats bobbed gently on the water, the air carrying the scent of sea. As she passed, Spyros appeared at the door of his shop, unlit cigarette in his mouth, sunglasses still firmly in place despite the sun having all but disappeared from the sky.

He waved to her. 'How was your day?'

Martha waved back, forcing a smile. She tried not to think about Janie and Harry. 'Good, thank you.'

'You were probably tired.'

Martha suddenly panicked. What did he know? 'Um, a little...'

'After your day on the water yesterday. Sun and sea can leave you a little crazy.' He gestured to the sky.

Relieved, she nodded. 'Oh yes, exactly. Definitely takes it out of you.'

'You're meeting Connie now?'

What was it with this place that everyone knew everyone else's movements? 'Yes, I am.'

Spyros had a small smile on his face. 'Have fun.' He disappeared back inside the shop.

'Martha!'

She heard her name and looked up to see Connie, sitting at her usual table.

Moving carefully through the tables, Martha took a seat beside her.

Connie kissed her on the cheek and poured her a glass of white wine, offering it to her. 'It's just us, Harry insisted on giving you a break from Milo. How was your day?'

Martha took the wine and clinked Connie's glass. 'Lazy.'

Connie laughed. 'That's what I like to hear. Too many people come and think they must do stuff to have a good time. But this is the place where you come to do nothing.'

'Well, in that case I've had a very productive day.' Martha took a sip of her wine, the flavour of lemon peel and jasmine filling her mouth. 'That is delicious. What is it?'

'Moschofilero,' said Connie.

'Mosco-what?'

'It's the grape, one of my favourites. I've ordered us some things already; I hope you don't mind.'

Martha shook her head. 'Not at all, thank you. How was your day?'

Connie sighed. 'Busy. I didn't close the shop until just now.'

'I nearly bought a dress from the shop just up there but...' Martha pointed back to the small boutique she'd been in.

'Too expensive?' Connie raised an eyebrow.

Martha nodded. 'It was quite.'

'It used to be a lovely shop but then the daughter took over a few years ago and she's filled it with expensive designer clothes and her markups are ridiculous.' Connie rolled her eyes.

'Janie? I just met her. She seemed to know all about me.'

'She knows about everyone.'

'She knew about me bringing Milo over.'

'I bet she did.' Connie took another sip of her wine. 'She was a friend of my daughter's. Not a very good one, as it turned out.'

'What happened?'

'Oh, I won't bore you.'

Despite herself, Martha felt instantly intrigued at the mention of Asya.

The waiter brought over a tray with bowls of bread, dips and olives and another shallow dish filled with olive oil the colour of gold. He placed them in front of the two women, topped up their water glasses and poured more wine for Connie. Martha picked up a piece of bread and swiped it into the top of a mound of tara-masalata. She took a bite and closed her eyes, savouring the salty tang. She looked out across the water, the sky changing colour seemingly before her eyes. Lights had started to glow in the trees, the island soundtrack of chorusing insects surrounding them.

'Can I talk to you about Harry?' Connie reached for some bread.

Martha nearly choked on her mouthful. 'Um, yes. Of course.' She wiped at her mouth and turned to face Connie.

'I just want you to know that whatever might or might not happen between you – and it's really none of my business – but for what it's worth I do so want Harry to be happy. And I saw him today, he came home very early...'

Martha blushed. The woman clearly knew where he'd spent the night. 'Oh.'

'Please, I don't wish to make you feel awkward, but he looked exactly that. Happy. I haven't seen him look like that for a long time. Things weren't always easy between us. In fact, there was a time after Asya went missing when I wondered whether we'd even have a relationship but eventually we found a way to make this work. He spends time here so I can spend time with my only grandson and for that I am truly grateful. But it's been a long time now and Harry still punishes himself over what happened.'

'Connie, can I ask what did happen?'

'Well, we'll never really know.' Connie sighed deeply. 'Her clothes were found on the beach where she often swam. But her body was never found. No one saw her, there were no witnesses. There was no note, nothing. One day she was there, the next she was gone.' Connie's gaze fell to the piece of bread she had in her hands. 'Asya was desperately unhappy, she'd come back to live here with me for a time after she and Harry split up. Milo was tiny. She'd struggled with depression for years, long before Milo was born, but she'd been pretty good for a while. It got bad again after he was born.'

Martha reached for Connie's hand. 'I'm so sorry.'

'Barely a moment goes by when I don't think of her. But I want those she left behind to be happy and I think you make Harry happy.'

Martha laughed nervously. 'Connie, I barely know him.'

'I know, but I can see it. In both of you. And I don't want what's happened in the past to stand in the way of the future. I want him to live with the happy memories – and there were some very happy ones – not the ending. Right now, he lives with the ghost of Asya.'

Martha couldn't quite believe what she was hearing. This was not the conversation she was expecting at all. Hours before she'd been told Harry had driven Asya to do whatever she'd done. She couldn't possibly know if it was true or not but, for the sake of her own heart, she'd decided not to find out. And now Connie was telling her that Harry deserved a chance to be happy. Would she be saying that if she thought he'd broken her daughter's heart? It didn't make sense. 'I don't know what to say.'

'You don't have to say anything. But I do want you to do what feels right and that's why I wanted to tell you this, so that you understand.'

Martha met Connie's gaze, seeing the tears in her eyes. She'd thought of nothing but Harry all day. Deep down, she wanted to believe he was the man Connie said he was. 'I'm not sure I'm ready for anything like this.'

Connie squeezed her hand. 'Well, that's up to you. But if you never try, you'll never know.'

14

———

By the time Martha got back to the house it was after eleven at night. She and Connie had sat and talked about everything from Asya to Milo and how she hoped he would always come and spend his summers with her for as long as he wanted to. Martha couldn't imagine how it must feel, the not knowing, but Connie talked about how she'd managed her way through grief for her missing daughter to a place where she was able to be grateful for the time they'd had. It was heartbreaking to hear.

After that initial discussion about Harry, he'd barely been mentioned again and for that Martha was grateful. She'd felt awkward talking about him with Connie, even though Connie clearly hadn't. As she lay in the hammock in the garden, the cool night air on her sun-kissed skin, she looked up at the stars and wondered – again – what the next day might hold. She'd not heard from Harry since he'd left her bed earlier that day. Maybe she wouldn't? Then what? There was no way she was going to message him, much as she wanted to. With every fibre of her body, in fact. She thought back to the morning, her body responding with a small shiver. Get a grip, Martha, she told herself. She was behaving like a lovesick teenager.

Her phone pinged and she rummaged beside her to find it. The glow of the screen lit up her face. She squinted and saw the message was from Liv, asking how it was going. Martha decided to call her, knowing Liv would still be up and looking at her screen waiting for the two blue ticks.

'Well, how is it?'

Martha laughed. It was lovely to hear her sister's voice. 'Amazing. How are you?'

'Details first, what's the house like?'

Martha glanced back at it. 'Well, I'm currently lying in the hammock in the garden. I can hear the sea; the beach is about a minute's walk. Less than that. And the beach is never that busy, you can only get to it by foot or by boat. The house is gorgeous, it's a converted barn, I think. Really sweet, very peaceful. Apart from the drilling from the building site next door in the morning.'

'Oh no, really?'

'It's fine, I've had a word. They've stopped.' Martha couldn't help but smile to herself.

'And are you quite happy on your own?'

Classic Liv, thought Martha.

'Yes, Liv. I am, promise. People have been very kind. I had a bit of an adventure getting here though.'

'What happened?'

'I ended up bringing a boy with me to the island who'd got stuck in Corfu. All the ferries had been cancelled but I'd found a taxi boat so he came with me. His family were so grateful, they've been lovely. Took me round the whole island by boat yesterday. It's the best way to see it. His grandmother is just the loveliest woman. She's lived on the island for years. Knows everyone, although everyone seems to know everyone, to be honest. I've just had dinner with her this evening.'

'Wow, you have been busy.' Liv laughed.

'How's Iris doing?'

'She's pretty good, actually. Back to answering my messages two days after I send them like nothing ever happened but when I last spoke to her, she sounded fine. Work is busy, I think, so probably a good thing. We all miss you though. Mum wanted to call you, but I thought you might like just to be left alone to enjoy your holiday, so I said I'd message and pass back any news.'

Martha wanted to say more but decided to keep Harry to herself, for now at least. 'Tell them I'm having a lovely time and I'll come down as soon as I'm back.'

'And you're really okay?'

'I promise I am more than okay. It's heavenly here. The island is so beautiful.' She felt a twinge of guilt at not being completely honest. 'Thank you, Liv. Send my love to Jimmy and the kids, too.'

'I will.'

They said their goodbyes and Martha slipped her phone gently back down the side of the hammock, moving her gaze up to the sky. As she adjusted to the light, the number of stars seemed to double before her eyes. She lay back and let her thoughts drift. Harry seemingly queue-jumped and suddenly there he was, looking down at her on the beach for the first time.

Again, her phone vibrated against her. Another message, this time from Joanie, asking if she was still awake. She immediately dialled Joanie's number, realising in that moment she was in fact dying to talk about what was going on. If nothing else Martha wanted to say it out loud so someone could tell her if she was being ridiculous or not. Joanie was the perfect person to confide in.

'Martha! How's it going?'

'Are you sitting down?'

'Hang on, let me refill my wine glass.'

Martha listened as Joanie did just that, clearly lighting a cigarette before telling Martha to go on.

And so Martha told her the whole story, about meeting Milo, then Connie, then Harry. And what had happened next, at the house.

'What are you going to do, then?' Joanie got straight to the point.

'What do you mean?'

'What do you mean, what do I mean? Martha, you've met someone who you're clearly mad about.'

'He lives in America, Joanie.'

'And Greece! What's not to love?'

'This isn't *Eat, Pray,* bloody *Love.* I have a job at home, I can't just meet a man and stay here forever.'

'Jesus, Martha, I'm not suggesting you do. Just make the most of it whilst you're there, for God's sake. He sounds fucking amazing, or rather amazing fuck—'

Martha quickly cut her friend off. 'Thank you, Joanie.'

'Sorry, but honestly, Martha, you haven't sounded like this for a long time.'

'That's what Connie said about Harry.'

'Well then, get on with it.'

Martha sighed. 'There's a... complication.'

'You said he wasn't married.' Joanie exhaled heavily.

Martha could picture her friend, smoking out of her flat window as she always did. 'No, of course not. He was with Milo's mother, Connie's daughter, for a long time but she's not... She went missing years ago.'

'Well, I'd gathered she wasn't around. What happened?'

'Harry said she disappeared; Connie thinks she drowned. Her

name was Asya and her body was never found. And then, at the house this morning, the cleaner came and, out of nowhere, told me everyone thinks Harry...'

'Harry what?'

Martha couldn't quite believe what she was about to say out loud. 'That he's a playboy. He broke her heart and basically made her do whatever she did.'

'Shit, Martha, really?'

'Told you it was complicated.'

'Do you think he is?'

Martha looked up at the stars. 'I hope not.'

'What did he say?'

'He told me right at the beginning when we met that she'd disappeared, almost like a warning that if I wanted to not get involved, he'd understand.'

'You need to have a conversation with him about it.'

Martha sighed. 'I know. I'm just putting it off. To be honest, I made my mind up earlier to get out now, not see him again.'

'This sounds more than a holiday romance, Martha.'

'This wasn't meant to happen. I was ready for some time on my own, no drama. And now, for the first time in my life, I've met someone who I feel like I'm supposed to be with. I literally can't stop thinking about him, Joanie.'

'You have got it bad.'

'I've not heard from him since this morning anyway so this might all be a fuss over nothing.'

'Ever the optimist.' Joanie laughed.

'Sorry.'

'Promise to let me know what happens?'

'You will be the first to know.'

Suddenly Martha heard a male voice in the background. It sounded horribly familiar.

'Sorry, am I interrupting something?'

'Must go...'

'Joanie, please don't say it's Ian.'

'Love you, bye.'

Joanie had gone before Martha had a chance to say anything about letting that creep back into her flat and, no doubt, her bed. But then, who was she to judge? Martha hardly knew the man she'd shared a bed with the night before.

Her phone was still in her hand when it pinged again. It was a message from Harry.

Hope you had a good supper with Connie. Milo & I are having a barbecue on the beach tomorrow evening. Would you like to come?

Martha stared at the message for a moment, trying to work it out. Did that mean he wanted to see her, or was it just Milo asking? And why so formal? No name signing off, not even a kiss. After what they'd done the night before she'd hoped for a kiss at least. She climbed out of the hammock and made her way back to the house, deciding to answer once she was in bed. Replying straight away would look far too keen, after all.

Before she'd even made it to the doors to her bedroom, she had another message. She glanced at the screen and opened it.

Thought I'd try and play it cool. I can't. Please come tomorrow, we'll pick you up at 6 x

Martha sighed with relief. Once in bed, she typed out a reply.

I'd love to. See you then x

She drifted into sleep to the sound of the waves rolling onto the shore, over and over and over.

Peering at her reflection in the mirror the next morning, Martha was secretly quite pleased with the light tan now developing on her face. Her hair had seemingly curated a style all its very own thanks to the effects of the sun and sea, but she didn't care. Pulling it back into a loose ponytail, Martha threw on a T-shirt and a pair of denim cut-offs over her swimming costume and headed down to the beach for her morning swim. Having woken early, she had it to herself. She slipped off her clothes and put on her swimming shoes before walking quickly over the stones and into the water. It wasn't until she was a few strokes in that she suddenly remembered about the jellyfish. A quick look around and she was happy, the water was clear. She floated on her back, her foot habitually reaching down every now and again. Then she stood and launched herself into the water, opening her eyes and looking out into the deep water beyond. She came up for air. Why did it still scare her? Martha really wished she could conquer the fear. Turning for the shore, she made her way back towards the beach to see a familiar figure waving at her. It was Milo.

She waved back, smiling. 'Hey, what are you doing here so early?'

'I went out on the boat early with Nico to get some fish. Yia-yia thought you might like some fresh peaches for breakfast—' he held up a bag like a prize '—so I said I'd bring them down to you.'

'That's so kind and exactly what I feel like. I love peaches.' She walked across the stones to meet him and took the proffered bag, peering inside. 'They look amazing.' She sat down on her towel and motioned for him to sit beside her. He did so and she handed him a peach.

'Thank you.' Milo took a bite as he sat down. 'So good,' he said, through a mouthful.

Martha did the same, catching the juice with her other hand.

They sat in comfortable silence for a few moments, eating their peaches, looking out across the perfectly flat sea. When he'd finished, Milo threw his stone into the water. 'Dad says you might come for a barbecue with us tonight.' Milo looked at her hopefully.

Martha nodded. 'I'd love to, if you'd like me to.'

'Yes, please.'

'You love it here, don't you?'

'I wish we could live here all the time, but we can't. Dad has got to work there.'

'Do you like living in America?'

'I guess.' Milo shrugged. 'I miss my mum, though.'

Martha bit into her peach, nibbling the last of the flesh from the stone. She swallowed and nodded slowly, trying to find the right words. 'I'm sure you do. It must be very hard without her. I'd miss my mum terribly too.'

'What's your mum called?'

'Penny.'

'Mine was called Asya.'

'That's a beautiful name.'

'I think so. But no one really says it. Only Yia-yia. Dad never says her name.'

Martha looked at him. 'Maybe he's worried about upsetting you?'

Milo kept his eyes on the horizon. 'Maybe. I just wish we could talk about her more. I don't really remember her.'

Martha could feel tears welling in her own eyes. The last

thing this boy needed was a relative stranger crying about his mother. She bit her lip. After a moment, she gently touched his arm. 'Milo, I think you should tell your dad what you've just told me. I think if he knew you wanted to know more, wanted to hear her name, he'd do just that. Sometimes adults make decisions because they think it's in your best interests, to protect you even. But if he knows how you feel, it might change things.' Martha looked at this beautiful boy in front of her, his blue eyes now looking right at her. 'Will you do that?'

Milo nodded.

Martha felt as though she'd wandered into territory that wasn't really hers; saying any more might do more damage than good. She changed the subject. 'Good, in that case how about we go back up to the house and, if you can wait five minutes, I'll get changed and walk back into the village with you. That peach was perfect but what I need now is coffee.'

'We could go and see Yia-yia. She'll be at the taverna having coffee soon,' said Milo.

'Sounds like a plan.'

They walked back up the beach together, looking forward to the day ahead of them.

* * *

In fact, it turned out to be one of the most perfect days Martha had ever had on any holiday, ever. After coffee with Connie at the taverna, she suggested taking Martha to a nearby hilltop town where there was a market that morning. Martha loved nothing more than a market on holiday and this one had everything: jewellery stalls, food stalls, clothes stalls and, best of all, Greek pottery stalls. Connie dropped her there so she could browse at leisure, then collected her in time for lunch on the way back at a small restaurant owned by friend of Connie's. Shaded from the burning heat of the sun by a thick canopy of vines overhead, they sat and ate overlooking the most stunning view down to the sea far below them. The mainland lay in the distance, boats dancing across the water with their sails full of wind. The women talked easily over an unhurried lunch, sharing a small carafe of wine and picking over plates of meze piled with halloumi flecked with chilli flakes, bowls of olives, houmous and whipped feta, roasted peppers, griddled aubergines and warm flatbreads as soft as pillows.

Connie's life fascinated Martha. She'd clearly enjoyed great success in her career, from what Martha had managed to prise out of her, but Connie's happiness seemingly came not from her achievements but from those around her. It was people and places that Connie clearly loved more than anything. Despite the tragedy of her daughter, her life on the island was a happy one, and her greatest love was obviously Milo.

For a fleeting moment, Martha wondered whether to mention what Milo had said to her that morning on the beach, but thought better of it. The last thing she wanted to do was overstep the mark and as much as she felt as though she'd known Connie for ever, it really had been only a matter of days.

After lunch, Connie dropped Martha back at the house and she spent the rest of the afternoon moving between the beach and the hammock in the garden, swimming and reading. She wrote postcards she'd bought that morning to her parents, one to Liv and Jimmy and two to Iris. The first said the house was awful and that she would've hated it, but Martha decided that was too flippant so wrote another, telling Iris she missed her and hoped she was okay.

Then, after falling asleep in the hammock, Martha woke with barely twenty minutes to get ready before Harry picked her up.

When she heard the familiar sound of the old Land Rover coming down the road towards the house she was still trying to figure out what to wear. She looked at her reflection in the long mirror in her bedroom, resolving to treat herself to that new dress before she left the island.

The thought of leaving gave her a jolt. She'd gone from having the weeks stretching ahead of her, feeling like a lifetime, to being almost halfway through. And somehow, despite resolving to spend the time on her own with as little human contact as possible, she'd met a man she was beginning to realise she was in danger of falling in love with.

She pulled at her crumpled blue cotton dress and wished she had brought her make-up with her. A slick of red lipstick was called for, but she'd just have to go without. Hearing the beep of the car outside, she grabbed her basket and made for the door.

Milo was standing on the doorstep with a wide grin on his face. 'Dad's gone a bit overboard on dinner, just to warn you.'

Martha laughed. She was still quite full after lunch; those sharing plates were deceptive. 'Well, that's lucky because I'm starving,' she lied.

'And one more thing. We're not going to the beach.'

'Really? Where are we going?'

'We're getting back on a boat, if that's all right with you.'

Martha looked down at the flip-flops on her feet. 'Do I need better shoes?'

'No, you'll be fine. Come on.'

She grabbed her sweater from the back of the sofa before following Milo out to the car. Harry waved hello and Martha smiled back, their eyes meeting for a second. She tried her best to ignore the butterflies in her stomach but knew her reddening cheeks were a giveaway.

'Did Milo tell you about the boat? Is that okay with you?'

'I'll have to put a brave face on, obviously.' Martha laughed. 'But yes, I think I'll cope.'

'You are going to love it!' Milo shouted over the noise of the engine.

Harry put the car into gear, and they began the steep climb up the hill. What had been the most perfect day was about to take a very unexpected turn.

15

_____

After a short drive back to the harbour where Martha had first arrived on the island, Harry parked the car by an old stone wall and sent Milo on ahead to open the cabin on the boat.

'Can you manage this one? I'll carry the cool box.' Harry handed Martha a basket, a loaf of bread sticking out of one side and a bottle of red wine at the other.

Martha took it from him. 'How was your day?'

Harry shut the door and put the key in his pocket. 'Pretty good. Got some work done this morning then spent the rest of the day up at the house.' He didn't let on that he'd spent much of it trying to steal glimpses of the garden below, hoping to see Martha. 'How about you? How was lunch?'

'Gorgeous. Although I'm not sure how I'm going to get my new bowls back home in one piece. Pottery probably isn't the best thing to buy here.'

'Martha, let's not talk about that.'

'About what?'

Harry looked around, then took Martha in his arms. He kissed her and she responded, without thinking. It was intense, urgent, as if they'd been kept from each other for days. His hands were in her hair, hers on his back.

Martha gasped. It felt so right. It felt like home.

'I have missed you, Martha. I know I sound ridiculous. But I really, really missed you today.'

She looked into his eyes, her gaze unflinching. 'I missed you too. Thought about you for most of it.' She shook her head. 'I wasn't going to tell you that. I'm breaking so many rules here.'

'Can we not talk about you going home?'

'Fine, I'll just pretend I'm staying here forever. Because that's not crazy at all.' Martha rolled her eyes at him.

'I'm serious, Martha.'

'Serious about what?'

'Serious about you not talking about going home. At least not tonight.' He kissed her again, then took her hand as they walked towards the boats moored up alongside the harbour wall.

'Which one is it?' Martha looked along the line of small fishing boats.

'That one.' Harry pointed to the left where Milo was standing on the deck of a beautiful wooden sailing boat with a painted sage-green hull.

Martha gasped. 'This is yours?'

Harry laughed. 'It's old. But yes, I bought it about five years ago and it took us a few summers to do up. It might not be the flashiest boat in the harbour, but we love it. Don't we, Milo?' He called up to his son.

'Shall I do the bow line?' Milo shouted back over his shoulder, crouching down as he unwound the rope from a cleat on the foredeck.

'Hang on, we've got to get everything aboard. Martha, if you go down there—' he pointed to the stairs leading down to the cabin '—and I'll pass these to you. Milo, can you go and check the fuel gauge? I think there's still enough breeze for us to have a quick sail.'

Soon they were heading out of the harbour under motor as Milo stood up by the mast, ready to pull up the mainsail on Harry's say-so. Martha sat to one side of the wheel, her bare feet up on the seat, with a cold beer in her hand. She was secretly relieved; boats had never been her strong point despite being brought up by the sea and though she was very happy to be on one, she was even happier when she didn't have to do anything.

Once the sails went up, Harry cut the engine and stood behind the wooden wheel, adjusting it every few seconds as they moved through the water. Milo sat on the other side, his legs dangling over the side. Martha loved the sound of the water as the hull cut through the waves, the wind gently hitting the sails. She'd thought she'd seen the best of the island that day with Nico, but this was something else.

They rounded a headland and, tucked behind another small island, a deserted bay came into view. Harry pointed ahead. 'That's where we're planning to have supper. All right with you?'

Martha looked up at him, smiling, her sunglasses shielding her eyes from the still-strong sun. 'Fine by me.'

'Milo, come and take the helm and I'll get the sail down. Martha, can you just bring the anchor up so it's ready? It's in the locker at the front. I'll come and help in a minute.' Harry picked his spot and instructed Milo to put the engine into neutral, then went and joined Martha, throwing the anchor overboard. Together they watched it catch on a small rock, then settle into the sand.

'Dad, can I swim before we eat?' Milo peered over the side of the boat.

'Sure,' Harry called. He turned to Martha, peeling off his shirt. 'Are you coming in?'

She too looked down at the clear blue water below, knowing it was too deep to touch the bottom. She could feel the panic rising in her chest.

They heard a splash. Milo's face appeared by the side of the boat, an enormous smile firmly in place. 'Martha, come in!' He dived back under.

She shook her head. 'I'm good, I'll just watch.'

Harry looked at her. He was about to say something, then stopped.

She felt so embarrassed. 'I can't.'

'What, swim? You can, I've seen you, remember?' Harry looked at her quizzically.

'Not when I'm out of my depth. Not since I was little. I nearly drowned once.' She couldn't believe she was telling him. She hadn't talked about it for years. She then remembered Asya, wishing she'd not said anything. 'Sorry,' she whispered.

'Don't be.' Harry climbed down the steps at the back of the boat. 'Listen, why don't you sit on here, at least have your feet in the water? I'll swim right here.'

She sat and watched as they swam, wishing she had the nerve to join them. What was she afraid of? Harry was right. She *could* swim. But no matter how much she tried to reassure herself, she just could not get into the water knowing it was deep.

Harry suggested Milo and he swam round the boat one last time before getting out and preparing dinner. Martha went down into the cabin to start unpacking, relieved to be able to wipe away the tears of frustration she'd been holding back. Hearing them climb aboard, she quickly pulled herself together, putting a smile back on her face. Harry appeared at the top of the steps, dripping water onto the deck.

'Please can you hand me a towel from that bag behind you? Then come up, let me do that.'

'You sure?'

'Absolutely, I'll put the table up.' He pulled at the board in the middle of the cockpit, turning it into a small table. Before long, it was covered with pots and bowls with fresh prawns, garlic mayonnaise, a tomato salad, a green salad, cheese and olives. 'Right, tuck into your starter.'

'Starter?' Martha looked at the table.

'We've got lobster.'

'I mean, this is awful. I'm sitting on a boat in the most heavenly place I've ever been, and you want me to eat lobster? I shall be making a formal complaint.' Martha laughed.

'I know, I'm so sorry. What can I say?' Harry passed her a glass of rosé. 'Here, just to make it better.'

She took the glass from him, their fingers touching. Both let their hands linger longer than they needed to. 'Okay, fine. I'll try and make the best of it.' She laughed and sipped her wine, the cool freshness coating her mouth. 'That's delicious. Is it Greek?'

'Of course. A friend of mine makes it. He's an incredible wine-maker. Just built a new winery.'

'On Paxos?'

'No, on the mainland. Peloponnese. Good, isn't it?'

Martha took another sip, then nodded. 'So good.'

The three of them feasted on the spread before them. They had the bay to themselves and the glow thrown by the setting sun bathed everything in a rich golden light. The water was calm and by the time Martha had pulled up the anchor (she'd insisted) the wind had dropped away to barely a whisper.

'We'll have to motor back, sadly. If I put the sails up, we'll still be out here at sunrise.' By the time they rounded the headland to make their way back to the harbour it was almost dark. Milo stood on the foredeck, looking out for buoys as instructed by Harry, leaving Harry and Martha to talk as he helmed. They spoke in low voices, the gentle hum of the motor blanketing their conversation.

'Tell me what happened, why you can't swim in deep water,' said Harry.

Martha told him the story, at least relayed what she'd been told all those years ago. 'It's so frustrating because, even though I don't remember it, it left me too scared to swim out of my depth. It's kind of humiliating, actually.'

'It's understandable,' said Harry.

'Anyway, I feel bad talking about nearly drowning when that's what happened...'

'To Asya?' Harry looked up ahead to see Milo still standing on the bow of the boat, searching the water. He said something so quietly, Martha had to ask him to repeat it.

'What did you say?' She shifted a little closer towards him.

'I said she didn't drown.'

There was a silence as Martha tried to make sense of what he was saying. Connie had implied Asya had drowned; Eleni had even said it was Harry that had driven her to it. She almost didn't want to ask the next question. 'What did happen, then?'

'She left me.' Harry kept his eyes on the horizon ahead. 'Us.'

'Wait. I thought... how do you know?'

'Because she told me. In a letter.'

'But you said she disappeared. You said she drowned.'

'I said she'd disappeared. I didn't say she drowned. That's what she wanted people to believe.'

'Why?' Martha's voice rose.

Harry called up to Milo. 'All good up there?'

'All good,' Milo called back.

'She asked me not to tell anyone. Not her mother, not Milo. Nobody. And I haven't. Until about thirty seconds ago, that is.' He exhaled, a long slow breath.

Martha was quiet for a moment, trying to take it all in. She looked up at Harry. 'Why tell me?'

'Because I trust you. And you knowing the truth is important to me.'

'But surely it's important to them too, to Milo and her mother, her friends.'

'I had to respect her wishes, Martha. She didn't want them to know.'

'Where did she go?'

'I've no idea. She just said she couldn't do this any more.'

'Do what, exactly?'

Harry shrugged. 'Live here. I'd been back that summer – we weren't together at that stage, hadn't been for about a year but we did our best to parent Milo together when I was here at least – and then one day she started talking about wanting to leave. I assumed she meant with Milo. What I didn't realise was she meant on her own. And then she left.'

There was a long pause filled with nothing but the sound of the engine and the sea around them. Finally, Martha spoke. 'Harry, I'm so sorry.'

'The day she left I found the letter. It was propped up on the kitchen table at the cottage I used to rent. Not even in an envelope, just folded in half. I honestly thought it was a shopping list. She said she wanted people to believe she'd drowned so that it was nobody's fault. She said she was sorry and asked that I didn't tell anyone. That was it.'

Martha thought for a moment. 'But wouldn't it be better if they knew she was still alive? One day she might change her mind and come back?'

'That's why I'm telling you. I have done what she's asked, for years. But I want you to know the truth in case she does. I know the rumour on the island was that I had something to do with her disappearance, that I drove her to it, but, to be honest, I didn't care what anyone said. All I cared about was Milo, protecting him, looking after him. And Connie, of course.'

'You really don't care about being accused of something you didn't do?'

'Milo was all that mattered; he still is.'

'And what if she does come back? What would you do then?'

Harry looked at Martha briefly. 'I used to think about that but now, if she walked back through the door tomorrow, we'd just have to cross that bridge. I've done what I think is right. I've respected her wishes. If she does ever come back, she'd have to respect mine.'

Martha gazed out into the darkness. 'Connie said you lived with the ghost of Asya.'

'I know, she's said the same to me many times, which is why it was sometimes so tempting to tell her what I knew. But I couldn't. I'm not sure it would have made things any easier, anyway. Maybe Asya was right, maybe it is easier if they all think she's never coming back. That way they don't ever have to know why she left.'

Martha felt winded by Harry's words. Here was a man prepared to be cast as the bad guy to protect the ones he loved from knowing the truth. Not only that, he'd had to carry a secret so enormous it must have felt unbearable at times. She tried to speak, but her mouth was dry.

'Here,' said Harry, handing her his tumbler.

She took a sip, the taste of whisky making her cough. 'You could have warned me.'

'Sorry.' He took the glass back. 'Listen, I left you yesterday morning knowing I had to tell you the truth. I want you to know. And now you do, I would understand if you wanted nothing more to do with me. I think I would if I was you. You didn't ask for any of this. But it's up to you.' He reached for her hand in the dark, squeezing it gently. 'I'll drop you back tonight, take Milo home and come by in the morning. If you decide you'd rather not see me again, I'd understand. But I really don't want to lose you. I'm sorry, I'd hoped this wouldn't happen.'

'What do you mean?'

'I'd hoped I wouldn't fall in love with someone. Again.'

'Harry, that's...' Martha couldn't believe he'd said he loved her. How could he possibly know so soon? She hadn't told anyone she'd loved them for years, not since Joe. She knew her feelings for Harry were unlike anything she'd ever known. It was as if he'd been waiting for her all along. But to say the word out loud so soon? The thought of it terrified her. Yet he was so matter-of-fact about it, it made Martha laugh. 'Are you sure?' It was all she could think of to say.

'I'm quite serious.'

'Sorry, I'm just quite surprised. Thank you.'

Harry laughed. 'So formal.'

'But... I still can't believe you've kept this to yourself all this time. That must be so hard to live with.'

'I did what I thought was best. That's all I can do.'

Milo appeared out of the darkness.

'Hey, you,' said Harry. 'You must be tired.'

'Kind of.' Milo rubbed at his eyes.

'Can you get ready to jump ashore? We'll come in alongside the landing pontoon for now. I'll move it in the morning.'

'Sure.' Milo walked towards the bow again.

Martha watched the boy as he walked back into the darkness. Thinking about what he must have been through made her want to wrap him in a hug and never let him go.

* * *

Sleep had not come easily that night. As Martha lay in her bed, listening to the world as it woke up slowly outside, she couldn't stop thinking about what Harry had told her. The fact that he'd had to live with this secret for so long was shocking and so terribly sad. And, of course, she couldn't help but wonder where Asya was now, whether she would in fact walk back into Harry's and Milo's lives one day. How desperate she must have been to fake her own death to leave her past behind. And not just her past; her own child.

And if that wasn't enough, he'd told her he loved her. And if Martha was completely honest with herself, she knew she loved him too. This wasn't the rush of a new love, nor was it simply lust. This was something quite different, meeting someone for the first time and feeling as though she'd known him all her life.

Martha tried her best to doze but felt restless. She got up, threw on her swimming costume, wrapped a sarong around her waist and made her way down to the beach. The sun was not yet up, the sea undulated softly. As she walked into the water, the coldness made her catch her breath. Quickly, she walked in up to her waist and moved forwards, strong strokes taking her out, away from the beach. She turned and swam the length of the bay, far enough out to swim freely. Her mind played imagined scenes in her head, from Asya placing the note on the table to her leaving a pile of clothes on the beach. It was like watching a film through her fingers: not wanting to see it but not being able to help herself.

As she made her way back towards the beach, Martha heard someone calling her name. Looking up, she saw Harry running towards her, Spyros just behind.

She started walking out of the water towards them. Looking at their faces, she knew something was wrong. 'Harry, what's happened?'

'It's Milo. Have you seen him?'

'No, not this morning. When did he go?'

Harry shook his head. 'We don't know exactly but he wasn't there when I went to wake him. He was supposed to leave early with Spyros on the boat.' His face was ashen.

Spyros looked at Martha. 'When he didn't show up, I called Harry straight away. Nico is out on the boat looking for him just in case he's gone to any of the bays we can't get to.'

Harry took Martha's hands. 'Spyros knows.'

'About what?' Martha was lost.

'About Asya. He was the one who took her to the mainland.'

Martha looked at Spyros. 'But you said...'

'That I hadn't told anyone. She knew she needed to leave the island without being seen if she was to disappear and so she asked Spyros to take her.'

Spyros shrugged. 'I'm sorry.'

'We just need to find Milo,' said Martha. 'Where else might he have gone?'

Harry looked around the bay. 'I was really hoping he'd come to you.'

'Did you check the house?' Martha glanced up towards it.

'Yes, nothing.' Harry ran his fingers through his hair. 'There's another place we need to look.' He looked at Spyros, who nodded at him.

'There's another bay he loves on the other side of the island,' said Spyros.

'Shall I come?' Martha looked at Harry.

'No, stay here in case he does turn up.'

'Okay, I'll ring you if he does.'

The three of them made their way back up to the house in silence. Martha wanted to say something reassuring but words seemed pointless. All that mattered was finding Milo. She watched the car disappear up the hill, then turned and went back to the hammock. She sat looking down towards the beach, looking back to the house every now and again, hoping to see Milo casually walk round the corner suggesting they go fishing. She realised in that moment how much she'd come to care for the boy. Closing her eyes, she said a silent prayer, asking whoever was listening to keep Milo safe. She messaged Connie, asking if there was anything she could do. Connie replied instantly, saying they had everyone they knew combing the island for him and that she'd let her know as soon as she had any news.

The next few hours crawled by. Martha tried to stay positive, but her mind kept taking her to places she didn't want to go. What if he'd learnt the truth about his mother from her and Harry's conversation on the boat the previous night? The thought of it made her feel wretched. How on earth was a young boy, not even ten years old, supposed to process any of that?

From her spot in the garden, the sounds of families arriving on the beach drifted up towards her on the gentle sea breeze. How strange that life carried on around as normal when all the people she cared about on the island were in such a desperate situation. She glanced at the time on her phone; it was already past ten o'clock. Milo had been gone for hours. Where was he?

Her phone was still in her hand when it rang, making her jump. It was Harry.

'Have you found him?'

'Not yet but he was seen on the coastal path earlier this morning. I think I know where he went. There's a path that hugs the edge of the cliff that comes out at the end of your beach. No one uses it now. It got too dangerous.'

'So should I go down there?' Martha put on her shoes as she spoke.

'Yes, you might be able to see him from the far end. If you do, call me.'

'Heading down there now.'

'I'm on my way.'

He rang off.

Martha quickly made her way down to the beach and scanned the people on it, hoping to spot Milo sitting on the sand. She then looked out across the bay, checking the faces of the people in the water. Everyone looked so happy and carefree. There was no sign of him. She started walking along to the far end of the bay where Harry had said the path came out. Picking her way carefully across the rocks, she rounded the corner. When she looked up at the cliff ahead, her heart jumped in her chest. There, in a hidden cove sitting on a ledge some way above the water, was Milo, hugging his knees.

'Milo!' Martha shouted at him, waving her arms.

He turned slowly towards her. He was obviously near enough to hear her but too far for Martha to see his face clearly.

'Go away!' Milo shouted back.

'Milo, everyone is so worried. Your father has been looking everywhere for you. Let me let him know you're all right.' She went to dial Harry's number.

'Don't!'

'Please, let me tell him you're safe.'

'I don't want to speak to him, ever again,' Milo shouted back.

Martha's heart sank, her worst fears about just what he'd overheard the night before seemingly confirmed. 'Listen, I'm coming to you.' Martha decided if she could make it to the small beach below, she could at least talk to him. Unwrapping her sarong, she dropped it on the sand. As she tucked her mobile phone in the folds, she sent Harry a message to say Milo was there, then climbed slowly down the rocks. Launching herself in, she swam as quickly as she could across the short stretch of shallow water between the rock and the beach. All she could think about was getting to Milo. As she walked across the small stretch of sand below, she looked up and saw scratches across his face and body. 'What happened?'

Milo turned to face her. He had dried blood smeared on his cheek and forehead. His voice shook. 'I fell. The path was all overgrown.'

Martha glanced up at the scrub above him. 'Thank goodness you landed there. Are you hurt anywhere else?'

Milo shook his head. 'Just a few cuts.'

'Well, we need to get you down from there. There's no way you can get back up.'

'I'm waiting for the tide to come in, then I can jump into the water.'

'Is it on its way in?'

He nodded. 'I reckon another hour and I'll be able to jump in.'

Martha looked back. She knew she had to stay with him but if she did, the water would be deeper by the time they swam back to the rock, and she'd be out of her depth. Turning back to Milo, she realised she had no choice. Leaving him wasn't an option. It was time to put her fear to one side. She sat down on the sand. 'What made you run?'

'I heard what Dad said last night.'

'What did you hear?' She was terrified about what he might say next. If he'd learnt the truth about his mother, what was she supposed to say?

'That you might leave.'

Martha couldn't hide her surprise. 'Is that what you heard?'

'Yes, I heard you cough and then I heard Dad say he'd understand if you didn't want to see him again. That he didn't want to lose you.'

'Did you hear anything else?' Martha could barely get the words out, the lump in her throat was so large.

'He said he loved you.'

Martha nodded, smiling. 'He did.'

'Do you love him?'

She looked at him, his face earnest. Such a simple question and yet so complicated. How could she love him? It was too soon. And yet she seemed to have thought of nothing but him from the moment they met. She wanted to be with him, know him. Her body physically ached for him. Her mind loved him. She loved him.

'Yes, I do.'

'Then why do you have to leave?'

'Because I... I'm just on holiday. This wasn't supposed to happen.'

He looked confused.

Martha sighed. 'Milo, I live in England. You live in America.'

'And here,' he said, correcting her.

'Yes, and here. And I love it here, I really do.'

'Then why don't you stay?'

'Because I have to get back to work.'

'But you're a teacher. You told me the name of your school. When we came over on the boat you said you had the whole summer off. So why can't you stay for the summer?'

Martha laughed. 'I can't do that! I have a flat, I have plans...' She didn't have any plans, other than to spend as little time as possible in her tiny flat, on her own, in London. Everyone else seemed to have plans. Not her.

'You said you needed a holiday, so stay here until you go back to work. You can teach me whatever it is you teach...'

'English Literature.'

'Exactly, teach me English Literature, whatever that is —' he pulled a face '—and in return I'll teach you.'

'Teach me what?' Martha tried to keep the smile from her lips.

'How to fish properly. We can go sailing more. All kinds of stuff. There's loads we can do. Please, Martha?'

She let the smile she'd been hiding spread across her face. 'Fine, if it makes you happy, I'll stay for a bit longer.' She looked out across the bay, the sun sparkling on the clear blue water, the warm wind on her salty skin. 'But I'll need to find somewhere to rent. I've only got the house until the end of next week.'

'Yia-yia will know somewhere, she knows everything.' Milo grinned at her. 'I can't wait to tell Dad you're staying.'

The sound of an engine came into earshot just as a small boat rounded the corner. Harry was behind the wheel, Spyros at the front. Martha waved as they came towards them, dropping speed as they edged the boat into the cove, Spyros searching the water for rocks below the boat as they did.

'Dad!' called Milo. 'Martha's staying!'

Spyros dropped the anchor overboard and Harry cut the engine, holding his hand to his ear.

'I'm staying!' Martha shouted across the water.

Harry's face broke into a huge smile. He peeled off his shirt, unhooked the boat's kill cord from his leg and swiftly dived into the water from the side of the boat. He swam towards them, came up the sand to Martha and stood beside her, reaching his hand down to pull her up. He looked up at Milo, clocking the cuts to his body. 'Are you hurt? What happened?'

'I fell,' Milo called down.

'Why did you go without telling me?'

Martha squeezed Harry's hand and stood beside him, whispering in his ear. 'He doesn't know.'

He gently squeezed it back.

'It doesn't matter now.' Milo looked at Martha. 'She's going to stay for a bit longer, aren't you?'

Harry looked at Martha, his eyes glistening. 'Really?'

'If you'd like me to, yes.'

He took both her hands. 'I'd love you to. You know that.'

'Just a few more weeks then, a month at a push. I do have to get back at some point. But Milo's persuaded me.'

'Right, well, we'd better get you down from there,' Harry called up to Milo. 'Hang on, I'll climb up.'

'No, Dad, we were going to wait until I can jump into the water.'

Harry looked at Martha. 'You were going to wait with him? But what about swimming back? It would have been too deep to...'

'Stand. I know. But I couldn't leave him.'

'Thank you, Martha.' Harry kissed her gently on the forehead. He turned back to Spyros. 'Are you happy to wait?'

Spyros lit his cigarette and nodded. 'Always.'

16

Connie hadn't moved from her seat at her kitchen table since Harry had left earlier that morning to go and find Milo. All she'd done was sit and call everyone she knew across the island to ask them to look for Milo. When she'd got the message from Harry that Milo was safe and that they were bringing him back on the boat from the hidden cove, she'd cried tears of relief. That boy was her world.

Details had been scant, Harry telling her he'd fill her in as soon as they were back, but Connie had known enough to be able to relax a little. Once she'd called round to let everyone know Milo had been found safe and well, she decided to head to the shop and open for a few hours. It would keep her busy, at least. The heat was intense that day; she knew there'd be plenty of women of a certain age seeking respite from the sun with a little light holiday shopping instead.

Sure enough, once Connie had hung out a few rails with scarves and baskets, the customers started coming in. After about an hour, the shop was so busy she didn't even notice Milo slipping in. He took a seat beside her behind her desk and tapped his grandmother gently on the shoulder, scratches showing across his face, arms and legs.

'Darling!' She hugged him tightly. 'Where did you go?'

Milo hugged her back hard. 'For a walk.'

'But why didn't you tell anyone? We've been so worried.' She took his face in her hands. 'Please don't ever do that again, understand?'

'Yes, Yia-yia. I'm sorry.'

Connie traced one of the scratches down the side of his face. 'You could have really hurt yourself. Your father said you'd been very lucky.'

Milo shrugged. 'I'm fine, honestly.'

He clearly didn't want to talk about whatever had been bothering him.

'Where's Harry?'

'He's with Martha. They're having a drink with Spyros at the taverna. Guess what, Martha's going to stay on for a bit longer.'

Connie nodded slowly. 'Is she? How do you know?'

'Because I asked her to.' Milo beamed.

'Well then, shall we have dinner all together tonight to celebrate?'

'At the taverna?'

'Yes, of course, where else?' Connie laughed. 'Go and tell them we'll all be in later.'

Milo hugged her again. 'Thank you, I will.'

She watched him as he sprinted off down towards the harbour, wondering what was going on in that head of his. Milo had always been pretty self-sufficient for a kid his age but to disappear off as he'd done that morning was so out of character. And now Martha was staying, and she hadn't seen Milo with a smile like that on his face for a very long time. A woman's voice pulled her away from her thoughts.

It was Janie. 'Hey, Connie, I see Milo's back. I'm so pleased.'

Connie immediately felt uncomfortable in the woman's presence. She nodded. 'He is, thank goodness.'

Janie sighed dramatically. 'Poor thing, it must be hard for him. And now Harry seems to have a new woman in his life—'

Connie cut her off. 'Janie, I don't know what you're trying to imply but please don't. Milo is fine, that's all that matters.'

'I was just saying...'

'I think I know what you were saying, and I'd appreciate it if you could refrain from making assumptions about things you know nothing about.' Connie stood up from behind the desk. 'If you'll excuse me, I have to go and get something from the back.'

Janie moved to one side. 'Of course, sorry.'

Connie moved through the shop and walked behind the screen at the back. Once hidden from view, she exhaled slowly. She waited a moment before coming back out. There was no love lost between the two of them, not since the day they'd met years before when Asya had introduced her to her mother. Then, when Asya had disappeared, Janie was suddenly everywhere Harry was, offering him friendship and, Connie suspected, more besides. The idea of Harry falling for Janie filled Connie with dread. Maybe that was why she was so keen on Martha? In which case, wasn't that all a bit unfair, putting pressure on someone she barely knew just to ensure Harry didn't have a relationship with someone Connie didn't like or, more specifically, trust? But she knew it was more than that. It wasn't just about Harry. This was about protecting Milo too. And Connie was prepared to do whatever it took to protect her grandson. Anything at all.

* * *

Martha, Harry and Spyros sat together around a table at the café, a small bottle of beer in front of each of them as they toasted Milo's safe return.

'I can't thank you enough,' said Harry, clinking his bottle against Martha's.

'Well, you might just regret saying that.'

'Why?' Harry raised an eyebrow.

'If I am to stay here for a bit longer, then I'll need somewhere to stay.'

Spyros got up from his chair and pretended to answer his phone.

Martha smiled. 'Subtle.'

'There is somewhere you can stay and I think you'll be quite happy about it.'

'Where?'

'Right where you are now.'

'At the house?' Martha couldn't believe it. 'How come? Surely it's booked out?'

'It is. But they won't mind you staying there.'

'How do you know?'

'Because it's me that's booked it.'

Martha shook her head. 'But I thought... Connie said she didn't know whose it was.'

'She doesn't. But I met the woman who owns it last year when I started building my house and she was worried about renting it out to guests only for them to turn up and realise they were next to a building site. So, I took it on for August and was going to rent it out but then decided I'd just move in. The owner won't be here until late autumn when the tourists have gone. Hopefully we'll have finished the building by then.'

Martha laughed, remembering Milo picking up the visitor's

book when they'd first walked into the house. 'So, I can rent The Hideaway from you?'

'You could, but I'd rather you were just my guest there.'

'What about Milo?'

'He wants to stay with Connie. This is the only time he sees her all year and he loves being near the village.'

Martha couldn't believe it. 'Are you sure?'

'I want you to stay. Here, with me. With us.'

'Harry, I'll have to go back home at some point.'

'I know. But not yet.'

She picked up her beer bottle and raised it to his again. 'I might be able to do a few more weeks, at least.'

* * *

Dinner that evening turned into a celebration of sorts, for the safe return of Milo and for Martha's news. Supper was fresh seafood, washed down with perfectly chilled white wine, and once dinner had finished, Spyros, Nico and other locals joined them at their table. As the moon hung over the harbour, casting its creamy light across the bay, Martha felt happier than she had done in a very long time. Every now and again, she and Harry would catch each other's eye across the table, the connection now impossible for either of them to ignore, let alone try and fight. Later that night, when Harry dropped Martha back to the house, she asked if he would like to come in for a coffee.

He left just before sunrise.

Soon after he'd gone, Martha fell into a deep sleep. It was after nine o'clock when she woke again. The sun was bright, the air already warm. She reached out across the bed to feel the space where Harry had been just a few hours before. Propped up against the pillows, she gazed out of the open doors to the garden below. The idea of being here for at least the next few weeks was wonderful but at the same time Martha couldn't quite drown out the quiet voice in her head telling her this was all just too good to be true. She reached for her phone and began typing out a long message to Joanie to tell her of her new plans. Martha smiled as she typed; she could just imagine her friend's response. As predicted, a matter of seconds after she sent the message Martha's phone rang.

'You're what?' Joanie's voice screeched.

'I know, I'm not sure what I'm doing either. But I'm doing it anyway.' Martha laughed.

'When will you be back?'

'I think I'll stay for a few more weeks at least. What date do we go back?'

Joanie groaned. 'To school? Can't remember. And anyway, I'm far more interested to hear how it's going with Harry.'

'Good, really good in fact. Honestly, Joanie, it all feels so natural. And I really feel like... myself here.'

'This sounds like a lot more than a holiday romance. What are you going to do?'

'Can we not talk about that?' Martha sighed.

Joanie laughed. 'I'm so happy for you, Marth.'

'Thank you.'

'Just promise me you will actually come back?'

'Ha, I promise.'

Martha got up and padded into the kitchen to make some coffee, only to find the packet was empty. Knowing she really needed a coffee that morning, Martha had a quick shower, threw on a T-shirt and her denim shorts, making a mental note to treat herself to a few more clothes now she was staying for a while, and set off for Loggos. As she walked down the hill, taking in the now familiar view with the bay below, the smell of the bakery on the corner lured her in.

Martha stepped into the cool of the shop and ordered a cappuccino to take away along with a heart-shaped piece of bread from a basket on the counter. She took a seat at a table just outside the door and sat watching the village come to life whilst she waited for her coffee.

Just then, a voice called her name. Martha looked up to see a woman smiling down at her.

'Hello, we met in the shop.'

'I remember. Janie, isn't it?'

'Yes, that's right. Can I join you?'

Martha gestured to the seat opposite her. 'Of course, please do. I ran out of coffee this morning, but I've been dying to have one from here. Perfect excuse.'

'Where are you staying?'

'At a house on Kipos Beach. Well, a stone's throw.'

The smile quickly faded from Janie's face. 'Oh, I see.'

'Do you know the house?'

Janie nodded. 'Very well.'

Martha felt uncomfortable. She glanced inside the shop, wishing her coffee would appear so she could finish it and go.

'In fact,' continued Janie, 'there was a time not so long ago when I thought I'd be living there.'

Martha couldn't hide the look of surprise on her face. 'Were you going to rent it from Harry?'

'Not exactly.' Janie pulled at her sleek dark hair, twisting it around in her long, slender fingers. 'Martha, this is a little awkward. I'm not sure what Harry's told you...'

Martha felt as if the ground underneath had shifted. Her stomach lurched. She stared at Janie, then opened her mouth to speak. No words came.

'I'm sorry, he obviously didn't say anything.' Janie laughed a small hollow laugh. 'Not that I'm surprised. We've been together on and off for years, when we're both here, that is. It's an arrangement that suits both of us.'

'I see.' Martha nodded slowly. 'And so now you're not... moving in?'

'So it would seem. I hate to be the one to tell you, but Harry doesn't have the best moral compass.'

This wasn't the first time Martha had been told this about Harry; Eleni had said as much. She should have known it was too good to be true; life just didn't work like that and she had been too stupid to see it. She wondered how many others had fallen for the island playboy over the years, thinking they were the only one. The sense of humiliation was excruciating.

'Well, thanks for the heads up, Janie.' Martha stood up. She was furious. With Harry, of course, but most of all with herself. She put a ten-euro note on the table between them. 'Here, the coffee's on me.' She gave Janie one last look. 'Nice to meet you.' She then turned and made her way back up the hill, walking as fast as she could. What had been her idea of paradise just a few moments before had become the place she least wanted to be. Tears started to fall and by the time she'd walked to the top of the hill, they were streaming down her face. She was shocked, angry and confused. Presumably everyone knew about Janie and Harry and no one had thought to mention it. Even if it was in the past, Harry should have told her.

Martha stopped at the top of the hill and took out her phone to call Harry and ask him what was going on. Looking at his name on the screen, she wondered who this man really was. How could she have been so naive? In that moment, she decided to save what little pride she had left by packing her bags and getting off the island as fast as she could. She didn't even want to have the conversation with him about Janie. It was too late for that. The warning signs had been there all along; now Martha needed to do something about it.

Once back at the house, Martha gathered her clothes and stuffed them into her bag, sweeping the bedroom for her belongings. She got her clothes from the line where she'd hung them up the day before, pulling at them with such force the pegs went flying into the air. She scribbled a note to Eleni, saying she'd had to leave early. Shutting the doors and windows, Martha felt as if she were waking up from a dream, one she'd been foolish enough to believe.

She locked the main door and left the key under the pot plant as instructed, then set off up the track towards the main road. She had no idea how long it would take her to walk but her plan, once at the harbour, was to board the first ferry she could. Once she was on her way, she'd change her flights. The mid-morning sun made the walk arduous, and Martha was sweating by the time she got to the main road. Setting off in the direction of the harbour, she ran over the events of the previous week. She'd been so consumed with the place, the people – with Harry – that she'd seemingly left her judgement behind. She didn't know anything about him, really. Except now she did. She knew she didn't trust him. If he'd not been honest about Janie, how could she be sure he was being honest about anything he'd told her? Martha shook her head as she walked, wanting to get the thoughts out of her head.

A car beeped its horn as it passed, making Martha jump. She stumbled on the uneven ground and fell to the floor, her bags around her. Picking herself up, she wiped at her face, feeling the grit on her skin. She carried on walking, only for another car to slow down behind her. She looked over her shoulder and glanced through the open window at the driver as it passed.

It was Spyros. 'Martha, can I give you a lift?'

Martha looked ahead, not wanting him to see that she was crying. 'No, it's fine, thank you.'

'Where are you going? Are you all right?'

'I've... just got to...' Martha didn't know what to say.

'Please, let me give you a lift. You don't have to say anything.' Spyros stopped the car and reached over to open the passenger door.

Martha got in. 'Thank you. I just need to get to the ferry terminal.'

'What happened?'

Martha sighed. 'Something's come up at home and I have to go.' She felt terrible for lying to Spyros. He'd been so kind to her since she'd arrived there. But in that moment, it seemed like the easiest way out. 'I'm so sorry.'

'Does Harry know?' Spyros glanced across at Martha.

'No, and I don't want him to know. Not until I've gone, anyway.'

'Why?'

'Honestly, it's best if I just go.'

Spyros shrugged. 'If you say so.'

They drove on in silence for a few moments. Martha thought it a little ironic that it was Spyros who'd got Asya off the island all those years ago and now here he was, driving another one of Harry's lovers – clearly that was all she was to him – to safety. She told herself it was for the best, a lucky escape. Better to get out now before any more was said and done.

'Harry will be very sad when he realises you've gone.'

'I'm sure Harry will find comfort elsewhere in no time.' Martha immediately regretted saying those words.

'Is this about Janie? I saw you with her this morning. You know, there is nothing between them. Not now.'

Martha looked at the sea far below them, the wind making

white horses on the waves further out. She thought back to the conversations she and Harry had had in the time they'd been together. In those quiet small hours spent in each other's arms she'd confided in him, trusted him. She'd thought he felt as she did. Spyros had just confirmed Harry and Janie had had a relationship and yet Harry hadn't mentioned Janie once. Even if he had ended it, it looked as if he'd only done that when Martha came along. If he'd done that to Janie with someone he'd only just met, surely it was only a matter of time before he did it again. Quite simply, Harry was not to be trusted.

But Martha didn't want to explain any of this to Spyros, thinking it was easier if she just went with her cover story. 'I'm sorry, but I'm needed back home.'

'What about Milo?'

Martha was so angry with Harry she didn't care about upsetting him. But Milo was a different matter and the thought of him being told she'd gone without so much as a goodbye was too much to bear. 'Will you please pass on a message for me?'

'Of course.'

Martha reached in her bag and grabbed her battered old notebook and a pen. She wrote him a note telling him she was sorry she had to go but that she'd loved spending time with him. 'Thank you,' said Martha, folding the piece of paper over and tucking it into the back of the car visor.

'I think you don't want to tell me but I'm sorry that you're sad, Martha. I wish I could help.'

'There is something you can do. Please can you tell Harry not to try and contact me? That would help.'

Spyros nodded slowly. 'If that's what you want.'

'It is.' Her heart felt heavy in her chest. 'Can I ask you something?'

'Anything.'

'I just want to know before I go. Do you think Asya might come back one day?'

'You know, when she left I always hoped one day she would, but now I don't think she ever will.'

'Why do you say that?'

He thought for a moment. 'She felt trapped. She loved Milo, of course, but having him changed her life so much, tied her to one place. And as much as Harry tried to support her when he was here, it wasn't enough. Not for her, anyway. She will always keep moving, I think.'

The thought of Asya making the decision to cut and run rather than stay filled Martha with sadness. She couldn't imagine making such a brutal decision but, then again, how was she to know what she would have done in the same situation? Motherhood wasn't for everyone. Maybe it wouldn't be for her? If Martha was honest with herself, she knew that was part of the reason for not wanting to marry Joe. The idea of settling down with him and having children, when she'd known she didn't love him as she'd felt she should, had made her cut and run too. And deep down, even though she knew it was one of the hardest decisions she'd ever made, it was also one of the best. She remembered, when she made it, the feeling was one of utter relief. It was as though a great weight had been lifted from her body, where once it had crushed her chest.

As for the one she was making right now, leaving without explanation, felt harder. In fact, she felt wretched. She reminded herself why she was doing it, Janie's words still fresh in her mind. Harry was not to be trusted. This was merely damage limitation.

They rounded the corner and started the descent down the winding road towards the harbour. Spyros pulled the car up beside the ferry booking office. 'Are you sure you won't change your mind?'

Martha nodded. 'I think this is best for all of us, Spyros.' She blinked her tears away and smiled at him through the window. 'Thank you for the lift.'

* * *

He watched as she went into the terminal, waving one last time before she disappeared into the building. Reaching for his phone, he went to type out a message to Harry. He remembered Martha's words, asking him not to say anything. Slowly, Spyros put the phone back in his pocket, lit a cigarette and reluctantly turned the car back up the hill.

17

It was just before midday when Harry finally stopped writing. He'd been on a deadline for a piece for the paper back home and had filed his copy with moments to spare. Closing his laptop, he shut the door of his small makeshift office and made his way across the garden to the main house. He found Connie at the table, her head in a book.

'Did you get it done?' She spoke without looking up.

'Yes, thank you. Where's Milo?'

'He's gone down to help Nico on the boat today. They're going out after lunch. He wanted to go and see Martha this morning, but I told him to leave her alone for a bit. Poor thing probably wants a bit of space.'

Harry sat down opposite her, a glass of water in his hand. 'He does adore her.' He drank the water and put the glass on the table. 'Connie, are you sure you're okay with all this?'

Connie smiled at him. 'I am. I'm happy for you, Harry.'

'Thank you.' He smiled back at her. He picked up his phone and checked the screen. 'I sent her a message suggesting we have a barbecue at the house later, but she's not replied. Probably down at the beach, swimming. Did you know she stayed with Milo yesterday even when she knew she would've had to swim out of her depth had we not arrived? She's scared of deep water, nearly drowned when she was little.'

'I didn't know that.' Connie looked at Harry, twisting the silver rings on her fingers. 'Well, I suppose I should think about going and opening up the shop if I want to catch them after lunch.'

Just then, Milo burst through the door. He was out of breath, barely able to speak. 'Dad, Martha's gone.'

Harry stood up, knocking over the empty glass. 'What do you mean? Gone where?'

'I'm sorry, Yia-yia, I know you said to not go this morning, but I just thought I'd run down to the beach and see if she was there so we could swim. Anyway, she wasn't there so I went up to the house to find her, but it's all locked up.'

'Are you sure?' Harry was bewildered. The last thing she'd said to him that morning when he'd slipped from her bed was asking for him to return just as soon as he could.

'Dad, why has she gone?' Milo was crestfallen.

Harry picked up his phone and stuffed it in his pocket. 'I don't know. But we'll go and find her. Come on.'

'Where are you going?' Connie followed them to the door.

'To the ferry terminal.' Harry glanced up at the clock on the wall. 'If we go now, we might just get there before the next one leaves.'

'Why would she just go like that?' Connie immediately thought of Janie, wondering if she'd had anything to do with it. Instinct told her she did but she decided to keep that to herself, for the time being at least.

'I don't know.' He put his hand on Connie's shoulder. 'We'll call when we find her.'

Soon they were roaring up the hill and out of the village,

hugging the coast and heading south towards the harbour. As the car hurtled along, Harry shouted instructions to Milo, telling him to message Spyros, Nico and anyone else they could think of who might be near enough to find her. 'Send Singing Spyros a message too, he's right there. He could go and check to see if she's in the terminal.'

'What do I tell him to do if he does find her?' Milo started typing out a text.

'Tell him to stall her. Whatever happens, don't let her get on the boat.'

They drove on and, after a few questionable overtaking manoeuvres, started the descent down the steep hill to the harbour. They could see the ferry was already taking on passengers as tourists scrabbled on deck to bag their seats in the shade. Harry threw the car into a parking space and ran towards the terminal, Milo close behind. They got to the building and opened the huge double doors to find the ticket hall deserted. Even the desks were closed.

'Please, no,' whispered Harry. He looked around the empty space.

'Dad,' said Milo, pulling at Harry's arm, 'look.' He pointed up ahead to the door where foot passengers walked on.

Martha stood on the other side of the glass door, at the back of the queue.

Harry ran over to the door and tried to open it, but it was locked. He knocked on the glass. Martha turned and saw him, then immediately looked away. He knocked again. 'Martha, please.'

She looked at him through the glass, her eyes reflecting the hurt she was feeling. She shook her head.

'Has something happened? Please tell me.'

She looked at Milo, now standing next to his father. They

shared the same shaped face, the same soulful eyes. She couldn't bring herself to say anything in front of the boy; he'd had enough to deal with to last a lifetime. 'I just need to go home.' She smiled gently at Milo. 'I'm so sorry.' She then looked at Harry, barely able to meet his gaze. 'Let me go, please.'

Harry watched as she turned and walked away.

'Harry!' A voice called out. It was Spyros. He walked across the hall and joined them just as Martha disappeared.

'I was too late,' said Harry, quietly.

'I'm sorry, Dad.' Milo squeezed his father's hand.

Spyros lifted his sunglasses. 'I'm sorry, I tried to stop her.'

'When?' Harry turned to him. Even Spyros looked close to tears.

'I passed her earlier. She was walking along the road.'

'You mean she was walking from the house to here?'

'Yes, I offered her a lift. I thought she was just coming into town but then she had all her bags with her. She said she had to get back; something has happened at home.'

'What did she say?' Harry asked.

'She didn't say what. But I did see her talking with Janie this morning.'

'Janie?' Harry felt sucker-punched.

Spyros looked at Milo, then back to Harry. He lowered his voice. 'I saw them having coffee. Well, sitting at a table. And I notice Martha left before her coffee came. She just got up and left. Then it was about half an hour later that I was driving past, so she must have gone straight back to the house to get her stuff.'

The ferry sounded its horn. Harry, Milo and Spyros went outside to watch it go, all three scanning the deck to see if they could see Martha, but she was nowhere to be seen. It moved slowly away from the shore and turned to make its way back to Corfu. No one said a word.

* * *

On the boat, Martha sat behind a pillar on the starboard side, out of view from anyone on the mainland. She couldn't bear the idea of Harry and Milo watching as she left. All that had seemed so hopeful and beautiful just hours before was now nothing but a memory to be filed away as far as Martha was concerned. Every time she doubted her decision, she reminded herself that she was doing this for the right reasons. How could you love someone if you didn't trust them?

The tears might have stopped but her heart ached in her chest. She watched the waves moving below her, the deep blue colour of the sea so different from the bright turquoise waters that lapped the shore on her beach. Not that it was her beach, she now realised. It would probably be Janie's beach tomorrow, once Harry moved her in. Now she'd gone, there was nothing stopping them. Perhaps that was how he operated. One out, one in.

Her phone vibrated in her pocket. It was a message from Harry. She opened her phone, found his contact number and blocked it. It took a matter of seconds. If only dealing with heartbreak were that easy. Martha started typing a message to Joanie, then deleted it, deciding it was better to just get home and then explain everything. Not that she was even sure what she would say. The last thing Martha wanted to do was confess that she'd fallen head over heels in love with a stranger on a beach and had basically agreed to live with him on the island, only to find out he was in another on-off relationship. And from the person he was in one with! No doubt Harry would have denied it or made it out to be casual but, either way, something had obviously happened between them – recently, too – and in all the conversations they'd had he hadn't even mentioned it.

Martha told herself she'd had a lucky escape. Except the last thing she felt was lucky right now. Just foolish.

* * *

The trip home went by painfully slowly. At times it just felt like one long queue to get home, from the one at the airport to rebook tickets – she'd managed to get on a flight that evening – to the queue at passport control once back in London. As if to add insult to injury, the face recognition technology hadn't worked. Martha suspected it had been due to her eyes being so swollen from crying, her tears ones of frustration as much as sadness.

It was two o'clock in the morning by the time she opened the door to her flat. The weather reflected her mood, rain lashing at the windows of her taxi as she had made her way back from the airport at vast expense, having missed the last train. She dropped her bags on the sofa and went into the kitchen, opening the fridge. Unsurprisingly it was empty. She settled for a cup of black tea (she'd forgotten to pick up any milk) and took it to the sofa. She fired up her laptop. The idea had been to watch a few episodes of something suitably shallow and distracting before trying to fall asleep but before she knew it, Martha had fallen down a rabbit hole. She hadn't been able to resist typing Harry's name into the search bar and soon found herself reading about Asya's disappearance, a small article on an American news website. A picture of a much younger Harry looked out at her, his face relatively unlined, his hair darker, his eyes bright blue. As she scrolled down, a picture of a beautiful dark-haired woman filled the screen. She was wearing a long white sleeveless dress and her feet were bare. She stood on some rocks, looking back to whoever was taking the photograph, a wide smile on her face. It was strange to be looking at a picture of her now, knowing what Martha knew. She hoped she was happy, wherever she was.

Shutting her laptop, Martha lay back on the sofa and closed her eyes. Her dreams took her back to the beach. She was in the sea, alone. One minute she could touch the bottom and the next, the sea floor dropped away. Below was just darkness but instead of panicking, Martha kept swimming. She got stronger with each stroke. Soon she was swimming far out from the shore. She heard a voice calling her name and looked over to the beach. At one end, Milo was waving at her, laughing. Behind him stood Harry, tending to a small fire on the beach, the smoke drifting up lazily. Martha wanted to swim towards them but at the same time, she wanted to keep swimming in the deep water, no longer scared of what lay beneath.

She woke to the sound of her phone ringing, a number she didn't recognise. Looking at it, she realised it was a call from abroad. She immediately declined the call. Now she was home, she wanted to distance herself from what had happened. It was time to get back to reality. Still holding her phone, she messaged Joanie, letting her know she was home. Martha waited for the ticks to turn blue, but a single grey tick told her that Joanie hadn't even seen it.

She went to scroll down to one of her sisters, maybe her parents, but something made her catch herself. Maybe she needed to lean into herself, work this one through alone. After all, that was why she'd agreed to take the holiday in the first place, to spend some time alone, happy in her own company. She'd barely managed half a day out there.

Martha remembered how she used to relish days spent alone. A visit to a gallery, a walk through a London Park, lunch as a solo diner. Looking out of the window, she saw the rain had finally stopped, the sun trying to find a way through the clouds. Grabbing her phone, she wrote a list in her phone notes of all the things she was going to do over the following month.

Finish *Jane Eyre* (again)
Go to the British Museum (free!)
Join a local swimming club
Don't sleep with anyone*
*unless it's Brad Pitt

If Martha was going to get over a holiday romance, she was going to do it her way.

* * *

Harry woke early and looked out of the open doors down to the beach. He had been utterly miserable since Martha had left and living in the house without her only seemed to make it worse. He'd tried calling her, desperate to know what had happened, but she'd obviously blocked his number.

After returning to the village, the first thing Harry had done was go to Janie's shop to ask what she'd said but the shop had been shut and there had been no sign of her. He'd thought about writing to Martha but had no address. And anyway, what would he say?

Harry went into the kitchen and started rifling through the drawers. He knew he had to put whatever was in his head down on paper. Finding an old pad and – eventually – a pen that worked, he took them to the table outside, sat down and started writing.

Martha,
I am so sorry. Please let me explain.

I know you spoke to Janie just before you left, and I don't know what was said but please know that the relationship I had with her had been over for a long time. It was only brief in the first place, a couple of summers here on the island. It's the only relationship I'd had since Asya, and I thought it was a casual arrangement on both our parts. Wrongly, as it turned out.

I'm not making excuses. I realise now I should have told you, but I honestly didn't think it was something that mattered to either of us. If the reason you left is because of something she told you, please know that at least.

I know my life isn't straightforward and I understand if you'd simply decided that spending any more time with me would just make yours more complicated. But one thing I do know is that when we were together, the world seemed like a wonderful place.

Yours,

Harry

He put the pen down and looked at the words on the page, running his fingers over her name. Then he picked up the paper and scrunched it up into a ball, tossing it into the long grass in the garden. He felt hopeless. Martha had left, clearly wanting nothing more to do with him, and there was very little Harry could do about it. Even talking to Janie seemed futile; the damage was done. He got up, his limbs heavy, and grabbed a towel from the line before walking down to the beach. All he wanted to do was empty his mind and if there was one place he could do that, it was in the water.

Harry swam out beyond the shallows and turned, treading water as he looked back at the island. This place had been his part-time home for so long. His son had been born here; people he loved had disappeared from here. Not once, but twice. Harry had had no choice but to let them go. It was what they'd both wanted.

The secrets he'd had to keep to protect others for so many years suddenly weighed heavy and he dived under the water, seeking silence from the noise in his head. When he came up for air, he saw a figure on the beach, waving at him. It was Milo. Harry swam back towards the shore and joined his son, now sitting on the stones, his body still showing the faint lines of scratches he'd got that day when he'd slipped on the cliff path.

'You're here early.' Harry was a little out of breath.

'Couldn't sleep.' Milo sighed.

'Me neither.'

'I miss her, Dad.'

'Me too. I wish we'd got there in time to talk to her.'

'I mean Mum.'

Harry swallowed. So rarely was her name spoken aloud.

'You never talk about her.' Milo looked at him. 'What was she like, Dad?'

Harry scanned the clouds above, then looked at Milo. 'She was... a beautiful person.' He meant it. 'I think she would have been very proud of you, that's for sure.'

'Do I look like her?'

'Yes, you do. Same-shaped face, same skin. Thank goodness you've got her skin and not mine.' He laughed.

'Can we have more photos of her at home, like Yia-yia's got?'

Harry nodded. 'Yes, of course we can. I've got lots in boxes at home. We'll go through them when we get back and put them in frames.'

'I'd like that,' said Milo.

Harry took his son's hand. 'You know she loved you very much. Still does, wherever she is.'

'You mean in heaven?'

Harry wondered whether this was the time for Milo to know the truth but, looking at his beautiful boy, he decided it wasn't up to him. Not yet, anyway. Telling him now would mean he'd always be wondering if she might return. At least this way he wouldn't have to live his life waiting for her to walk through the door. Maybe it wasn't the right decision but, for now, Harry felt it was the right one.

He squeezed his son's hand. 'Wherever she is, I know she loves you.'

'Dad, I think you need to find Martha.'

'You do?'

Milo nodded. 'I miss her too.'

'So do I, but, for whatever reason, she decided to go. I wish she hadn't more than anything in the world, but as hard as it is, we must respect her decision.' Harry ran his hands over his face, not wanting Milo to see the tears that threatened to fall. After a moment he stood, holding out his hand to Milo. 'Come on, let's go and get some breakfast. I'm starving.'

They wandered back up to the house. Milo gently touched his pocket. Inside was a scrunched-up piece of paper, one he'd found in the garden on his way to the beach. He'd read it quickly before putting it carefully in his pocket. Now all he had to do was figure out how to get the letter to its intended recipient.

18

FOUR MONTHS LATER

'Take a seat, please.' Mrs Browning gestured to the empty chair on the opposite side of the desk.

'Thank you,' said Martha. She sat with her hands in her lap, trying her best to look calm and composed. It was nearly the end of December, time for her end-of-term review, her first as the new head of the English department. She couldn't help but feel nervous, given the rocky start. Despite her having come into the job with years of teaching experience, heading up the department meant managing peers as well as pupils and, as it turned out, the pupils were far better behaved. The politics and power plays from some of the other teachers and behaviour of some of the more entitled parents had been tiresome. But in the last few weeks Martha had felt as if she was making progress and, most importantly, her students were turning in good work.

'So, how do you think your first term in the job has gone?' Mrs Browning fixed Martha with her knowing gaze, a small smile on her face.

'I think well, given there's been a lot to learn. It's quite a leap from my old job but I've loved the challenge,' said Martha. The challenge had involved ridiculously long hours, marking work until the small hours of the morning, helping her students as they tried to navigate adolescence as best as she could and all for a pay packet that sometimes left her wondering why she didn't quit and sign up for something a little more lucrative and a lot less exhausting. But the fact was she loved her job and couldn't imagine doing anything else. Seeing the joy in a student's face when they finally wrapped their head around the words on the page in front of them, giving them a different perspective on the world, made it all worth it.

Mrs Browning nodded. 'It is a challenge indeed, but I have to say, Martha, I've been very pleasantly surprised at how you've risen to it. I wasn't entirely sure which way it was going to go, to be honest.'

Martha stifled a laugh. 'Really?'

'Yes. When I offered you the job last summer, I knew it was a lot to take on. But you came back this term more determined than I've ever seen you.'

Martha thought back to the start of term. Throwing herself into her new job had been part of the strategy to get over her heartbreak and there were certainly days when she barely thought about Harry, consumed by work as she was. But as soon as she stepped out of the school building, her mind had room to remember. And the memories were still painful; it had been months, but it didn't seem to be getting any easier. She constantly wondered whether she'd done the right thing, getting out before she got hurt. The truth was it still hurt. The only person she'd confided in was Joanie, who'd been brilliantly supportive. But she couldn't bring herself to tell her family. They'd only worry about her and, really, she just wanted to move on. Except she couldn't. She was still in love with Harry and it infuriated her.

Mrs Browning was looking at Martha, clearly waiting for her to say something.

'Well, thank you, I guess.' Martha smiled, hoping it wasn't obvious she'd slightly zoned out.

'Right, here's your written review.' Mrs Browning pushed an envelope across the desk. 'And whilst I remember, there's another letter for you in there too. It arrived earlier today and landed on my desk.'

'Thank you.' Martha picked the large envelope up and put it in her bag. She stood up and shook her boss' hand across the desk.

'Thank you, Martha. Keep up the good work.'

As she took the train home, watching the familiar stream of houses and gardens and extensions and trampolines pass by, Martha felt relieved. She smiled to herself, pleased with what she'd been told. But more than that, she was happy to have proved herself wrong. In truth, Martha hadn't thought she deserved the job when it had been offered to her. Her greatest challenge had been believing in herself.

Walking back to her flat, Martha felt guilty for swerving the end-of-term drinks. She was so exhausted, all she wanted to do was get home, order takeaway, and put her feet up in front of Netflix. As soon as she got in, Martha changed out of her work clothes and made straight for the sofa with a glass of wine in hand. Her phone rang just as she sat down.

'Martha, where are you?' Joanie shouted above the music in the background. She was in a bar and wasn't going to let Martha off the hook easily. 'It's the end of term! Come for a bit, at least. We're going dancing later. You need a night out.'

Martha looked down at her outfit: an old shirt, tracksuit bottoms, thick socks and sliders. It was certainly a look, but not one that anyone needed to see.

'I'm sorry, I've already made plans involving the sofa and hours of mindless TV.' Martha grimaced, knowing Joanie would deploy her best tactic to get Martha out. Guilt.

'Please, you need to come and support me. I'm the only fun one here!'

Martha laughed. 'I need more than that.'

'Okay, fine. If you come, even just for a drink, I'll treat you to dinner.'

Martha thought about the no-fuss but ultimately unsatisfying dinner for one she had ahead of her: a giant bag of lime Doritos and a pot of salsa. An hour before she'd been congratulating herself on her achievements but when it came to her work–life balance, it was woefully one-sided. Perhaps it was time she pulled herself out of her work vortex and headed back out into the real world.

'Where?' Martha knew if Joanie said the little place in Chinatown, there was no way she could say no to their dumplings.

'Dim sum at the usual?'

Damn, Joanie was good. 'I'll meet you there in an hour.'

'You won't regret it, I promise!'

Martha laughed. 'You always say that.'

* * *

The bar was heaving, the music loud and for a moment Martha wondered what on earth had possessed her to say yes. But as she moved through the crowd and clapped eyes on Joanie, the greeting she received from the assembled group around the table made it all worthwhile. Soon she was seated with a large gin and tonic, bought by Ian, who was predictably all over Joanie.

'I thought that was over,' whispered Martha in Joanie's ear.

'It is,' replied Joanie, smiling sweetly. 'But he's buying the drinks so be nice.'

The gin started to do its work, making Martha feel a little more relaxed and less bothered about the thumping music. But after another round, she signalled to Joanie that she was starving and, given she'd only come for the food, it was time for Joanie to deliver on the promise.

They said their goodbyes and the two friends made their way towards Chinatown, arm in arm, discussing their colleagues, specifically who Ian would end up going home with now Joanie had taken herself out of the running. As they navigated the narrow pavement, the December wind whipping around them, a flash of colour on a doorway caught Martha's eye.

'Hey, we've been there before, haven't we?' She pointed at the painting of the pink chihuahua on the door.

'I thought I'd never find this place again! It's a sign, Martha.'

'A sign for what?'

'A sign that we need tequila, obviously.'

'Joanie, no. You said dim sum. I am here for the dumplings. Not tequila.' She shook her head, but it was no good. Joanie was pushing at the door with one hand, pulling Martha with the other.

'Just one tequila, I promise.'

They went down the narrow stairs into the basement bar. To their surprise, it was almost empty. The barman turned round, smiling. 'You're keen, it won't get going in here for another hour or so. Hey, I know you.' He pointed at Martha.

'Hi,' said Joanie. 'I'm Joanie, this is Martha, and we'd like two margaritas, please.'

He looked at Martha, still smiling. 'You don't remember me, do you?'

Martha nodded. She did indeed remember him, but she

hadn't quite appreciated his youthful beauty last time round. 'Of course, how are you?' She tried desperately to remember his name.

He stretched his hand over the bar to shake Martha's. 'It's Art,' he said.

Martha took his hand, mortified at the turn of events. 'Yes, of course, hi.' She could feel herself turning red as she spoke.

Joanie looked from one to the other. 'Oh my God, I can't believe I'd forgotten about that!' She burst out laughing.

'I hadn't,' said Art as he set about making the margaritas as requested. He was still smiling.

'Okay, you two, can you please stop it? I'm so embarrassed.' Martha sat on the bar stool.

'Why? I would so not be embarrassed,' said Joanie, taking the seat next to her.

'Thanks,' said Art. He was laughing now too.

'Seriously, stop.' Martha had her head in her hands.

'Sorry, you'll have to excuse my friend. She's usually way more friendly than this.'

'You're not helping.' Martha raised her eyebrow at her friend.

'Well, for what it's worth, I had a lovely time,' said Art as he poured tequila into a cocktail shaker.

Martha watched as he shook the cocktails. He really was very handsome. But also, about half her age. Maybe not quite, but not far off. 'Thank you, I guess.'

He put the two drinks on the bar. 'These are on the house.'

'Really?' Joanie and Martha spoke in unison.

'Just don't tell anyone.' He winked at Martha.

Martha took a sip, the salt and snap of tequila hitting her palate with considerable force. 'I won't.'

'So, how have you been?' Art called over his shoulder as he put the bottle on the back bar.

'Oh, you know, fine. Busy.' Martha licked some salt from her finger.

Joanie nearly choked on her drink. 'Wow, you really have forgotten how to talk to boys.'

'What do you mean?'

'Art just asked you how you are, Martha. And if you're hoping to engage in a proper conversation with another human being that might lead to more, then we have work to do.'

Martha looked horrified. 'Oh no, I'm not...' She looked at Art. 'I'm not being rude. It's just...'

'She had her heart broken, Art. And much as I've tried to help her get over it, she's proving very resistant. She's been like this...' Joanie pulled a miserable face '...for months. There's no getting through to her.'

'Was it me?' Art grimaced.

'No, not you. No offence,' said Martha.

'None taken,' said Art, hand on his heart.

'Are you going to tell him the story, or shall I?' Joanie took another sip of her drink. She rolled her eyes at Art. 'Prepare yourself.'

'Oh, you don't want to hear it, I'm sure.'

'I'm all ears.' Art leaned on the bar.

Martha sighed. 'I fell in love on holiday in Greece this summer with someone who lives in America.' It was a relief to say it out loud to a stranger. She was tired of pretending it wasn't a problem. Despite wishing otherwise, she knew she was hopelessly in love with a man she hadn't seen for months and would probably never see again.

'Can't you just track him down? Surely you can find him on the Internet.'

'He has a ten-year-old son and his wife, well, not wife but ex-girlfriend and mother of his son, might or might not reappear at any moment. So, it's complicated.'

'Shit,' said Art.

'Exactly.' Joanie stroked her friend's arm gently. 'Not exactly ideal.'

Art shrugged. 'I realise it's complicated but surely, if you love someone, it doesn't matter what the circumstances are. You make it work.'

Martha and Joanie looked at him, both with an eyebrow raised.

'What can I say? I'm a barman, I've heard it all.' He laughed.

'Maybe, but right now I'm just trying to forget him,' said Martha.

'Well, if you need me, you know where I am.'

'Thank you, Art, that's very kind,' said Martha, slightly blushing.

'You're welcome.' He nodded, a faint smile on his perfect lips.

Joanie looked at her watch. 'Right, finish that up. Our table's booked for five minutes' time.' She finished her drink and put her empty glass on the bar. 'Thank you so much for the margaritas.'

'My pleasure, have a good night.' He waved as they left the bar.

'Ready for dumplings?' Joanie took Martha's arm once more.

'Always,' replied Martha.

'I'm sorry to do that to you but I really think you need to talk about it. You can't keep it buried inside there—' Joanie tapped Martha's head '—forever. It's got to come out for you to move on.'

Martha pulled her coat around her. 'I need to get over it, that's what I need to do.' She took Joanie's hand and together they headed towards the bright lights of Chinatown.

19

The run-up to the end of term was always so frantic and full of Christmas festivities, but Martha always looked forward to returning home to be with her family at Christmas. It usually felt like returning to a haven, where they would spend time as a family around the table, in front of the fire, walking on the beach when the weather allowed. It was always joyous. But this year was different. She'd had to navigate the whole run-up to Christmas with her heart still in pieces. And if ever there was a time of year guaranteed to make you feel more alone than ever, it was this one. As she boarded the train, a bag stuffed with hastily bought presents over one shoulder, she was feeling decidedly un-festive. Everyone else's happiness jarred with her own unhappiness.

Martha made her way through the carriage, scanning for a window seat at a table. She had to walk almost the entire length of the train but eventually she found a spare seat in the quiet zone of the train. She felt as if she'd won the lottery. Settling herself in for the journey, she stowed her bags above and placed her train picnic on the table. She'd even had the foresight to pick up some magazines too, though she felt guilty for not having read any more of *Jane Eyre* since putting it on her to-do list back in the summer. She'd been carrying a copy in her handbag ever since Greece. Rooting around, she pulled it out and placed it on top of the magazines.

As she did so, a white envelope fell out onto the table. Picking it up, Martha studied the writing on the front. It was addressed to her at school. This was the letter Mrs Browning had given to her at the end of term when she'd had her review. She remembered putting the bigger envelope in her bag and this smaller one must have fallen out into the pages of her book. She'd then clearly forgotten all about it. She was used to getting the odd letter from an overbearing parent every now and again, but the writing was obviously that of a child rather than a parent.

Martha opened the envelope, bracing herself for a prank letter from a student. She'd had a few of those in her time. She took out the piece of paper and unfolded it, noticing how it had obviously been screwed up at one point or another. Nothing prepared her for the words on the page she now held in her hands. Even after reading the first few sentences, she still couldn't believe it. The handwriting didn't match that on the envelope. Even though she'd never seen it before, she knew instantly whose it was.

She scanned the letter, rereading over and over. She hardly dared breathe.

It was Harry telling her that when they'd been together, the world had seemed a wonderful place. When had he written it? And why had he only just sent it? It didn't make sense. She picked up the envelope again, looking at the writing. Of course, it was Milo's writing! He must have found the obviously discarded letter and somehow figured out how to get it to her. Milo knew where she worked, she remembered telling him on the boat, but had he really remembered? Reading Harry's words again, she wondered for the millionth time whether she'd left the island too quickly, whether she should have asked Harry straight out. Instead, she'd got spooked.

She folded the paper in half and slid it carefully back into the envelope. The journey went by painfully slowly; the magazines and train picnic remained untouched. All Martha could think about was Harry, Milo and the life she might have had if only she hadn't been too scared to jump.

* * *

By the time the train pulled into Martha's stop, it was completely dark. She climbed down, juggling the bag of presents and her overnight bag, and scanned the people waiting on the platform. Her father wasn't in his usual spot, so she walked up towards the exit, assuming she'd bump into him on his way down.

'Martha!'

She looked up to see Liv standing at the far end. As soon as Martha saw Liv's face, she knew something was up.

'Where's Dad?' Martha heard the panic in her own voice.

'He's fine, but he's had a small stroke.'

'Why didn't anyone tell me?'

'Mum thought it was best to tell you when you were here.' Liv reached for Martha's bag. 'Here, let me take one.'

'When did it happen?'

'Last weekend. It was only a small one but still, it was a shock. Especially for Mum.'

'How's he doing?'

'Home and resting. He was only in hospital for a few days, thank goodness. He couldn't wait to get out.'

'I can imagine. And Mum?'

'She's pretty shaken. She found him in the garden, thought he'd just fainted.'

Martha couldn't believe it. Her parents had been together for so long, the thought of one without the other was unbearable. She knew they were getting old but just couldn't imagine a world without them. 'Is he going to be all right?'

'According to the doctors, he's going to be absolutely fine, I promise.'

'I wish I'd known.'

'We just didn't want you to worry.' Liv spoke gently.

'I know, but I wish you didn't all keep things from me.'

'Hey, Martha, this isn't like you. What's going on?' Liv stopped and turned to face her sister. 'Talk to me, what's going on?'

Martha pulled herself up. 'Sorry, I'm... it's been a long term. I'm glad I'm here.' She put a smile on her face. The last thing she wanted to do was snap at her sister.

'So are we. Dad's so happy you're coming home.'

As they drove down the familiar roads, Martha thought how lucky she was to have parents who loved her and a family that wanted her home for Christmas. It made her feel guilty to think she hadn't wanted to come.

Martha walked into the house to find her mother, Iris, Jimmy and the kids around the table, all wrapping presents. Carols played from the old radio on the dresser, the unmistakeable smell of her mother's famous lasagne coming from the oven.

'Darling! You're here,' cried Penny, the first to jump up.

'Hi, Mum. Hi, everyone.'

'Hey, Marth!' Iris waved from her seat and blew her a kiss.

'Hi,' said Jimmy, a child on each knee.

Martha dropped her bag down. 'Can I go and see Dad?'

'He's in the sitting room,' said her mother. 'Take him this.' She handed Martha a cup of tea. 'He wanted something stronger, but he'll have to make do with this for now.'

Martha took the mug from her mother and went down the hall. She found her father asleep in his chair by the fire. She put the mug down gently on the table beside him and looked at his face, so familiar but suddenly old. She was used to seeing him up and about, always busy doing something. Now he looked pale and tired. He opened one eye.

'Hello, you.'

'Hi, Dad. How are you?'

'Never better.' He chuckled at his own joke.

'I wish I'd known.'

'I know, but your mother worries. Anyway, I'm fine. All that matters is that you're here and home and we're going to have a lovely Christmas all together. If your mother doesn't insist I can only drink tea, that is.'

Martha smiled. 'I'm sure you'll be allowed a whisky later; it is Christmas Eve after all.'

The fire crackled in the hearth. 'How was your end-of-term review?'

'You remembered?'

'Of course.' He nodded.

'Good, actually. Better than they expected.'

'You'll be running that school before you know it.'

Martha shook her head. 'I hope not. Head of department is enough for me. But I have been thinking; I've been there for almost seven years. I think I need to try somewhere different. Out of London, even.'

'Quite right. Spread your wings. If you never try, you'll never know.'

Martha remembered Connie saying the same thing to her, pulling her back to Greece – and Harry – in an instant.

Iris' head popped round the door. 'Supper's ready!'

'Coming,' her father replied. 'Martha, help me up, will you?' He held out his hand for Martha to take. When she did, he squeezed it softly. 'It's lovely to have you back, Martha. We haven't seen you for so long, we've been worried about you.'

'I just needed to sort myself out a bit.' She shrugged and smiled at him. 'But I'm here now.'

* * *

The last of the lasagne had been fought over – the crispy bits were always decided by a game of rock, paper, scissors between the sisters – and the conversation had turned to plans for the following day.

'We've got B & Bs staying in the barn tonight, so I'll just have to sort them out with some breakfast things in a basket in the morning,' said Liv. 'Then we'll be over in time to help get lunch ready.'

'Are we swimming in the morning, Martha?' Iris looked at her sister hopefully.

It was a family tradition, one that they all used to do, but now it was just the sisters, John and Penny watching from the shore. Martha shivered at the thought of it but if she tried to back out, she'd never hear the end of it. 'Do I have a choice?'

Iris and Martha cleared the table, and everyone moved into the sitting room, ready for the annual Christmas Eve game of charades. Without fail, watching their father act out *The Cruel Sea* reduced the entire family to tears every year. As they settled into their usual spots on the various sofas, the dogs settling at John's feet, there was a knock at the door.

'We're not expecting anyone, are we?' Penny went to get up.

'I'll go,' said Iris.

'Who's she got coming over?' John wondered aloud as Iris left the room.

Liv rolled her eyes. 'God knows.'

Martha laughed.

They set about writing out names of various films, songs and books, always the same ones, before screwing up the bits of paper and putting them into an empty bowl.

Before long, Iris came back into the room. 'It's someone for you, Martha.'

'Who?' Martha stepped over one of the dogs and followed Iris. She glanced at her watch. It was well after nine, quite late to be calling on anyone on Christmas Eve in her opinion.

It took a few seconds for Martha's brain to engage. There, in the doorway, stood Harry, with presents under his arm. 'What are you doing here?' She was so shocked, her voice was barely a whisper.

'Hello.' Harry smiled at her, nervously. 'I'm sorry to show up like this. But...' Harry looked at Iris, still standing just behind Martha.

Iris looked at Martha, who nodded gently and smiled. 'Oh sorry, I'll go.' Iris gently put her hand on Martha's shoulder. She'd obviously got the hint.

Martha and Harry held each other's gaze for a moment.

'I don't know what to say.' Martha took in his face, those eyes. She'd thought about him every day since she'd left the island, sometimes it had felt like every minute of every day. He'd been in her dreams, her thoughts, and now he was here. But still, it didn't make sense. 'How did you find me?'

'I asked the owner of The Hideaway hoping we could find you that way but they couldn't tell me, data protection and all that. So, Milo and I pieced it together. We had the name of the village and we knew the house was near the beach. You'd told me about the local pub too, so we found you on Google Earth. Or rather, the house. Then when we got here earlier today, we asked if anyone knew you in the local pub. Turns out everyone knows this family.'

Martha was stunned. 'Are you telling me you've come from America?'

Harry nodded. 'I know, it's a long shot but we figured it was the only one we had. We've been planning it for a while.'

'We?'

Harry nodded his head towards the car in the drive. Martha looked over to see Milo sitting in the passenger seat. 'But... that's... crazy,' she whispered, wondering if she was about to wake up.

'Yes, it is. Listen, I need you to hear me out just for a minute. You don't owe me a thing but please let me say this. Martha, I don't know what happened to make you leave so suddenly but whatever Janie said—'

Martha cut him off. 'It's okay, I know what you're going to say.'

'You do?'

'Milo sent me your letter.'

'He did?' Harry looked bewildered. 'Damn, that kid.' He laughed gently.

Martha took a deep breath. 'This time, I'm jumping.'

'You're what?'

She stepped forward.

'Can I put these down first?' Harry placed the presents on the doorstep. He then took her face in his hands. They looked at each other for a moment then kissed. Suddenly, a voice came from the car.

'Can I come out now, Dad?' Milo's face appeared at the window, grinning.

'Milo!' Martha waved.

He leapt out of the car and ran straight into Martha's arms.

'Martha, is everything all right?' It was Liv. She looked at Harry. 'Oh, it's you!'

Harry nodded. 'Hello.'

'Wait, you know each other?' Martha looked from Harry to Liv.

'They're staying in the barn,' said Liv. 'I didn't know you knew each other!'

'I thought you looked familiar,' said Harry, 'but I didn't want to spook Martha.'

'Oh, I'm definitely spooked.' Martha grabbed Harry's hand. 'In a good way. And this—' she gestured to Milo with her other hand '—is Milo.'

Milo smiled and waved at Liv. 'Hi.'

'Who's here, darling?' Martha's mother appeared behind Liv.

'Mum, this is Harry and Milo. I met them in the summer.' Martha looked at her mother.

Iris reappeared, looking at Martha in surprise. 'You didn't say anything about this?'

'I know, I'm sorry. I had to figure this one out myself. And I thought I had.' Martha turned back to Harry. 'So, what's the plan?'

'For goodness' sake, Martha, where are your manners? Invite them in!' Penny gestured for them to come into the house.

Harry looked at Martha. 'Are you sure?'

To her surprise, she found herself nodding. 'I guess we've gone straight to you meeting the family.' Martha laughed. 'Are *you* sure?'

'Never been surer.' Harry smiled and followed her inside, Milo beside him.

* * *

Later that night, Harry and Martha sat on the bench outside the house, wrapped in old coats grabbed from the back door. The game of charades had been suspended whilst Martha's family insisted on a potted history of how she'd met Milo and Harry. The three of them had sat together on the sofa, Harry and Martha either side of Milo, recounting the story between them. Once done, charades had resumed. The new arrivals had thrown themselves into the game with gusto, winning over the crowd with ease.

'So, was I wrong to come?' Harry winced.

Martha sighed. 'I thought I'd left the island because of what Janie had said. But perhaps I used it as an excuse. I mean, I could have just asked you. I know you have a past. We all do. I took the opportunity to go, telling myself you weren't to be trusted but the truth is I didn't think I could take on everything that loving you would involve.'

'You mean Milo?'

'Not just that. You live on the other side of the world. You're, well, a bit older than me.'

'Ouch.' Harry laughed.

'Sorry. But the annoying thing is it turns out I do love you.'

'You do?'

'You know I do. I just didn't want to get hurt. Again. But I did anyway. Leaving you behind was the hardest thing I've ever had to do. And I'm someone who's called their own wedding off at the last minute.' Martha turned to him again. 'Harry, what are you doing here?'

'I was utterly miserable when you left. I couldn't leave it there; I had to try and make you see that we could absolutely have a life together.'

'What about Asya?'

Her name hung in the air like wood smoke. 'One day I will tell

Milo about her. Not yet though, it's too much for him to live with knowing she's out there but not with us. But when he's old enough he might want to try and find her, and that's up to him.' Harry sighed, his shoulders dropping. 'I let her go all those years ago because it was the right thing to do. Letting you go wasn't. Not without a fight, anyway.'

Martha looked up at the moon. It was time to trust the universe. She looked back at Harry. 'Fine, I'm in.'

'You are?'

'Yes,' she whispered. 'Take that as my answer before I change my mind.'

Harry kissed her again. 'Thank you.'

'I have no idea how we're going to make this work, but I guess we have to figure that out together, right?'

'If we need to move, we'll move. Milo and I have already talked about it.'

'Wow, you really have been planning this!'

Harry nodded. 'By the way, do you want the present we've got for you?'

Martha had forgotten all about it. She nodded.

'Back in a moment.' Harry disappeared inside, then came back with Milo, who handed her a small gift-wrapped box.

Martha unwrapped it to find a key on a small keyring with a seashell attached. She held it up in the moonlight. 'What's this?'

'It's for The Hideaway. We bought it,' said Harry.

'You did?' Martha looked up at him, eyes wide.

Harry nodded. 'Someone made me an offer on the one I was building, so I went to the owner and made them an offer. Turns out every house has its price. I think it was always meant to be ours.'

Milo beamed beside his father.

'I don't know what to say.' Martha turned the key over slowly in her hand.

'Just don't say you've tired of it.'

'I will never tire of that place.' She laughed. 'When can we go?'

Harry took her hand. 'Just say the word.'

* * *

Christmas Day had turned out to be quite different from the one Martha had been expecting. For a start, she'd woken up next to Harry. Far from being a day she just had to get through, everything felt different with him by her side. Both he and Milo, who'd stayed over in Liv's old room, had joined Martha and Iris for their annual Christmas Day swim. 'It's more of a quick dip, really,' Martha had promised Harry. Despite the December sun, the sea was icy cold and they'd managed only a few minutes in the water before heading back up to the house to warm up with tea, bacon, scrambled eggs and hot buttered toast around the kitchen table, ready for them on their return thanks to Penny.

The sisters then took over the cooking of Christmas lunch with Jimmy, Harry and Milo helping as instructed. The first bottle of Crémant was opened just after eleven, the Christmas playlist was on repeat and by the time they sat down together around the table together to eat, the festive spirit was in full flow. Martha watched as Milo chatted away easily to her father at one end of the table, Harry to her mother at the other end, all wearing paper hats at jaunty angles, cracker debris covering the table.

Iris squeezed Martha's hand. 'You look so happy.'

'I am. I still can't believe he's here but I'm very glad he is.'

'You deserve it, Martha.' Iris smiled, tears in her eyes. 'He's wonderful. Milo too.'

Looking up, Harry caught Martha's eye. She smiled instantly.

Later, as the lights were dimmed and the Christmas pudding was brought to the table, the blue flames flickering as the fire burnt off the alcohol in the brandy, there was much excitement over who would get the slice with the lucky coin in. Everyone tucked in, digging around with their spoons.

'I've got it!' Milo held it up in his fingers. He was clearly thrilled.

'So now you have to make a wish,' said Penny. 'But don't tell anyone what it is.' She winked at him.

Milo closed his eyes and thought for a moment. Then he opened them. 'Done it.' He looked at Harry, then Martha, beaming.

'Nice, Milo. Real subtle,' said Harry, laughing softly. He looked at Martha again, now laughing at something her sister had said. She looked more beautiful than ever.

John tapped his glass. A hush went around the table. He stood up slowly. 'Now I've got you all round the table I'd just like to say a few words if I may.'

There were protests from the sisters, as always. Their father's Christmas Day speeches were legendary in that they always ended with him in tears as he toasted his family.

'I'll keep it short. I want to say that nothing means more to me than having the people I love around this table. It's been quite a year for us as a family but here we all are, together. So, make the most of every moment you have together with the ones you love because, really, that's all that matters. To you, darling Penny...' he raised his glass to her '...and to you all.' He looked around the table. 'Look after each other.'

'Cheers,' chorused the table, the sisters rolling their eyes at each other as they always did. But her father's words had landed differently with Martha this year. She realised she'd always taken them slightly for granted. Suddenly it all made sense.

She found herself tapping her glass. Before she changed her mind, Martha stood up. 'Can I say a few words too?'

Everyone fell silent. She felt their eyes on her, even the children's.

'So, I know Harry and Milo being here is something of a surprise to you all and I'm sorry I didn't give you any warning. The thing is, I nearly lost them. But they refused to let me go and for that I'm so grateful because that really would have been a terrible waste.' She smiled at them both. 'So, here's to them, or us, I should say.' She raised her glass to Harry, then Milo. 'Thank you for not letting me go.'

'Tears all round,' said Martha's mother, laughing as she wiped her eyes.

Iris sprang up from her chair and went to hug Martha, then Milo and Harry. Everyone else soon followed.

Outside, snow began to fall.

ACKNOWLEDGEMENTS

As ever, I didn't write this book alone and have so many people to thank. I'm going to start with my brilliant Boldwood family, especially Sarah Ritherdon for being the best editor a writer could wish for. Thank you to Amanda Ridout, Nia Beynon, Marcela Torres, Clare Fenby, Jenna Houston, Ben Wilson, Isabelle Flynn, Sue Lamprell, Sandra Ferguson and the whole team for their endless support over the last five years, I'm honoured to be a small part of the huge success story that Boldwood has become. Also, huge thanks to Alice Moore for yet another beautiful cover and to Emma Powell for reading the audiobook far better than I ever could.

None of this would happen without the love and support (and cocktails!) I'm lucky enough to have with my very special agent Heather Holden Brown. Huge thanks to Heather, Elly James and the rest of the team at HHB for always looking after me and my books with such dedication.

To my brilliant Paxos gang, thank you for giving me the inspiration to set part of the story on this ridiculously beautiful island. When I first visited, I hadn't planned to write about it but it's the kind of place that never leaves you. I hope anyone else who knows and loves Paxos feels I've done it justice.

I'm enormously grateful to my brilliant friends Alie, Bella, Gemma, Charlotte, Claudia and Amanda for their honest feedback as this story took shape. And to all those who asked after the book even when it felt like I'd been writing it FOR EVER, I thank you too. I'm extremely lucky to have wonderful readers and followers and your messages about my books and how you've enjoyed them are hugely appreciated.

To my husband Ross, thank you for your constant love support and encouragement. I couldn't do any of this without you. Only love.

Finally, to my sister, Alex. Tim would be so proud of you.

ABOUT THE AUTHOR

Helen McGinn is a much-loved wine expert and international wine judge. She spent ten years as a supermarket buyer sourcing wines around the world. Now, she's the drinks writer for the Daily Mail and regularly appears on TV's Saturday Kitchen and This Morning.

Sign up to Helen McGinn's mailing list here for news, competitions and updates on future books.

Visit Helen's website: www.knackeredmotherswineclub.com

Follow Helen on social media:

 facebook.com/knackeredmotherswineclub

 x.com/knackeredmutha

 instagram.com/knackeredmother

ALSO BY HELEN MCGINN

This Changes Everything

In Just One Day

This Is Us

The Island of Dreams

LOVE NOTES

LOVE IN EVERY CHAPTER

WHERE ALL YOUR ROMANCE
DREAMS COME TRUE!

THE HOME OF BESTSELLING
ROMANCE AND WOMEN'S
FICTION

 WARNING:
MAY CONTAIN SPICE

SIGN UP TO OUR
NEWSLETTER

https://bit.ly/Lovenotesnews

Boldw∞d

Boldwood Books is an award-winning fiction publishing company seeking out the best stories from around the world.

Find out more at www.boldwoodbooks.com

Join our reader community for brilliant books, competitions and offers!

Follow us
@BoldwoodBooks
@TheBoldBookClub

Sign up to our weekly
deals newsletter

https://bit.ly/BoldwoodBNewsletter

Printed in Great Britain
by Amazon